DARK GRAPHIC NOVELS

CHILLING TALES OF HORROR

DARK GRAPHIC SHORT STORIES

TEXT AND ILLUSTRATIONS
PEDRO RODRÍGUEZ

Enslow Publishers, Inc.
40 Industrial Road
Box 398
Berkeley Heights, NJ 07922
USA
http://www.enslow.com

Translated from the Spanish edition by Stacey Juana Pontoriero. Edited and produced by Enslow Publishers, Inc.

Library of Congress Cataloging-in-Publication Data

Rodríguez, Pedro, 1973-
   [Historias para no dormir. English]
   Chilling tales of horror : dark graphic short stories / text and illustrations Pedro Rodríguez.
      v. cm. — (Dark graphic novels)
   Summary: Presents adaptations, in graphic novel format, of seven classic horror stories. Includes a brief biography of each author.
   Includes bibliographical references.
   Contents: The hand / Guy de Maupassant — Sir Dominick's bargain / Joseph Sheridan Le Fanu — The house of nightmare / Edward Lucas White — The vampyre / John William Polidori — House B on Camden Hill / Catherine Crowe — The body snatcher / Robert Louis Stevenson — The black cat / Edgar Allan Poe.
   ISBN 978-0-7660-4085-4
   1. Horror tales. 2. Graphic novels. [1. Graphic novels. 2. Horror stories. 3. Short stories.] I. Title.
   PZ7.7.R638Chi 2012
   741.5'946—dc23
                              2011034194

Future edition:
Paperback ISBN 978-1-4644-0105-3

Originally published in Spanish under the title *Historias para no dormir*.
© Copyright 2012 Parramón Paidotribo—World Rights.
Published by Parramón Paidotribo, S.L., Badalona, Spain.
Production: Sagrafic, S.L.
Text and illustrations: Pedro Rodríguez

Printed in Spain

012013 EGEDSA, Barcelona, Spain

10 9 8 7 6 5 4 3 2

To Our Readers: We have done our best to make sure all Internet Addresses in this book were active and appropriate when we went to press. However, the author and the publishers have no control over and assume no liability for the material available on those Internet sites or on other Web sites they may link to. Any comments or suggestions can be sent by e-mail to comments@enslow.com or to the address on the back cover.

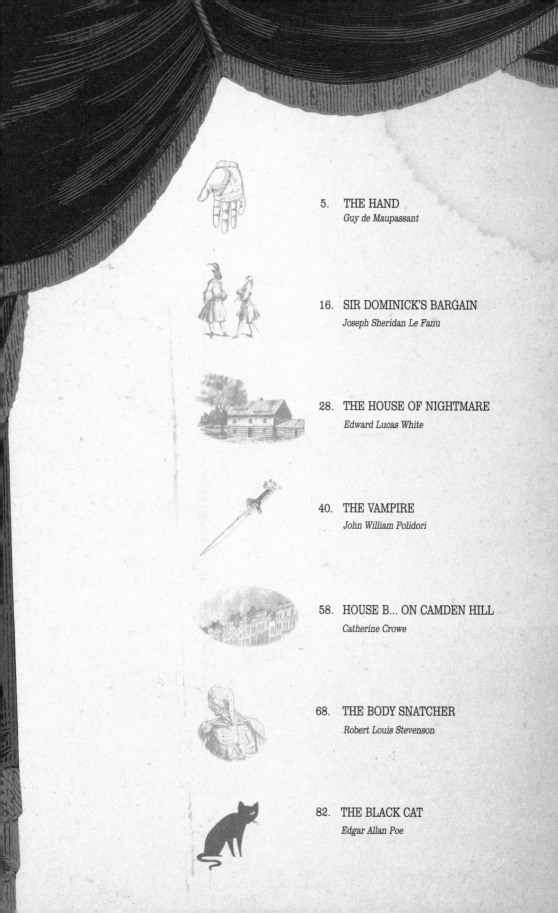

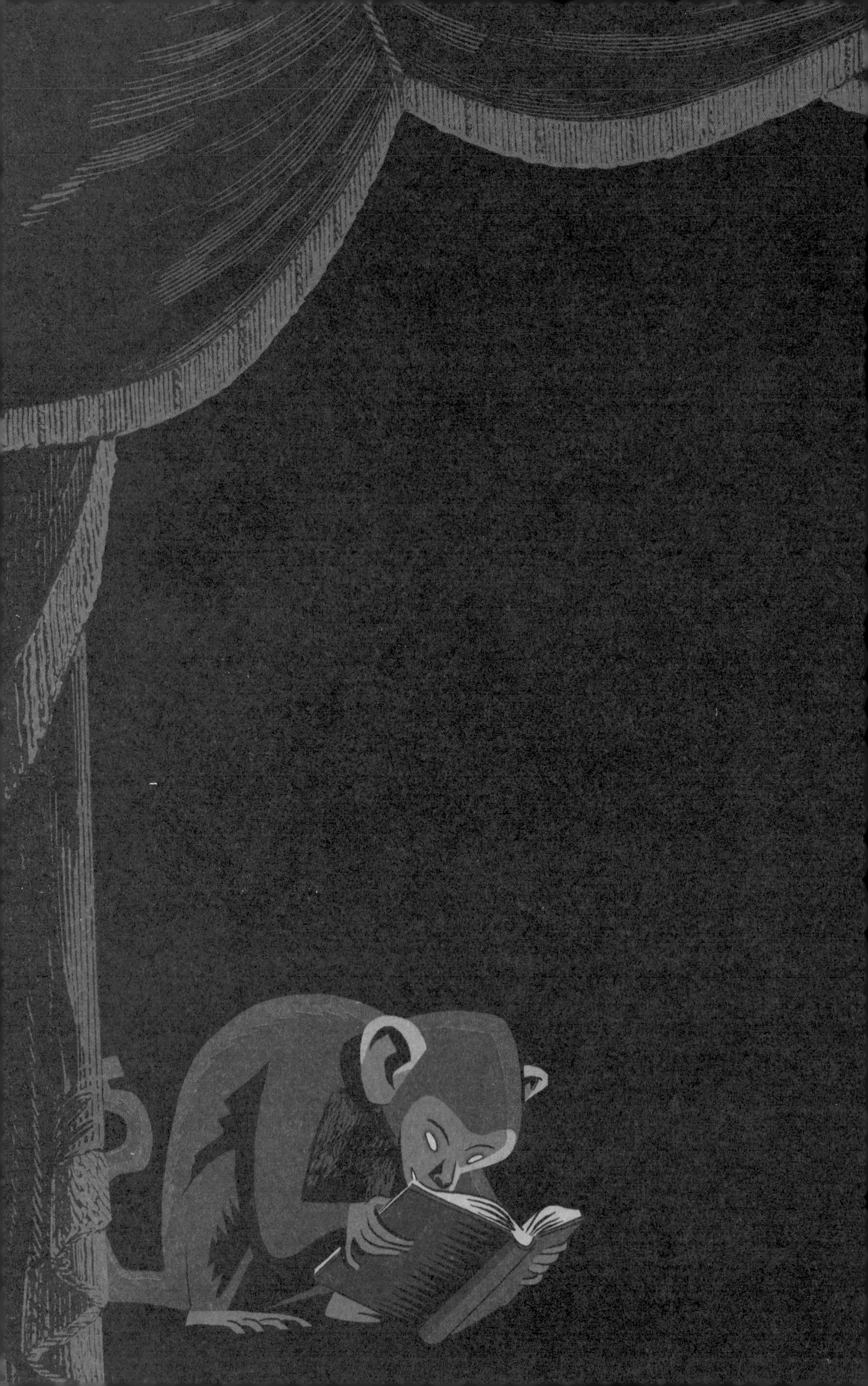

GUY DE MAUPASSANT

THE HAND

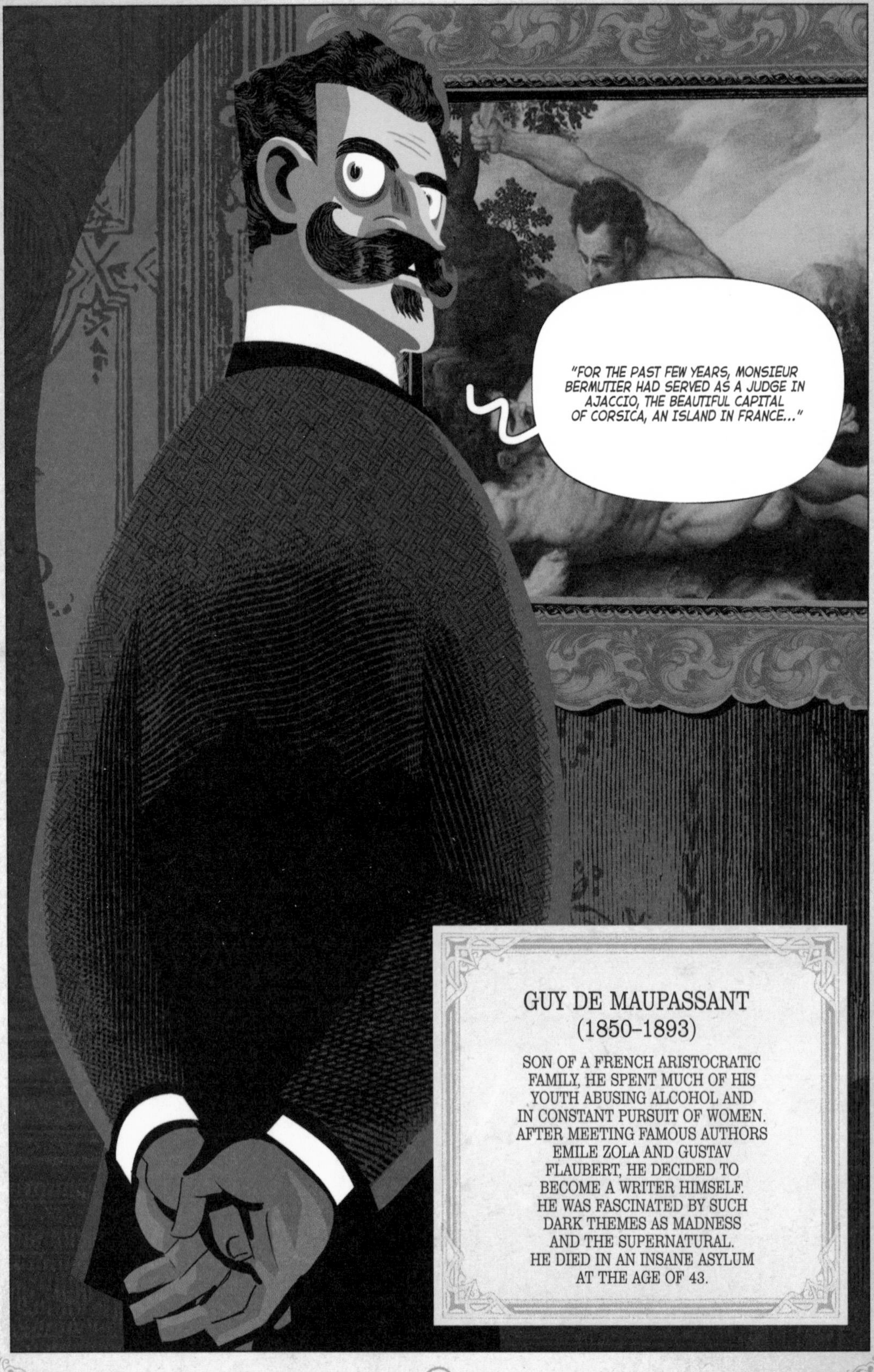
"FOR THE PAST FEW YEARS, MONSIEUR BERMUTIER HAD SERVED AS A JUDGE IN AJACCIO, THE BEAUTIFUL CAPITAL OF CORSICA, AN ISLAND IN FRANCE..."
GUY DE MAUPASSANT
(1850–1893)
SON OF A FRENCH ARISTOCRATIC FAMILY, HE SPENT MUCH OF HIS YOUTH ABUSING ALCOHOL AND IN CONSTANT PURSUIT OF WOMEN. AFTER MEETING FAMOUS AUTHORS EMILE ZOLA AND GUSTAV FLAUBERT, HE DECIDED TO BECOME A WRITER HIMSELF. HE WAS FASCINATED BY SUCH DARK THEMES AS MADNESS AND THE SUPERNATURAL. HE DIED IN AN INSANE ASYLUM AT THE AGE OF 43.

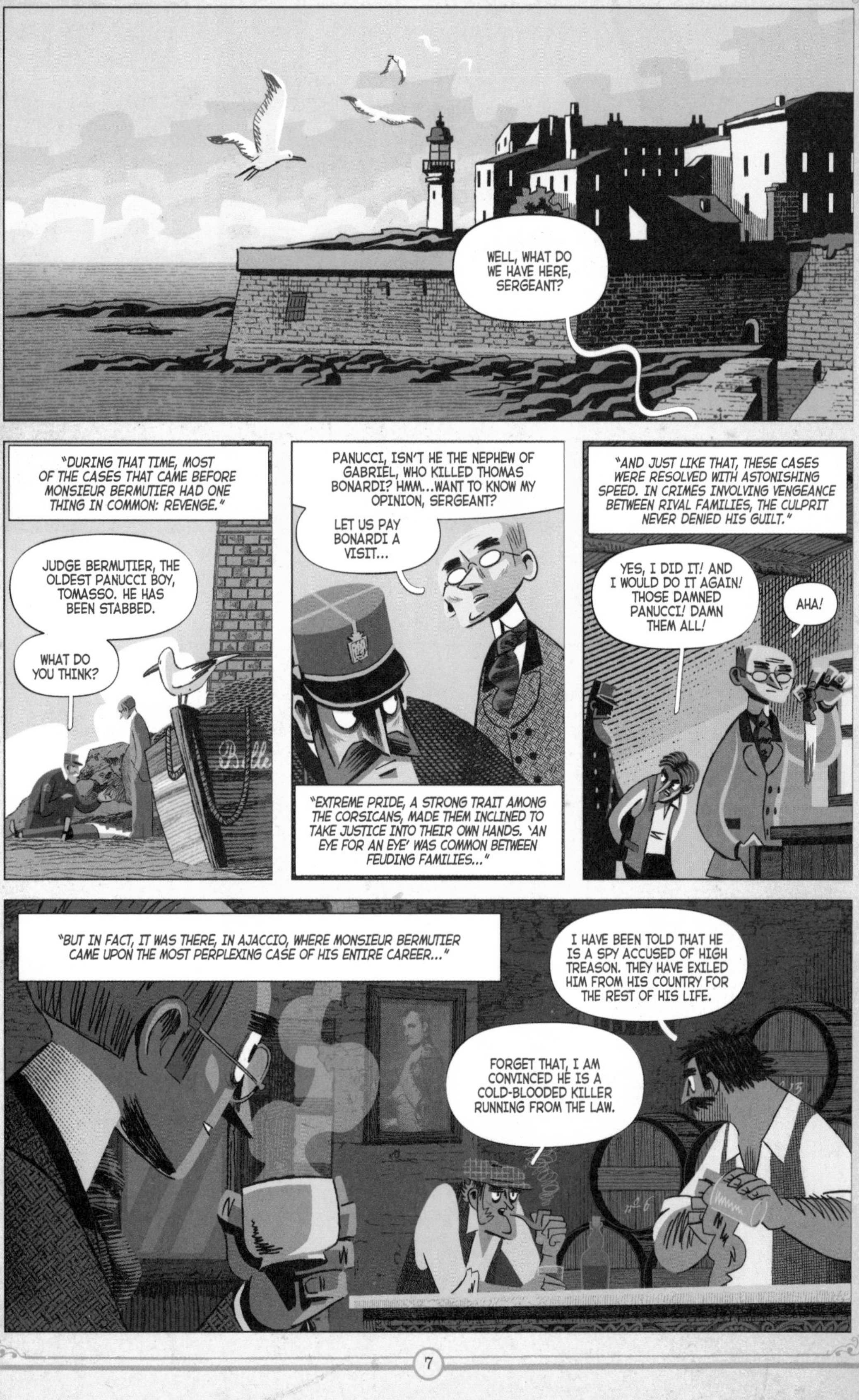
WELL, WHAT DO WE HAVE HERE, SERGEANT?
"DURING THAT TIME, MOST OF THE CASES THAT CAME BEFORE MONSIEUR BERMUTIER HAD ONE THING IN COMMON: REVENGE."
JUDGE BERMUTIER, THE OLDEST PANUCCI BOY, TOMASSO. HE HAS BEEN STABBED.
WHAT DO YOU THINK?
PANUCCI, ISN'T HE THE NEPHEW OF GABRIEL, WHO KILLED THOMAS BONARDI? HMM...WANT TO KNOW MY OPINION, SERGEANT?
LET US PAY BONARDI A VISIT...
"EXTREME PRIDE, A STRONG TRAIT AMONG THE CORSICANS, MADE THEM INCLINED TO TAKE JUSTICE INTO THEIR OWN HANDS. 'AN EYE FOR AN EYE' WAS COMMON BETWEEN FEUDING FAMILIES..."
"AND JUST LIKE THAT, THESE CASES WERE RESOLVED WITH ASTONISHING SPEED. IN CRIMES INVOLVING VENGEANCE BETWEEN RIVAL FAMILIES, THE CULPRIT NEVER DENIED HIS GUILT."
YES, I DID IT! AND I WOULD DO IT AGAIN! THOSE DAMNED PANUCCI! DAMN THEM ALL!
AHA!
"BUT IN FACT, IT WAS THERE, IN AJACCIO, WHERE MONSIEUR BERMUTIER CAME UPON THE MOST PERPLEXING CASE OF HIS ENTIRE CAREER..."
I HAVE BEEN TOLD THAT HE IS A SPY ACCUSED OF HIGH TREASON. THEY HAVE EXILED HIM FROM HIS COUNTRY FOR THE REST OF HIS LIFE.
FORGET THAT, I AM CONVINCED HE IS A COLD-BLOODED KILLER RUNNING FROM THE LAW.

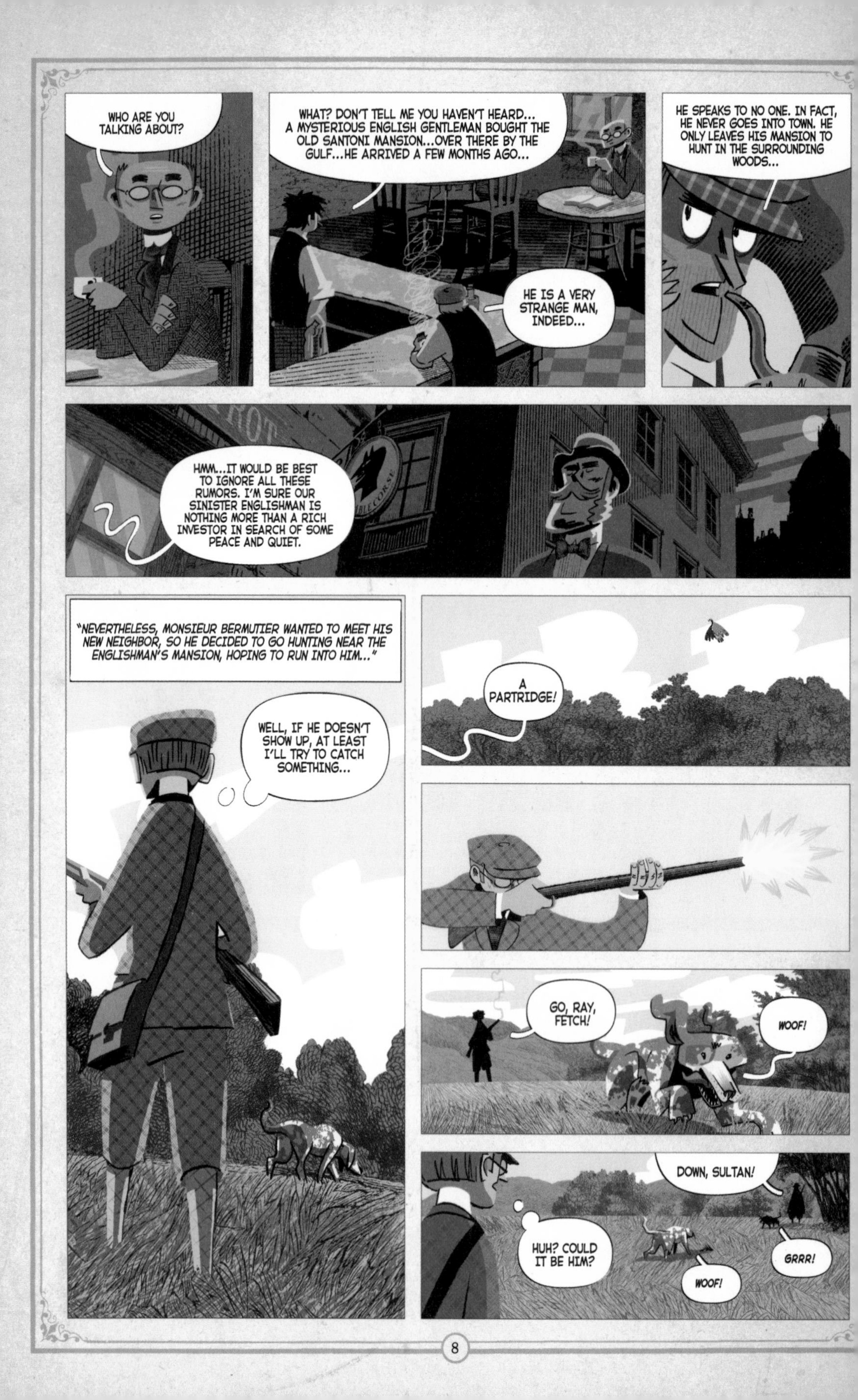
WHO ARE YOU TALKING ABOUT?
WHAT? DON'T TELL ME YOU HAVEN'T HEARD... A MYSTERIOUS ENGLISH GENTLEMAN BOUGHT THE OLD SANTONI MANSION...OVER THERE BY THE GULF...HE ARRIVED A FEW MONTHS AGO...
HE IS A VERY STRANGE MAN, INDEED...
HE SPEAKS TO NO ONE. IN FACT, HE NEVER GOES INTO TOWN. HE ONLY LEAVES HIS MANSION TO HUNT IN THE SURROUNDING WOODS...
HMM...IT WOULD BE BEST TO IGNORE ALL THESE RUMORS. I'M SURE OUR SINISTER ENGLISHMAN IS NOTHING MORE THAN A RICH INVESTOR IN SEARCH OF SOME PEACE AND QUIET.
"NEVERTHELESS, MONSIEUR BERMUTIER WANTED TO MEET HIS NEW NEIGHBOR, SO HE DECIDED TO GO HUNTING NEAR THE ENGLISHMAN'S MANSION, HOPING TO RUN INTO HIM..."
WELL, IF HE DOESN'T SHOW UP, AT LEAST I'LL TRY TO CATCH SOMETHING...
A PARTRIDGE!
GO, RAY, FETCH!
WOOF!
DOWN, SULTAN!
HUH? COULD IT BE HIM?
WOOF!
GRRR!

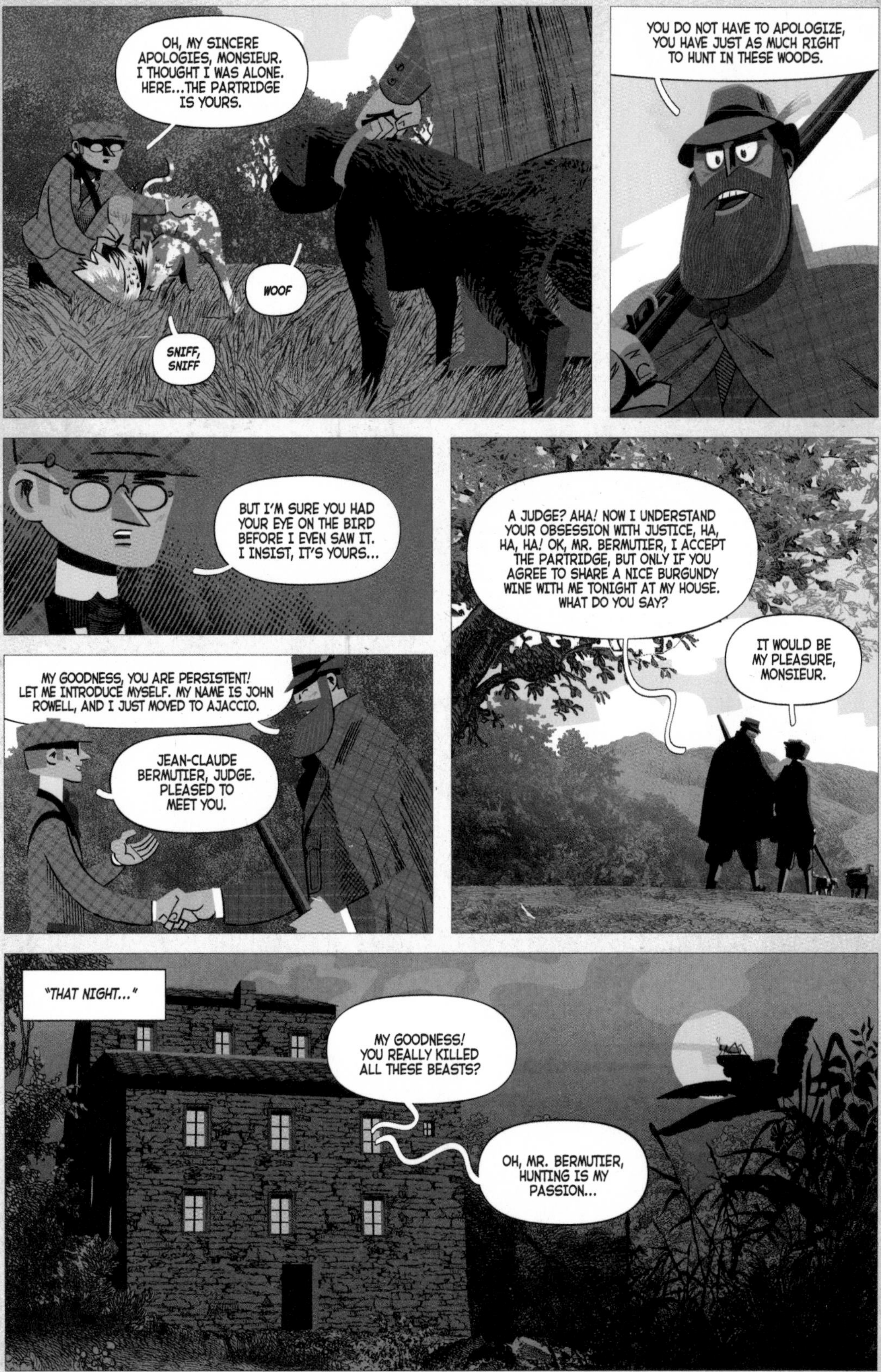
OH, MY SINCERE APOLOGIES, MONSIEUR. I THOUGHT I WAS ALONE. HERE...THE PARTRIDGE IS YOURS.
WOOF
SNIFF, SNIFF
YOU DO NOT HAVE TO APOLOGIZE, YOU HAVE JUST AS MUCH RIGHT TO HUNT IN THESE WOODS.
BUT I'M SURE YOU HAD YOUR EYE ON THE BIRD BEFORE I EVEN SAW IT. I INSIST, IT'S YOURS...
MY GOODNESS, YOU ARE PERSISTENT! LET ME INTRODUCE MYSELF. MY NAME IS JOHN ROWELL, AND I JUST MOVED TO AJACCIO.
JEAN-CLAUDE BERMUTIER, JUDGE. PLEASED TO MEET YOU.
A JUDGE? AHA! NOW I UNDERSTAND YOUR OBSESSION WITH JUSTICE, HA, HA, HA! OK, MR. BERMUTIER, I ACCEPT THE PARTRIDGE, BUT ONLY IF YOU AGREE TO SHARE A NICE BURGUNDY WINE WITH ME TONIGHT AT MY HOUSE. WHAT DO YOU SAY?
IT WOULD BE MY PLEASURE, MONSIEUR.
"THAT NIGHT..."
MY GOODNESS! YOU REALLY KILLED ALL THESE BEASTS?
OH, MR. BERMUTIER, HUNTING IS MY PASSION...

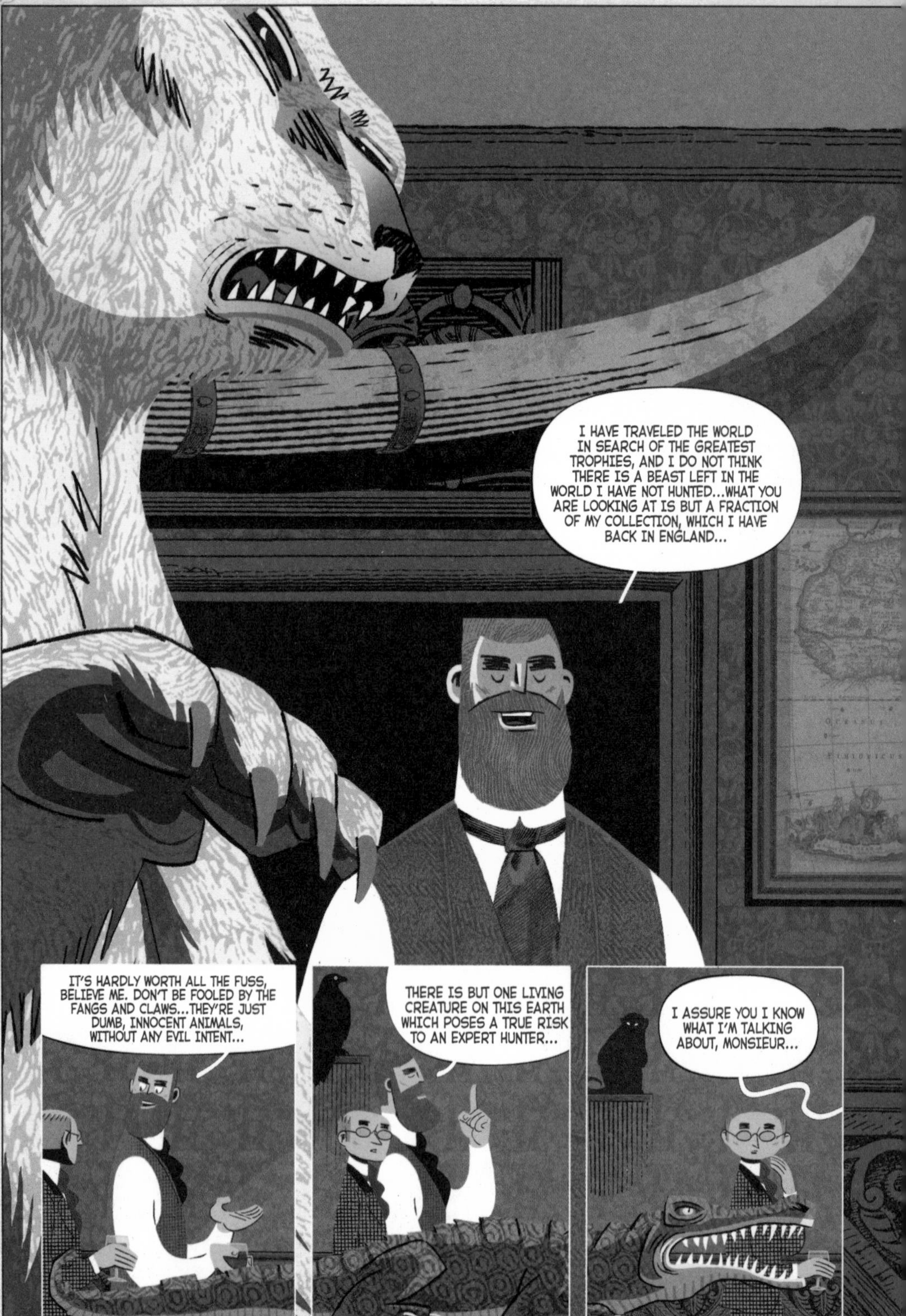
I HAVE TRAVELED THE WORLD IN SEARCH OF THE GREATEST TROPHIES, AND I DO NOT THINK THERE IS A BEAST LEFT IN THE WORLD I HAVE NOT HUNTED...WHAT YOU ARE LOOKING AT IS BUT A FRACTION OF MY COLLECTION, WHICH I HAVE BACK IN ENGLAND...
IT'S HARDLY WORTH ALL THE FUSS, BELIEVE ME. DON'T BE FOOLED BY THE FANGS AND CLAWS...THEY'RE JUST DUMB, INNOCENT ANIMALS, WITHOUT ANY EVIL INTENT...
THERE IS BUT ONE LIVING CREATURE ON THIS EARTH WHICH POSES A TRUE RISK TO AN EXPERT HUNTER...
I ASSURE YOU I KNOW WHAT I'M TALKING ABOUT, MONSIEUR...

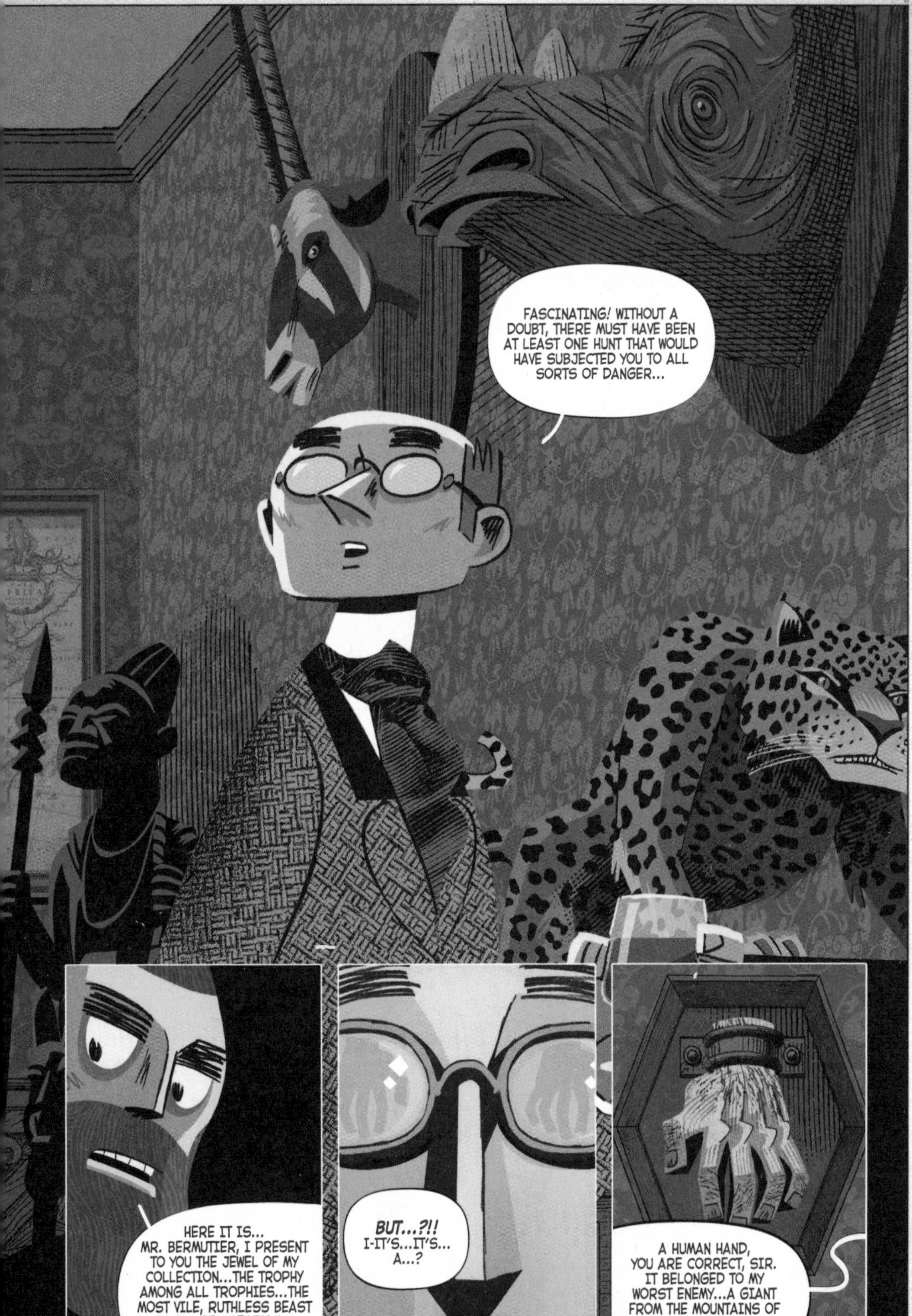
FASCINATING! WITHOUT A DOUBT, THERE MUST HAVE BEEN AT LEAST ONE HUNT THAT WOULD HAVE SUBJECTED YOU TO ALL SORTS OF DANGER...
HERE IT IS... MR. BERMUTIER, I PRESENT TO YOU THE JEWEL OF MY COLLECTION...THE TROPHY AMONG ALL TROPHIES...THE MOST VILE, RUTHLESS BEAST IN ALL OF CREATION...
BUT...?!! I-IT'S...IT'S... A...?
A HUMAN HAND, YOU ARE CORRECT, SIR. IT BELONGED TO MY WORST ENEMY...A GIANT FROM THE MOUNTAINS OF NORTH AMERICA...

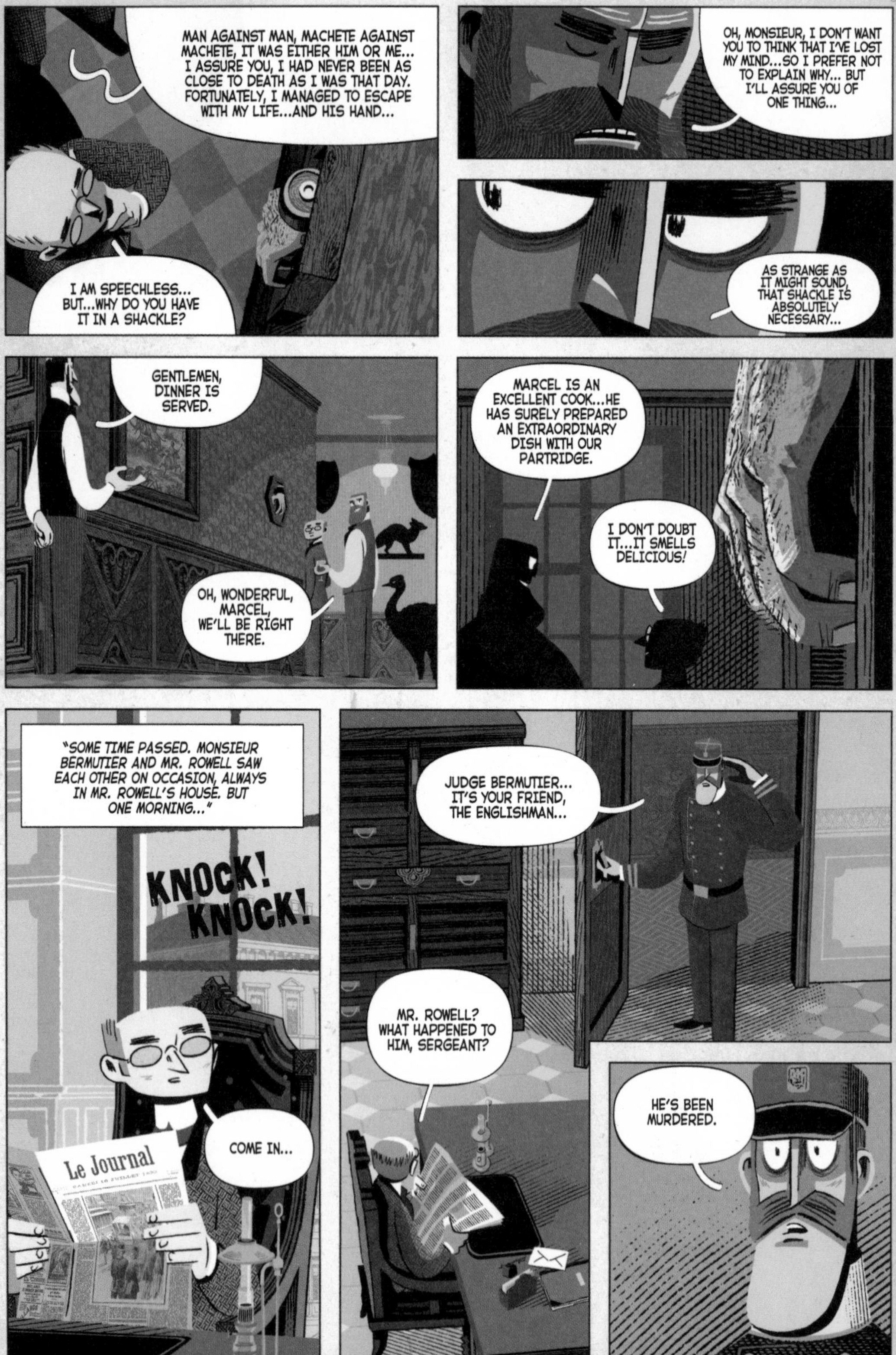
MAN AGAINST MAN, MACHETE AGAINST MACHETE, IT WAS EITHER HIM OR ME... I ASSURE YOU, I HAD NEVER BEEN AS CLOSE TO DEATH AS I WAS THAT DAY. FORTUNATELY, I MANAGED TO ESCAPE WITH MY LIFE...AND HIS HAND...
I AM SPEECHLESS... BUT...WHY DO YOU HAVE IT IN A SHACKLE?
OH, MONSIEUR, I DON'T WANT YOU TO THINK THAT I'VE LOST MY MIND...SO I PREFER NOT TO EXPLAIN WHY... BUT I'LL ASSURE YOU OF ONE THING...
AS STRANGE AS IT MIGHT SOUND, THAT SHACKLE IS ABSOLUTELY NECESSARY...
GENTLEMEN, DINNER IS SERVED.
OH, WONDERFUL, MARCEL, WE'LL BE RIGHT THERE.
MARCEL IS AN EXCELLENT COOK...HE HAS SURELY PREPARED AN EXTRAORDINARY DISH WITH OUR PARTRIDGE.
I DON'T DOUBT IT...IT SMELLS DELICIOUS!
"SOME TIME PASSED. MONSIEUR BERMUTIER AND MR. ROWELL SAW EACH OTHER ON OCCASION, ALWAYS IN MR. ROWELL'S HOUSE. BUT ONE MORNING..."
KNOCK! KNOCK!
COME IN...
Le Journal
JUDGE BERMUTIER... IT'S YOUR FRIEND, THE ENGLISHMAN...
MR. ROWELL? WHAT HAPPENED TO HIM, SERGEANT?
HE'S BEEN MURDERED.

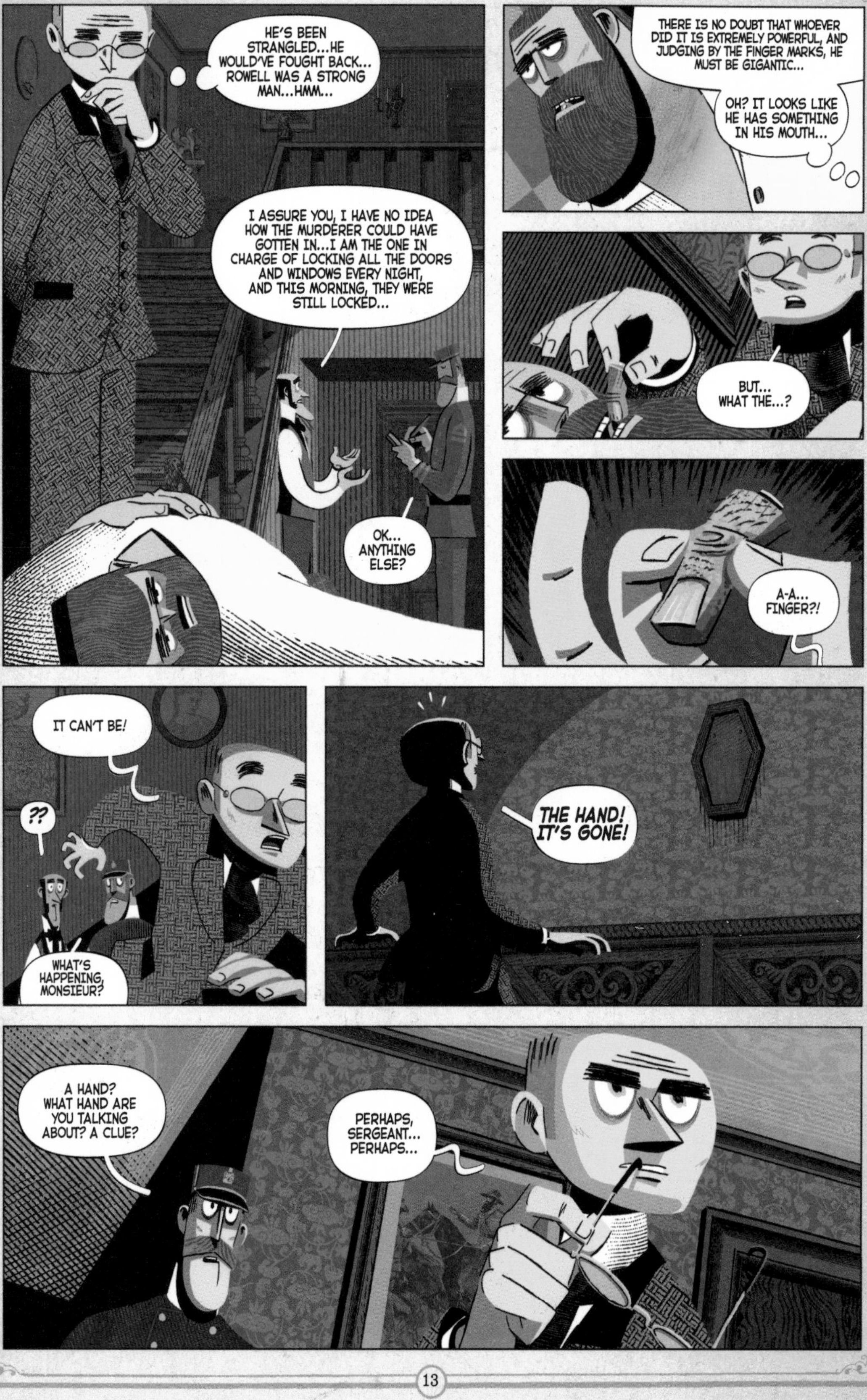
HE'S BEEN STRANGLED...HE WOULD'VE FOUGHT BACK... ROWELL WAS A STRONG MAN...HMM...
I ASSURE YOU, I HAVE NO IDEA HOW THE MURDERER COULD HAVE GOTTEN IN...I AM THE ONE IN CHARGE OF LOCKING ALL THE DOORS AND WINDOWS EVERY NIGHT, AND THIS MORNING, THEY WERE STILL LOCKED...
OK... ANYTHING ELSE?
THERE IS NO DOUBT THAT WHOEVER DID IT IS EXTREMELY POWERFUL, AND JUDGING BY THE FINGER MARKS, HE MUST BE GIGANTIC...
OH? IT LOOKS LIKE HE HAS SOMETHING IN HIS MOUTH...
BUT... WHAT THE...?
A-A... FINGER?!
IT CAN'T BE!
??
WHAT'S HAPPENING, MONSIEUR?
THE HAND! IT'S GONE!
A HAND? WHAT HAND ARE YOU TALKING ABOUT? A CLUE?
PERHAPS, SERGEANT... PERHAPS...

"THE MURDER REMAINED UNSOLVED, WITH NO WITNESSES OR SUSPECTS...AND THE MYSTERIOUS DISAPPEARANCE OF THE HAND. BERMUTIER BECAME OBSESSED WITH THE CASE, AND IT BECAME A WAKING NIGHTMARE. BUT TIME PASSED, AND EVENTUALLY LIFE WENT BACK TO NORMAL. BERMUTIER GAVE UP TRYING TO SOLVE THE MYSTERY AND RETURNED TO HIS DAILY ROUTINE. UNTIL ONE DAY..."

MONSIEUR BERMUTIER! YOU HAVE TO SEE THIS!

A CEMETERY WORKER JUST BROUGHT IT IN...

IT BETTER BE IMPORTANT, SERGEANT, I'M VERY BUSY...

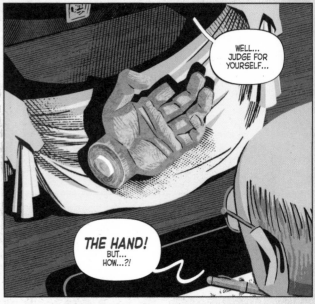

WELL... JUDGE FOR YOURSELF...

THE HAND! BUT... HOW...?!

THEY FOUND IT THIS MORNING... ON SIR ROWELL'S GRAVE. A TRULY SUPERNATURAL CASE, DON'T YOU THINK?

OH, YOU KNOW I DON'T BELIEVE IN THE SUPERNATURAL...HOWEVER STRANGE AN EVENT MAY BE, THERE IS ALWAYS A RATIONAL EXPLANATION, ALTHOUGH THIS ONE APPEARS IMPLAUSIBLE...THE DISCOVERY OF THE HAND COMES TO SUPPORT MY THEORY ON THE CASE THAT HAS BEEN ON MY MIND FOR SO LONG...

WANT TO HEAR IT?

OK...SUPPOSE FOR A MOMENT THAT SIR ROWELL NEVER SUCCEEDED IN KILLING THE OWNER OF THE HAND...A DUEL WITHOUT A VICTOR, ALTHOUGH SIR ROWELL DID MANAGE TO CUT OFF HIS ADVERSARY'S HAND. HE RAN, LEAVING HIS RIVAL INJURED...

YOU FOLLOW?...

HE LEFT HIM WITH ONE HAND AND WITH ONLY ONE THING ON HIS MIND...

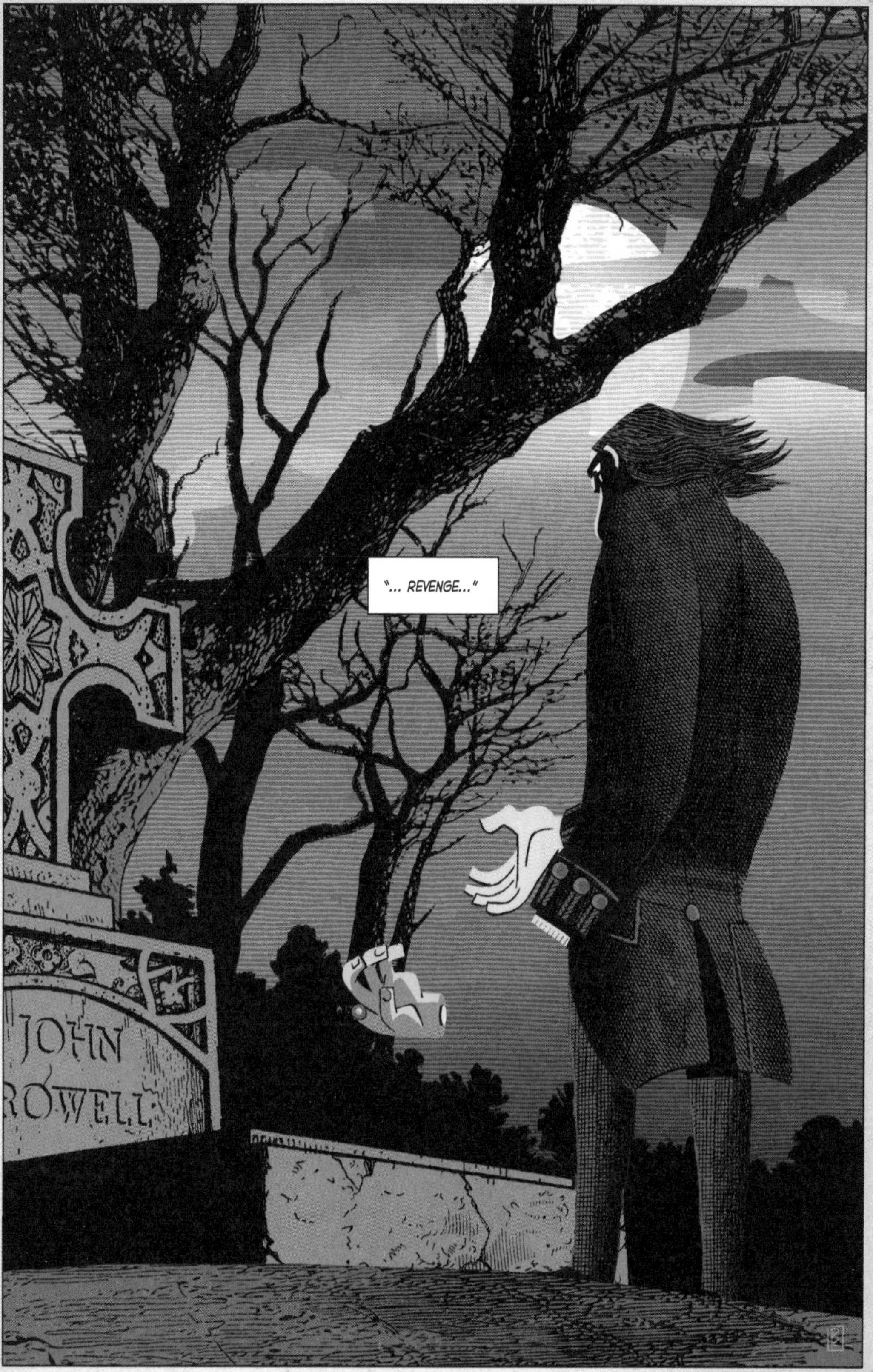
"... REVENGE..."
JOHN
ROWELL

JOSEPH SHERIDAN LE FANU

SIR DOMINICK'S BARGAIN

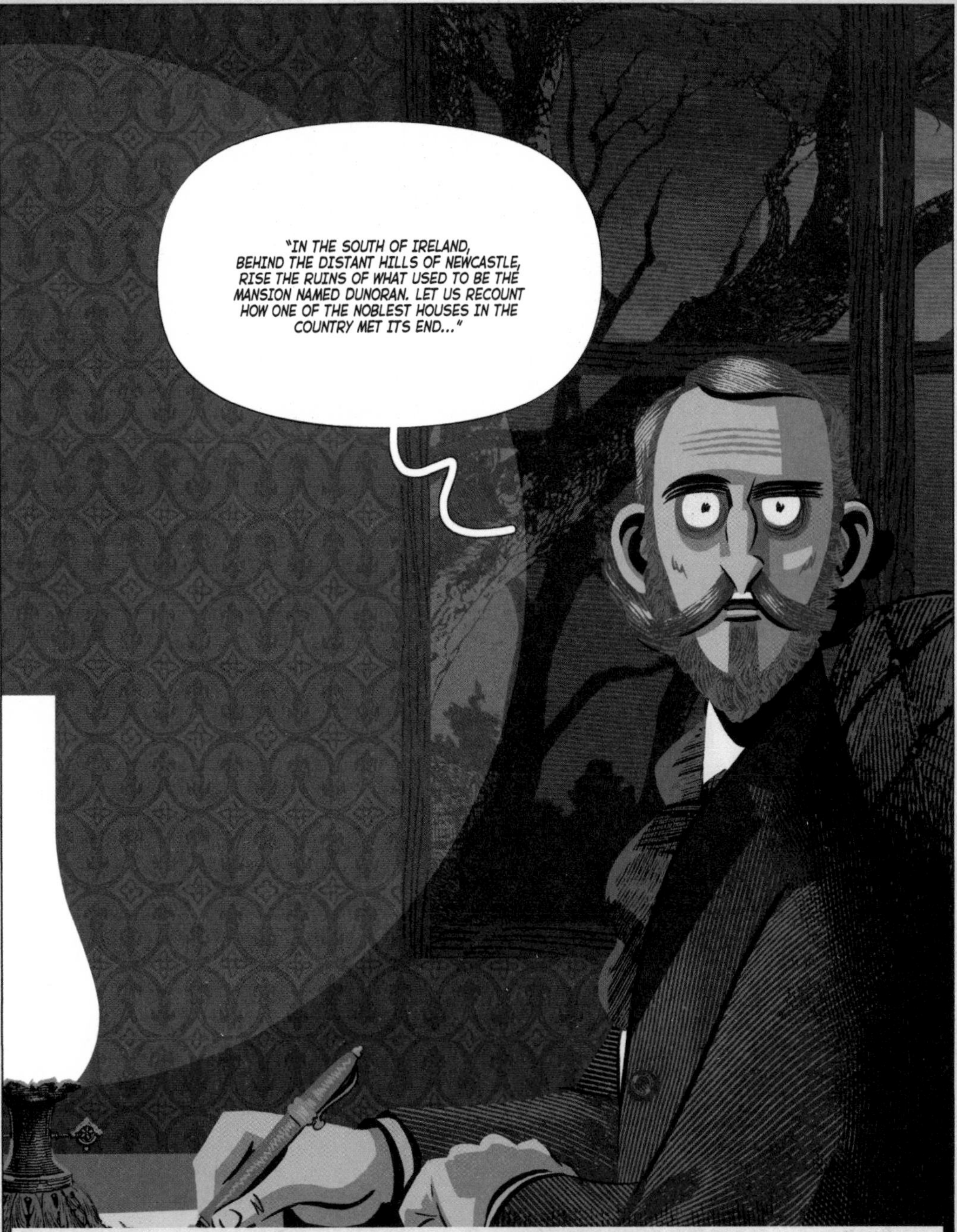
"IN THE SOUTH OF IRELAND, BEHIND THE DISTANT HILLS OF NEWCASTLE, RISE THE RUINS OF WHAT USED TO BE THE MANSION NAMED DUNORAN. LET US RECOUNT HOW ONE OF THE NOBLEST HOUSES IN THE COUNTRY MET ITS END..."

JOSEPH SHERIDAN LE FANU
(1814–1873)

THIS IRISH JOURNALIST ALSO WROTE NOVELS AND SHORT STORIES. AFTER THE DEATH OF HIS WIFE, HE WITHDREW FROM SOCIETY AND WAS NICKNAMED "THE INVISIBLE PRINCE." HIS WORK INFLUENCED ANOTHER GREAT IRISH WRITER: BRAM STOKER (THE AUTHOR OF *DRACULA*).

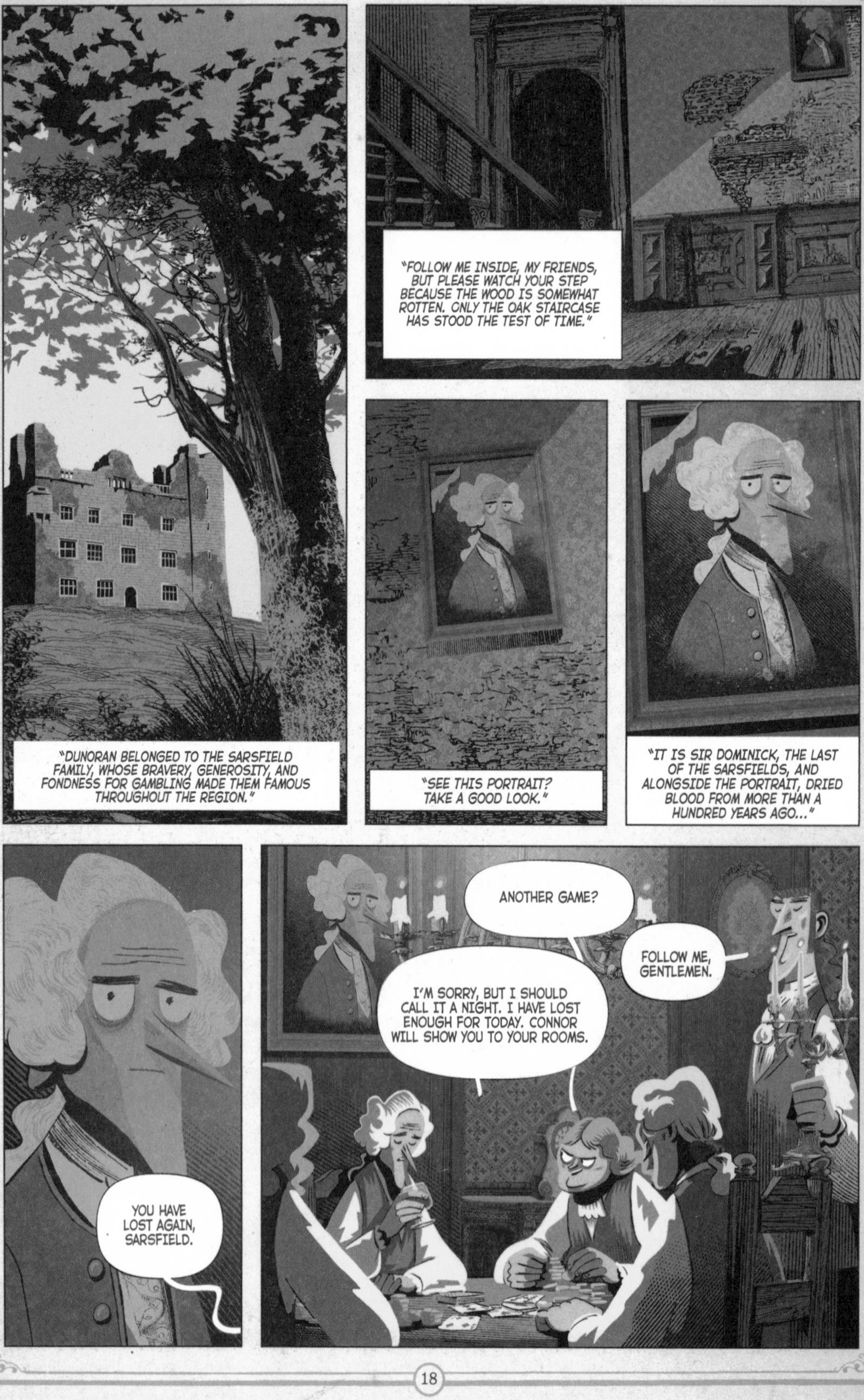
"DUNORAN BELONGED TO THE SARSFIELD FAMILY, WHOSE BRAVERY, GENEROSITY, AND FONDNESS FOR GAMBLING MADE THEM FAMOUS THROUGHOUT THE REGION."
"FOLLOW ME INSIDE, MY FRIENDS, BUT PLEASE WATCH YOUR STEP BECAUSE THE WOOD IS SOMEWHAT ROTTEN. ONLY THE OAK STAIRCASE HAS STOOD THE TEST OF TIME."
"SEE THIS PORTRAIT? TAKE A GOOD LOOK."
"IT IS SIR DOMINICK, THE LAST OF THE SARSFIELDS, AND ALONGSIDE THE PORTRAIT, DRIED BLOOD FROM MORE THAN A HUNDRED YEARS AGO..."
YOU HAVE LOST AGAIN, SARSFIELD.
ANOTHER GAME?
I'M SORRY, BUT I SHOULD CALL IT A NIGHT. I HAVE LOST ENOUGH FOR TODAY. CONNOR WILL SHOW YOU TO YOUR ROOMS.
FOLLOW ME, GENTLEMEN.

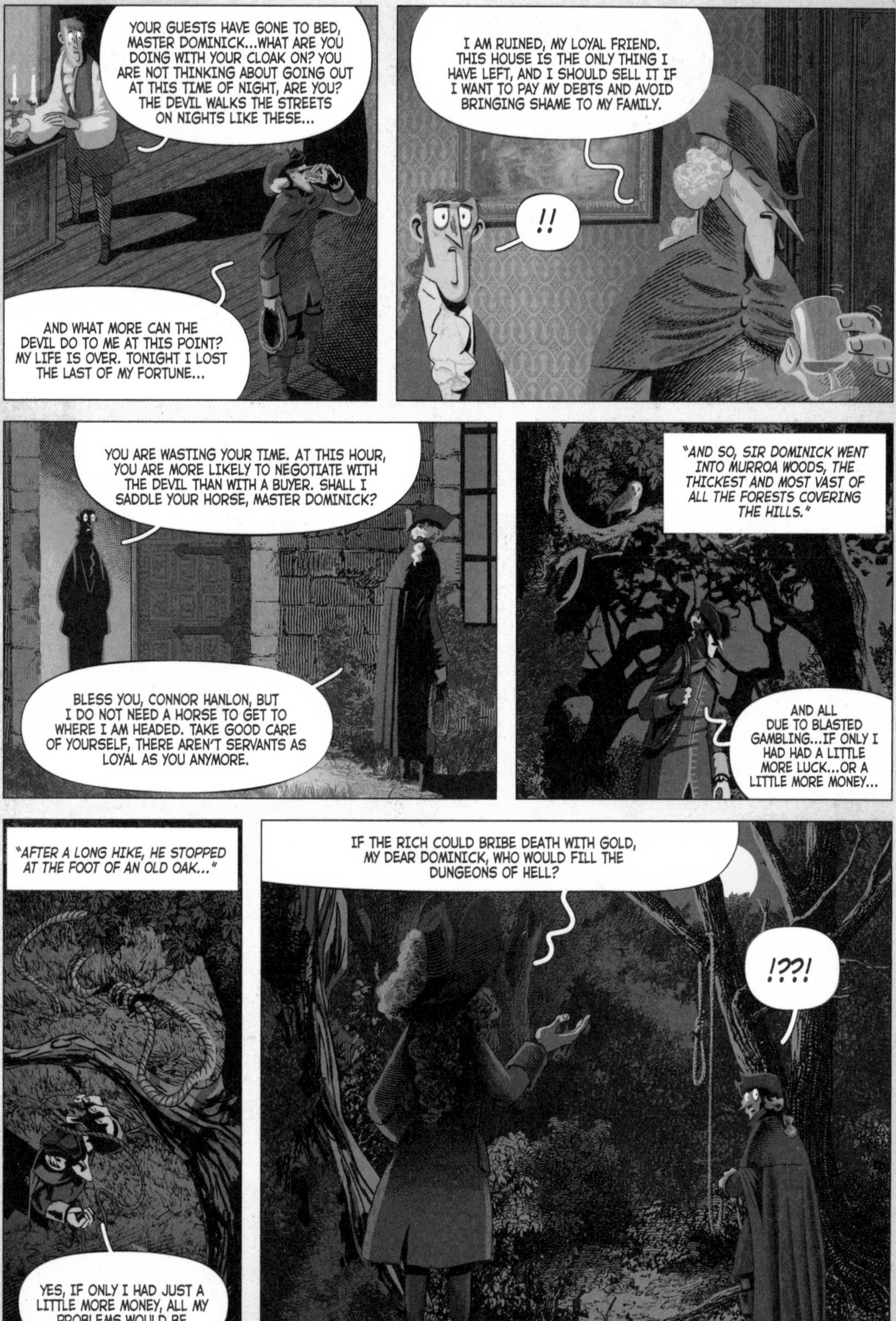
YOUR GUESTS HAVE GONE TO BED, MASTER DOMINICK...WHAT ARE YOU DOING WITH YOUR CLOAK ON? YOU ARE NOT THINKING ABOUT GOING OUT AT THIS TIME OF NIGHT, ARE YOU? THE DEVIL WALKS THE STREETS ON NIGHTS LIKE THESE...
AND WHAT MORE CAN THE DEVIL DO TO ME AT THIS POINT? MY LIFE IS OVER. TONIGHT I LOST THE LAST OF MY FORTUNE...
I AM RUINED, MY LOYAL FRIEND. THIS HOUSE IS THE ONLY THING I HAVE LEFT, AND I SHOULD SELL IT IF I WANT TO PAY MY DEBTS AND AVOID BRINGING SHAME TO MY FAMILY.
!!
YOU ARE WASTING YOUR TIME. AT THIS HOUR, YOU ARE MORE LIKELY TO NEGOTIATE WITH THE DEVIL THAN WITH A BUYER. SHALL I SADDLE YOUR HORSE, MASTER DOMINICK?
BLESS YOU, CONNOR HANLON, BUT I DO NOT NEED A HORSE TO GET TO WHERE I AM HEADED. TAKE GOOD CARE OF YOURSELF, THERE AREN'T SERVANTS AS LOYAL AS YOU ANYMORE.
"AND SO, SIR DOMINICK WENT INTO MURROA WOODS, THE THICKEST AND MOST VAST OF ALL THE FORESTS COVERING THE HILLS."
AND ALL DUE TO BLASTED GAMBLING...IF ONLY I HAD HAD A LITTLE MORE LUCK...OR A LITTLE MORE MONEY...
"AFTER A LONG HIKE, HE STOPPED AT THE FOOT OF AN OLD OAK..."
YES, IF ONLY I HAD JUST A LITTLE MORE MONEY, ALL MY PROBLEMS WOULD BE SOLVED...
IF THE RICH COULD BRIBE DEATH WITH GOLD, MY DEAR DOMINICK, WHO WOULD FILL THE DUNGEONS OF HELL?
!??!

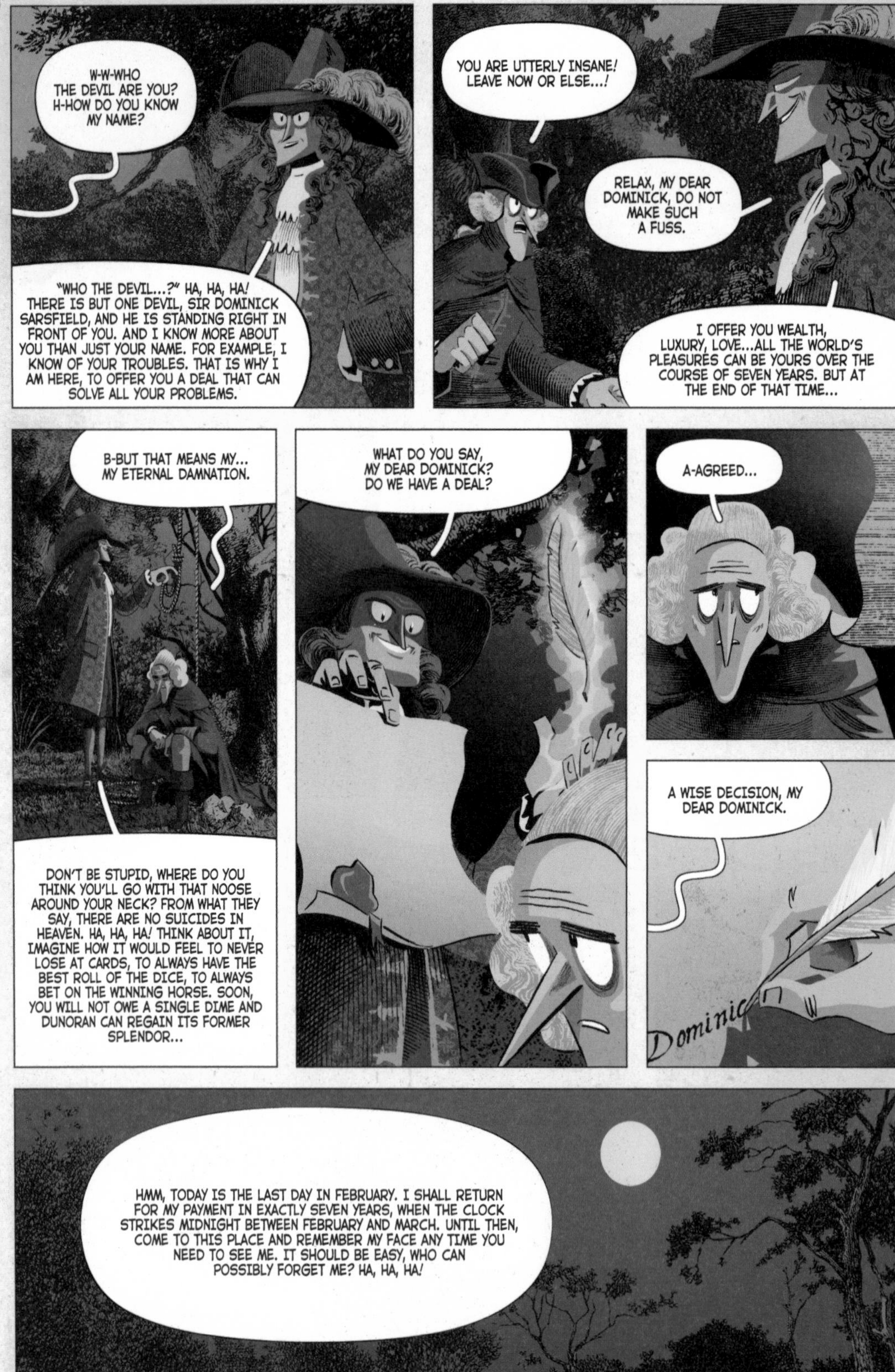
W-W-WHO THE DEVIL ARE YOU? H-HOW DO YOU KNOW MY NAME?
"WHO THE DEVIL...?" HA, HA, HA! THERE IS BUT ONE DEVIL, SIR DOMINICK SARSFIELD, AND HE IS STANDING RIGHT IN FRONT OF YOU. AND I KNOW MORE ABOUT YOU THAN JUST YOUR NAME. FOR EXAMPLE, I KNOW OF YOUR TROUBLES. THAT IS WHY I AM HERE, TO OFFER YOU A DEAL THAT CAN SOLVE ALL YOUR PROBLEMS.
YOU ARE UTTERLY INSANE! LEAVE NOW OR ELSE...!
RELAX, MY DEAR DOMINICK, DO NOT MAKE SUCH A FUSS.
I OFFER YOU WEALTH, LUXURY, LOVE...ALL THE WORLD'S PLEASURES CAN BE YOURS OVER THE COURSE OF SEVEN YEARS. BUT AT THE END OF THAT TIME...
B-BUT THAT MEANS MY... MY ETERNAL DAMNATION.
DON'T BE STUPID, WHERE DO YOU THINK YOU'LL GO WITH THAT NOOSE AROUND YOUR NECK? FROM WHAT THEY SAY, THERE ARE NO SUICIDES IN HEAVEN. HA, HA, HA! THINK ABOUT IT, IMAGINE HOW IT WOULD FEEL TO NEVER LOSE AT CARDS, TO ALWAYS HAVE THE BEST ROLL OF THE DICE, TO ALWAYS BET ON THE WINNING HORSE. SOON, YOU WILL NOT OWE A SINGLE DIME AND DUNORAN CAN REGAIN ITS FORMER SPLENDOR...
WHAT DO YOU SAY, MY DEAR DOMINICK? DO WE HAVE A DEAL?
A-AGREED...
A WISE DECISION, MY DEAR DOMINICK.
Dominic
HMM, TODAY IS THE LAST DAY IN FEBRUARY. I SHALL RETURN FOR MY PAYMENT IN EXACTLY SEVEN YEARS, WHEN THE CLOCK STRIKES MIDNIGHT BETWEEN FEBRUARY AND MARCH. UNTIL THEN, COME TO THIS PLACE AND REMEMBER MY FACE ANY TIME YOU NEED TO SEE ME. IT SHOULD BE EASY, WHO CAN POSSIBLY FORGET ME? HA, HA, HA!

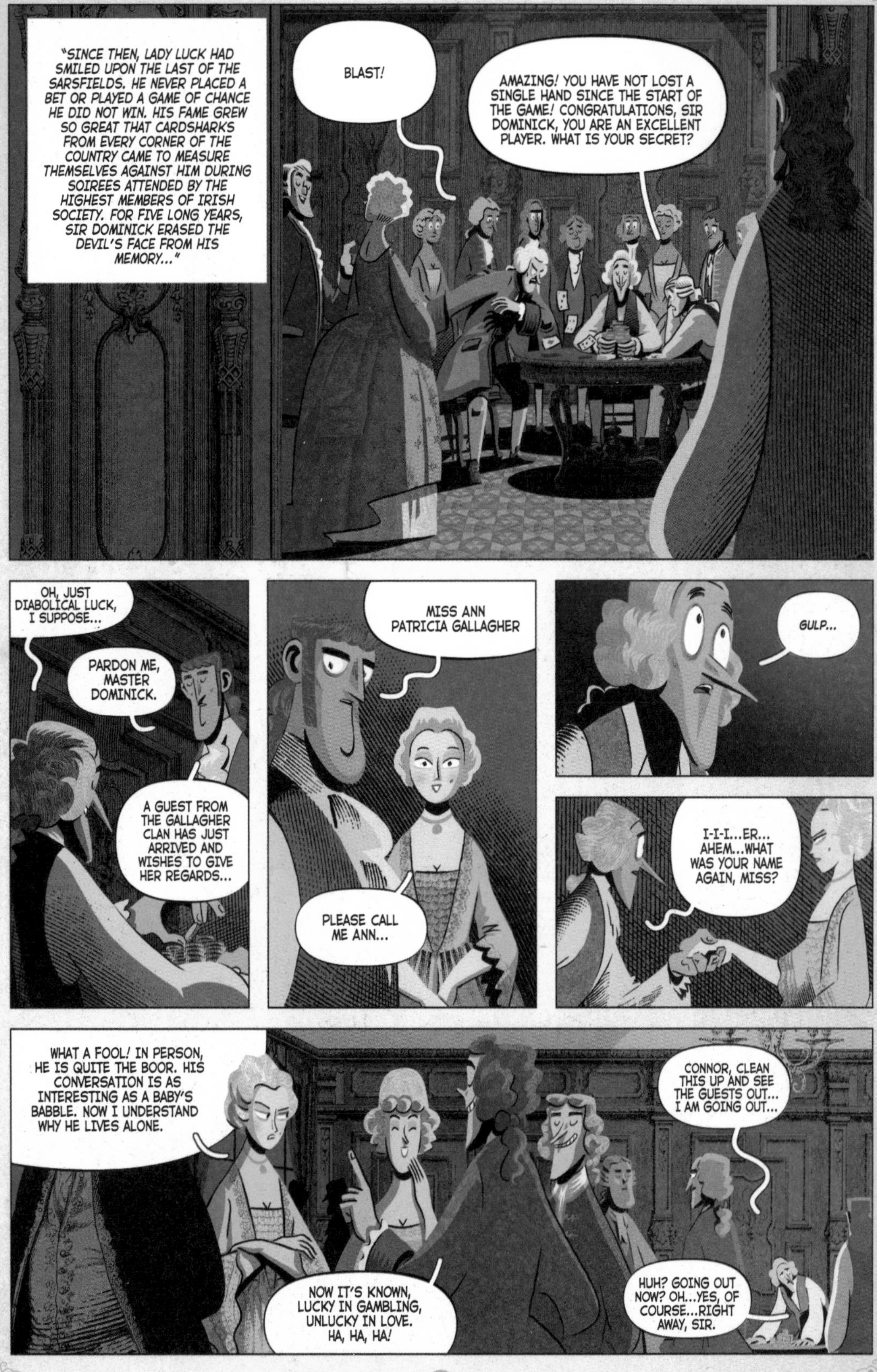
"SINCE THEN, LADY LUCK HAD SMILED UPON THE LAST OF THE SARSFIELDS. HE NEVER PLACED A BET OR PLAYED A GAME OF CHANCE HE DID NOT WIN. HIS FAME GREW SO GREAT THAT CARDSHARKS FROM EVERY CORNER OF THE COUNTRY CAME TO MEASURE THEMSELVES AGAINST HIM DURING SOIREES ATTENDED BY THE HIGHEST MEMBERS OF IRISH SOCIETY. FOR FIVE LONG YEARS, SIR DOMINICK ERASED THE DEVIL'S FACE FROM HIS MEMORY..."
BLAST!
AMAZING! YOU HAVE NOT LOST A SINGLE HAND SINCE THE START OF THE GAME! CONGRATULATIONS, SIR DOMINICK, YOU ARE AN EXCELLENT PLAYER. WHAT IS YOUR SECRET?
OH, JUST DIABOLICAL LUCK, I SUPPOSE...
PARDON ME, MASTER DOMINICK.
A GUEST FROM THE GALLAGHER CLAN HAS JUST ARRIVED AND WISHES TO GIVE HER REGARDS...
MISS ANN PATRICIA GALLAGHER
PLEASE CALL ME ANN...
GULP...
I-I-I...ER... AHEM...WHAT WAS YOUR NAME AGAIN, MISS?
WHAT A FOOL! IN PERSON, HE IS QUITE THE BOOR. HIS CONVERSATION IS AS INTERESTING AS A BABY'S BABBLE. NOW I UNDERSTAND WHY HE LIVES ALONE.
NOW IT'S KNOWN, LUCKY IN GAMBLING, UNLUCKY IN LOVE. HA, HA, HA!
CONNOR, CLEAN THIS UP AND SEE THE GUESTS OUT... I AM GOING OUT...
HUH? GOING OUT NOW? OH...YES, OF COURSE...RIGHT AWAY, SIR.

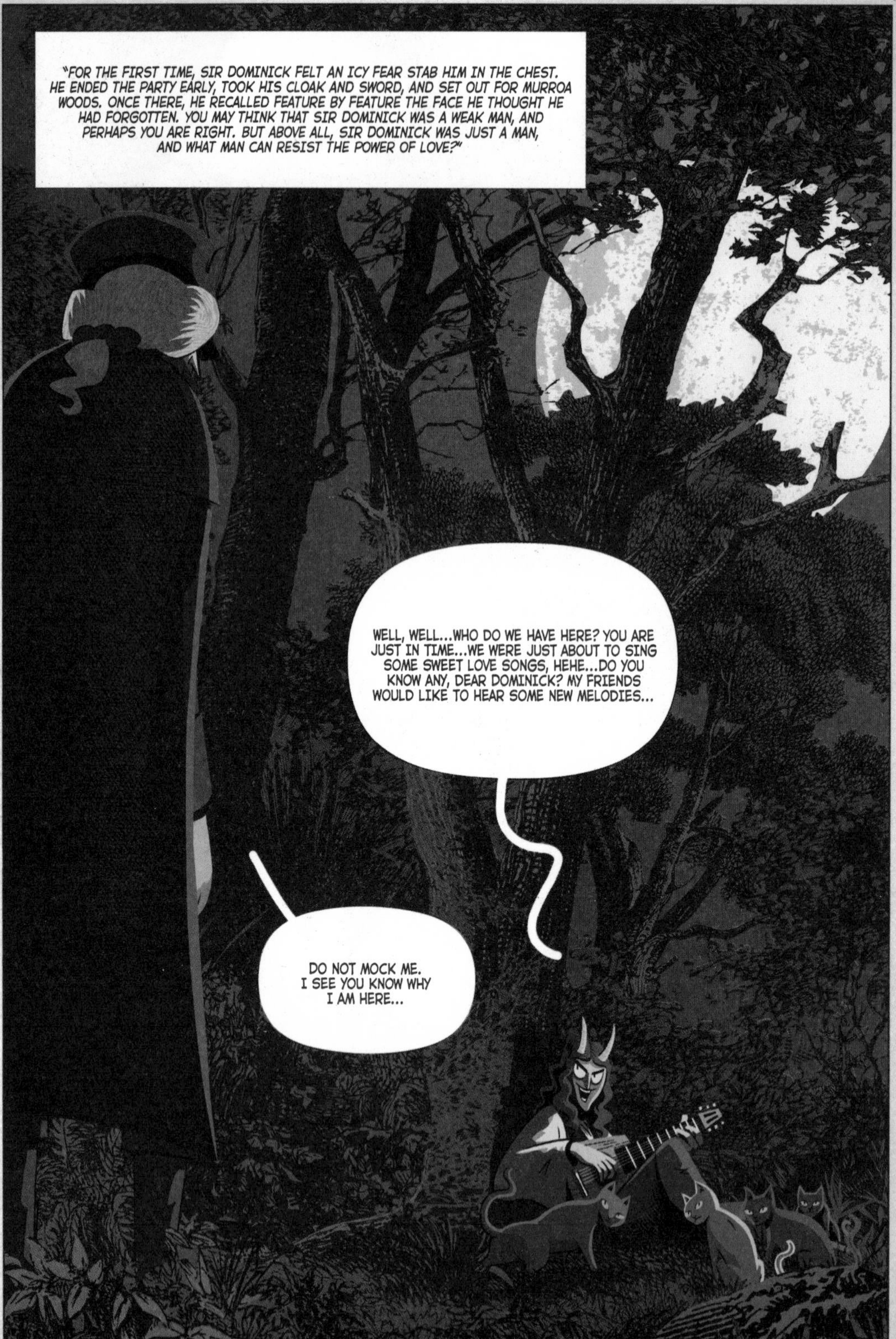
"FOR THE FIRST TIME, SIR DOMINICK FELT AN ICY FEAR STAB HIM IN THE CHEST. HE ENDED THE PARTY EARLY, TOOK HIS CLOAK AND SWORD, AND SET OUT FOR MURROA WOODS. ONCE THERE, HE RECALLED FEATURE BY FEATURE THE FACE HE THOUGHT HE HAD FORGOTTEN. YOU MAY THINK THAT SIR DOMINICK WAS A WEAK MAN, AND PERHAPS YOU ARE RIGHT. BUT ABOVE ALL, SIR DOMINICK WAS JUST A MAN, AND WHAT MAN CAN RESIST THE POWER OF LOVE?"
WELL, WELL...WHO DO WE HAVE HERE? YOU ARE JUST IN TIME...WE WERE JUST ABOUT TO SING SOME SWEET LOVE SONGS, HEHE...DO YOU KNOW ANY, DEAR DOMINICK? MY FRIENDS WOULD LIKE TO HEAR SOME NEW MELODIES...
DO NOT MOCK ME. I SEE YOU KNOW WHY I AM HERE...

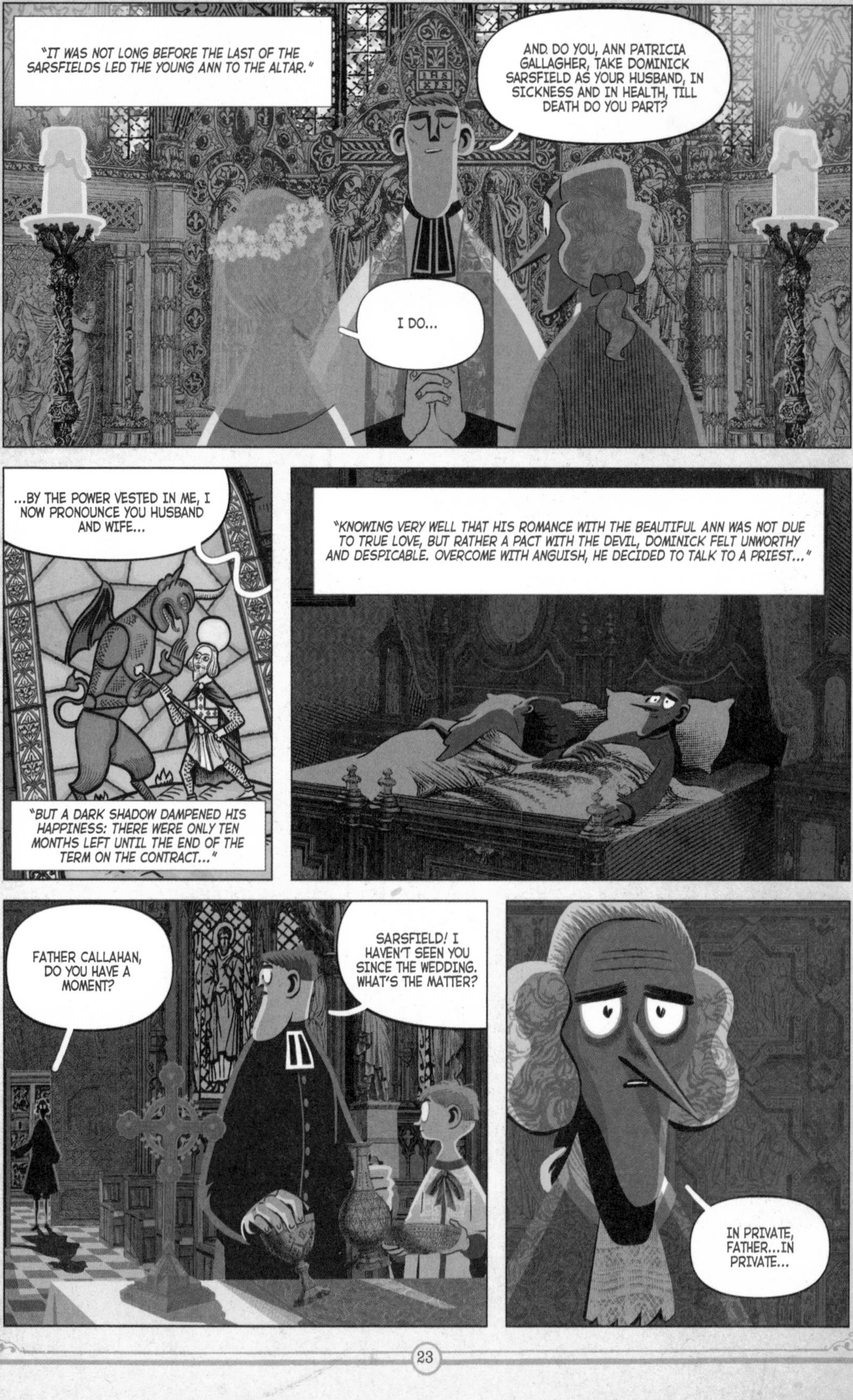
"IT WAS NOT LONG BEFORE THE LAST OF THE SARSFIELDS LED THE YOUNG ANN TO THE ALTAR."
AND DO YOU, ANN PATRICIA GALLAGHER, TAKE DOMINICK SARSFIELD AS YOUR HUSBAND, IN SICKNESS AND IN HEALTH, TILL DEATH DO YOU PART?
I DO...
...BY THE POWER VESTED IN ME, I NOW PRONOUNCE YOU HUSBAND AND WIFE...
"BUT A DARK SHADOW DAMPENED HIS HAPPINESS: THERE WERE ONLY TEN MONTHS LEFT UNTIL THE END OF THE TERM ON THE CONTRACT..."
"KNOWING VERY WELL THAT HIS ROMANCE WITH THE BEAUTIFUL ANN WAS NOT DUE TO TRUE LOVE, BUT RATHER A PACT WITH THE DEVIL, DOMINICK FELT UNWORTHY AND DESPICABLE. OVERCOME WITH ANGUISH, HE DECIDED TO TALK TO A PRIEST..."
FATHER CALLAHAN, DO YOU HAVE A MOMENT?
SARSFIELD! I HAVEN'T SEEN YOU SINCE THE WEDDING. WHAT'S THE MATTER?
IN PRIVATE, FATHER...IN PRIVATE...

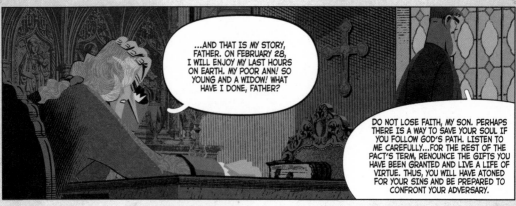

...AND THAT IS MY STORY, FATHER. ON FEBRUARY 28, I WILL ENJOY MY LAST HOURS ON EARTH. MY POOR ANN! SO YOUNG AND A WIDOW! WHAT HAVE I DONE, FATHER?

DO NOT LOSE FAITH, MY SON. PERHAPS THERE IS A WAY TO SAVE YOUR SOUL IF YOU FOLLOW GOD'S PATH. LISTEN TO ME CAREFULLY...FOR THE REST OF THE PACT'S TERM, RENOUNCE THE GIFTS YOU HAVE BEEN GRANTED AND LIVE A LIFE OF VIRTUE. THUS, YOU WILL HAVE ATONED FOR YOUR SINS AND BE PREPARED TO CONFRONT YOUR ADVERSARY.

YOU ARE NOT ALONE, MY SON. WE WILL DO THIS TOGETHER. I AM A SERVANT OF GOD. PERHAPS THAT WILL INTIMIDATE HIM AND HE WILL NEVER SHOW TO COLLECT. IF THAT HAPPENS, HE WILL LOSE HIS HOLD OVER YOU AND YOU WILL BE FREE FOREVER...

"FOLLOWING THE PRIEST'S ADVICE, SIR DOMINICK GAVE UP GAMBLING, GREED, AND HIS UNSAVORY ACQUAINTANCES. THE MOST PAINFUL OF ALL WAS GIVING UP LADY ANN..."

I-I-I DON'T UNDERSTAND, MY LOVE, WHY ARE YOU DOING THIS? HAVE YOU STOPPED LOVING ME?

OF COURSE I STILL LOVE YOU, MY ANGEL. THERE IS JUST SOMETHING I HAVE TO DO... AND I HAVE TO DO IT ALONE. YOU WILL BE BETTER OFF AT YOUR PARENTS' HOUSE. ON THE FIRST OF MARCH, YOU WILL BE BACK HERE WITH ME AND THEN NOTHING CAN COME BETWEEN US. I GIVE YOU MY WORD...

I DON'T KNOW WHAT YOU HAVE GOTTEN YOURSELF INTO, DOMINICK, BUT IF THIS IS WHAT YOU WANT...THIS IS HOW IT WILL BE. UNTIL THE FIRST OF MARCH...

MAY GOD HEAR YOU, MY LOVE...MAY GOD HEAR YOU...

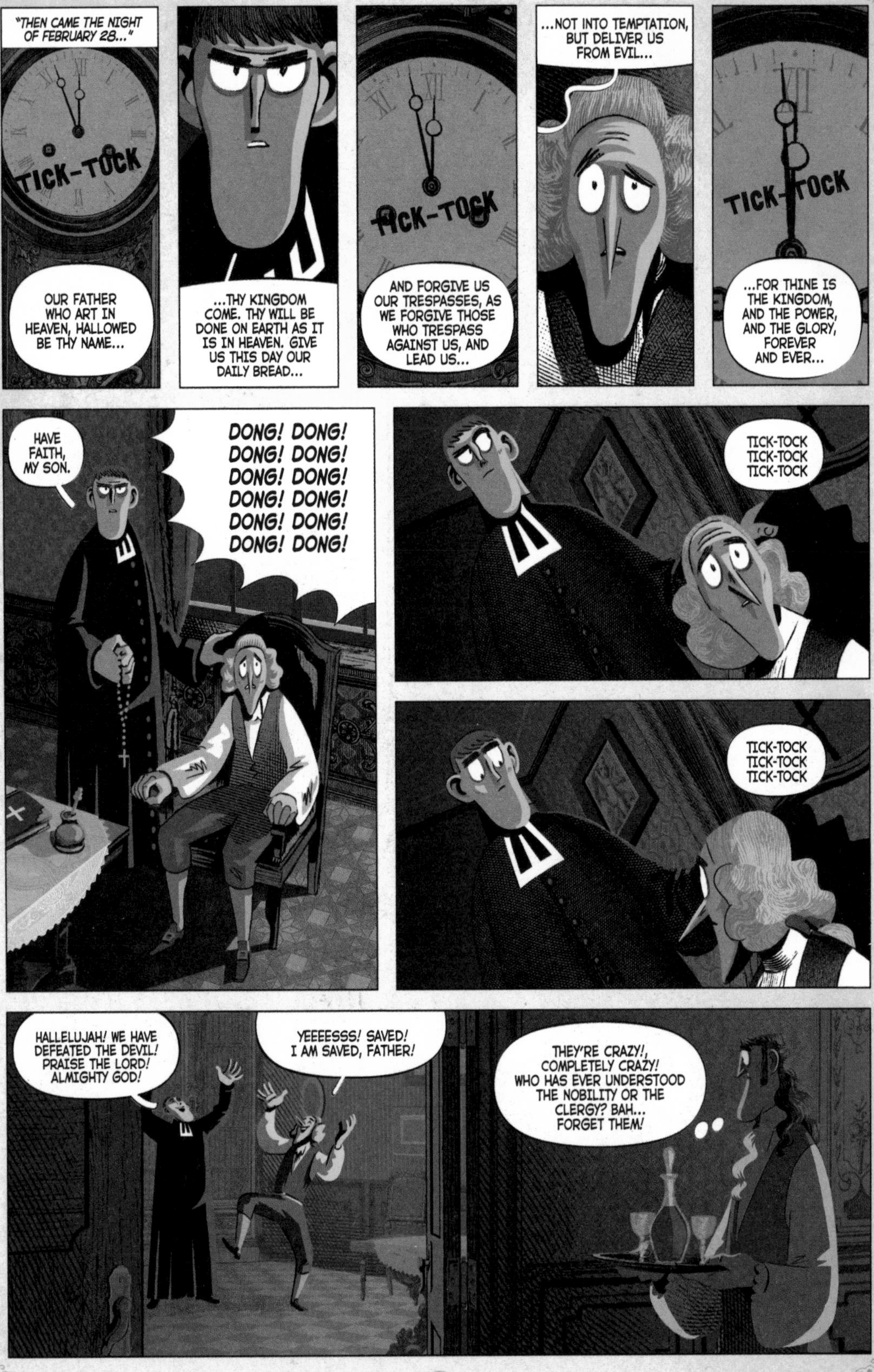
"THEN CAME THE NIGHT OF FEBRUARY 28..."
TICK-TOCK
OUR FATHER WHO ART IN HEAVEN, HALLOWED BE THY NAME...
...THY KINGDOM COME. THY WILL BE DONE ON EARTH AS IT IS IN HEAVEN. GIVE US THIS DAY OUR DAILY BREAD...
TICK-TOCK
AND FORGIVE US OUR TRESPASSES, AS WE FORGIVE THOSE WHO TRESPASS AGAINST US, AND LEAD US...
...NOT INTO TEMPTATION, BUT DELIVER US FROM EVIL...
TICK-TOCK
...FOR THINE IS THE KINGDOM, AND THE POWER, AND THE GLORY, FOREVER AND EVER...
HAVE FAITH, MY SON.
DONG! DONG! DONG! DONG! DONG! DONG! DONG! DONG! DONG! DONG! DONG! DONG!
TICK-TOCK TICK-TOCK TICK-TOCK
TICK-TOCK TICK-TOCK TICK-TOCK
HALLELUJAH! WE HAVE DEFEATED THE DEVIL! PRAISE THE LORD! ALMIGHTY GOD!
YEEEESSS! SAVED! I AM SAVED, FATHER!
THEY'RE CRAZY!, COMPLETELY CRAZY! WHO HAS EVER UNDERSTOOD THE NOBILITY OR THE CLERGY? BAH... FORGET THEM!

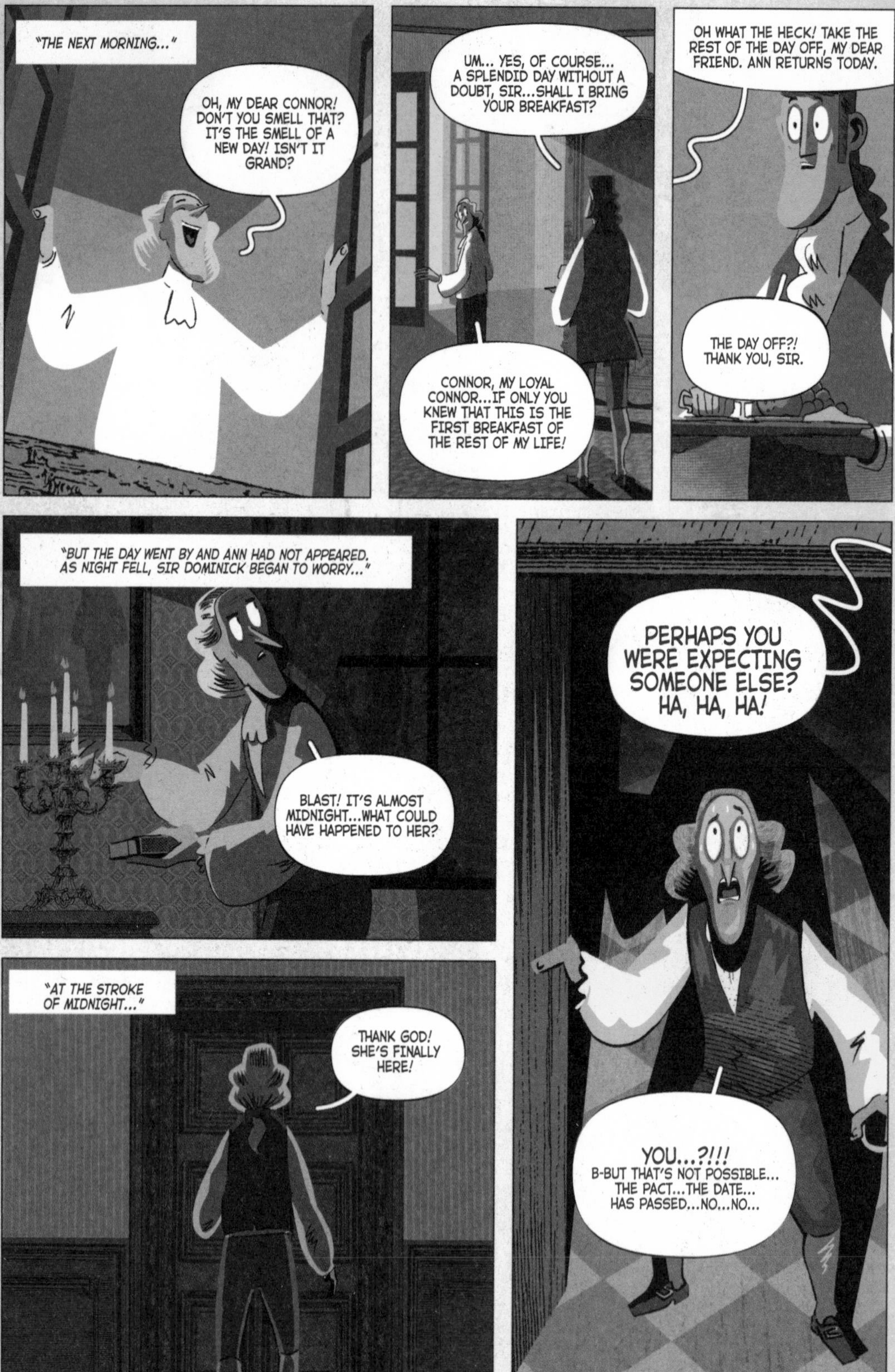
"THE NEXT MORNING..."
OH, MY DEAR CONNOR! DON'T YOU SMELL THAT? IT'S THE SMELL OF A NEW DAY! ISN'T IT GRAND?
UM... YES, OF COURSE... A SPLENDID DAY WITHOUT A DOUBT, SIR...SHALL I BRING YOUR BREAKFAST?
CONNOR, MY LOYAL CONNOR...IF ONLY YOU KNEW THAT THIS IS THE FIRST BREAKFAST OF THE REST OF MY LIFE!
OH WHAT THE HECK! TAKE THE REST OF THE DAY OFF, MY DEAR FRIEND. ANN RETURNS TODAY.
THE DAY OFF?! THANK YOU, SIR.
"BUT THE DAY WENT BY AND ANN HAD NOT APPEARED. AS NIGHT FELL, SIR DOMINICK BEGAN TO WORRY..."
BLAST! IT'S ALMOST MIDNIGHT...WHAT COULD HAVE HAPPENED TO HER?
"AT THE STROKE OF MIDNIGHT..."
THANK GOD! SHE'S FINALLY HERE!
PERHAPS YOU WERE EXPECTING SOMEONE ELSE? HA, HA, HA!
YOU...?!!!
B-BUT THAT'S NOT POSSIBLE... THE PACT...THE DATE... HAS PASSED...NO...NO...

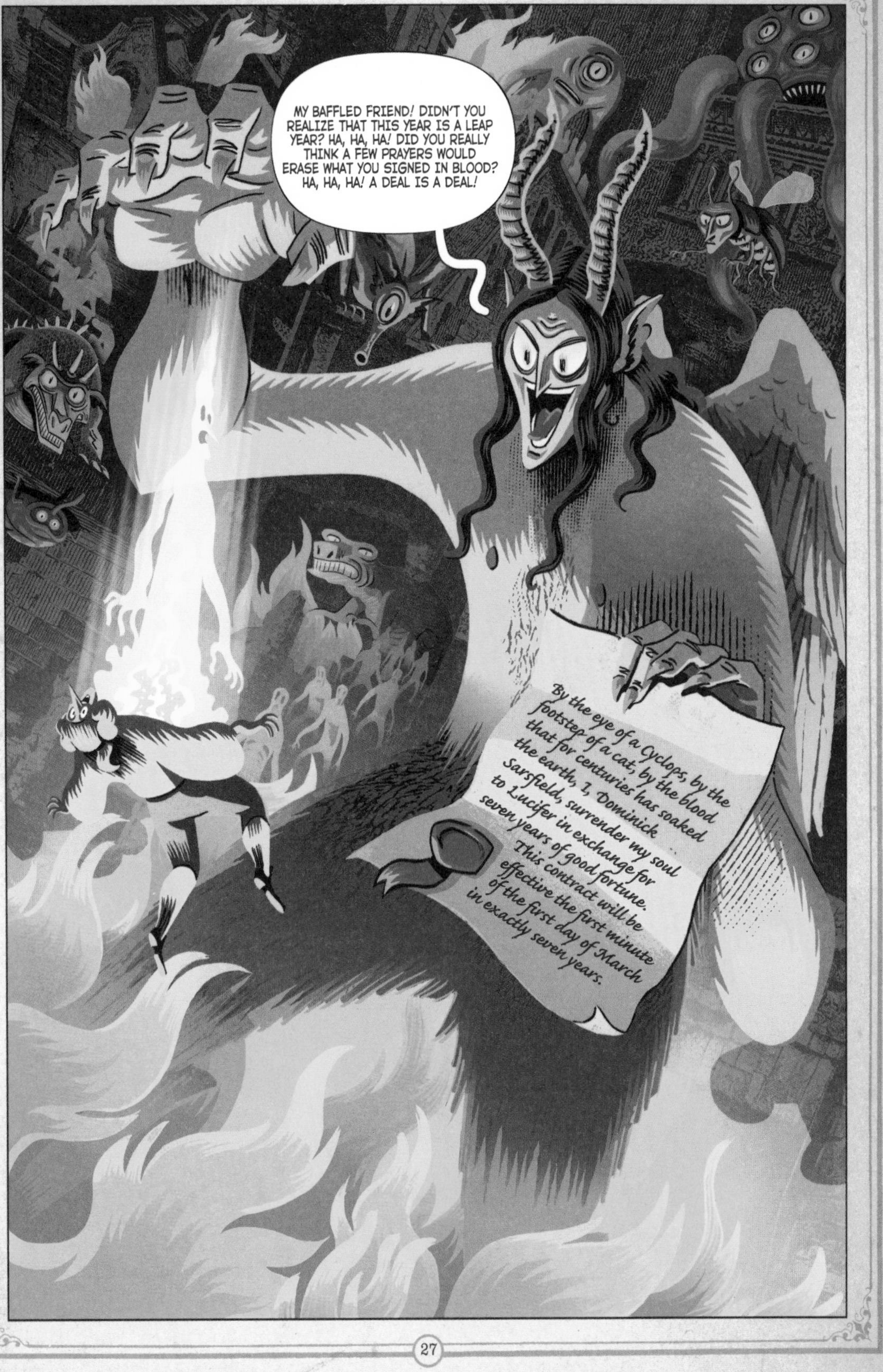
MY BAFFLED FRIEND! DIDN'T YOU REALIZE THAT THIS YEAR IS A LEAP YEAR? HA, HA, HA! DID YOU REALLY THINK A FEW PRAYERS WOULD ERASE WHAT YOU SIGNED IN BLOOD? HA, HA, HA! A DEAL IS A DEAL!
By the eye of a Cyclops, by the footstep of a cat, by the blood that for centuries has soaked the earth, I, Dominick Sarsfield, surrender my soul to Lucifer in exchange for seven years of good fortune. This contract will be effective the first minute of the first day of March in exactly seven years.

EDWARD LUCAS WHITE

THE HOUSE OF NIGHTMARE

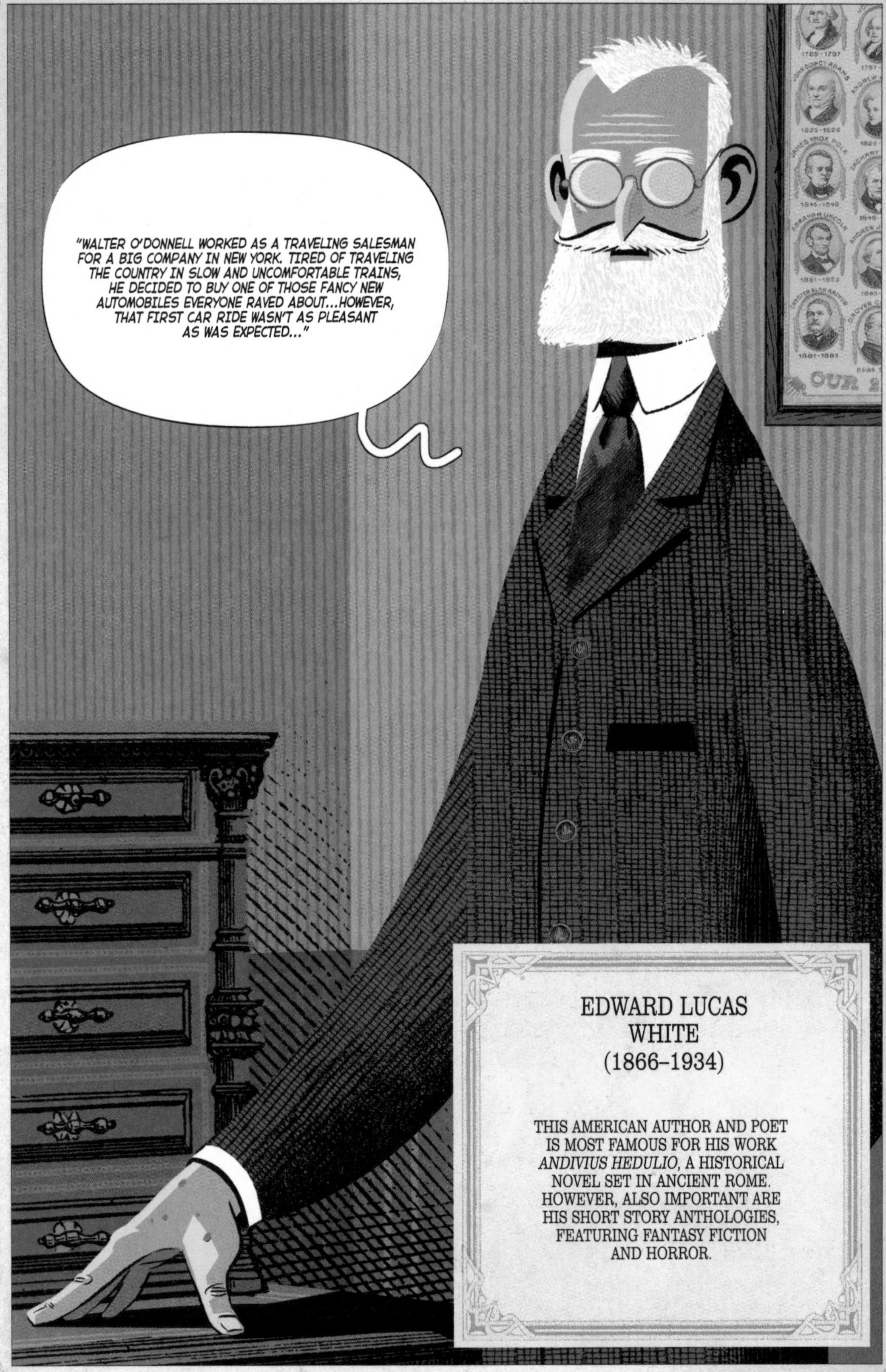
"WALTER O'DONNELL WORKED AS A TRAVELING SALESMAN FOR A BIG COMPANY IN NEW YORK. TIRED OF TRAVELING THE COUNTRY IN SLOW AND UNCOMFORTABLE TRAINS, HE DECIDED TO BUY ONE OF THOSE FANCY NEW AUTOMOBILES EVERYONE RAVED ABOUT...HOWEVER, THAT FIRST CAR RIDE WASN'T AS PLEASANT AS WAS EXPECTED..."
EDWARD LUCAS WHITE (1866–1934)
THIS AMERICAN AUTHOR AND POET IS MOST FAMOUS FOR HIS WORK *ANDIVIUS HEDULIO,* A HISTORICAL NOVEL SET IN ANCIENT ROME. HOWEVER, ALSO IMPORTANT ARE HIS SHORT STORY ANTHOLOGIES, FEATURING FANTASY FICTION AND HORROR.

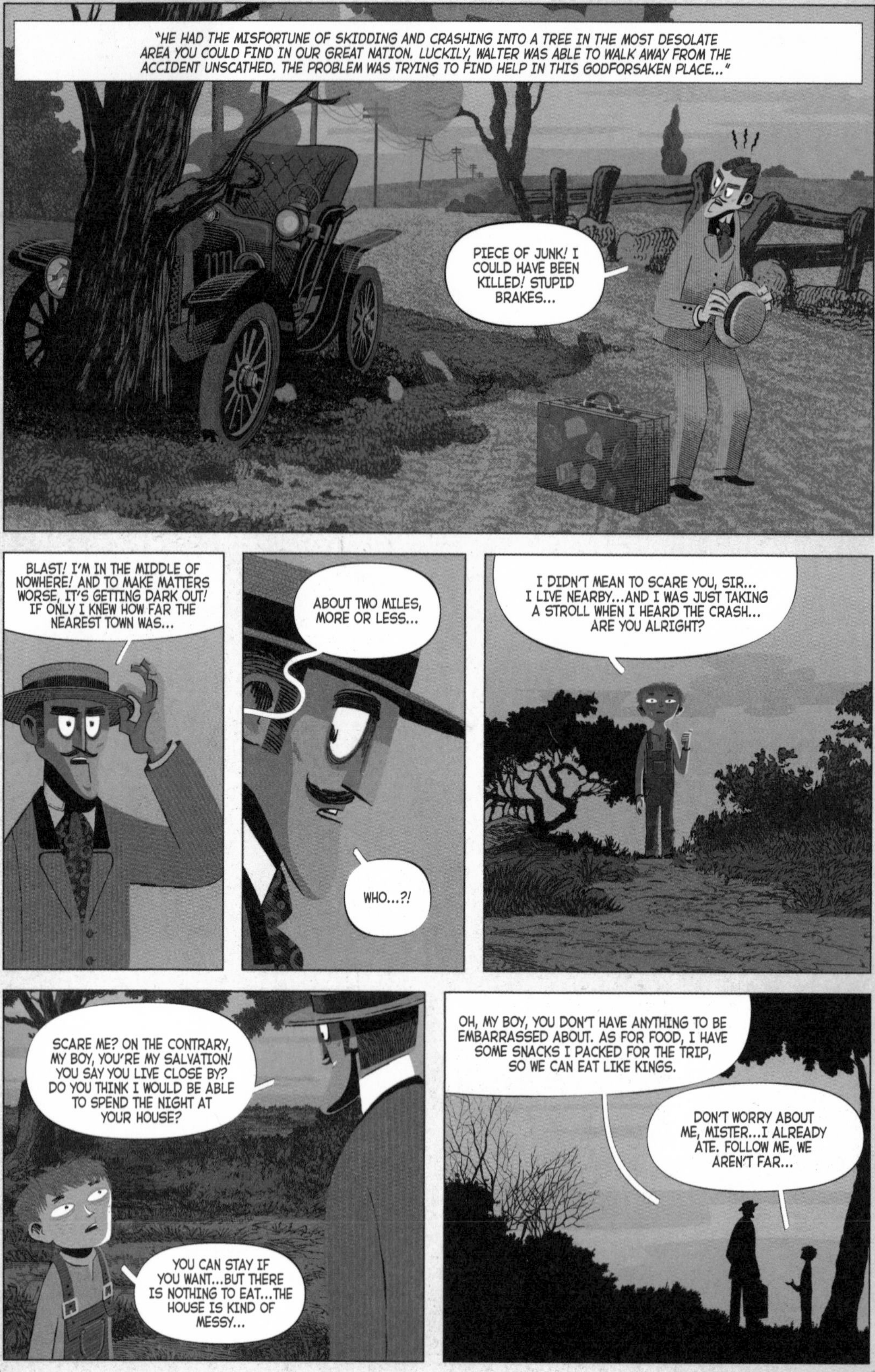
"HE HAD THE MISFORTUNE OF SKIDDING AND CRASHING INTO A TREE IN THE MOST DESOLATE AREA YOU COULD FIND IN OUR GREAT NATION. LUCKILY, WALTER WAS ABLE TO WALK AWAY FROM THE ACCIDENT UNSCATHED. THE PROBLEM WAS TRYING TO FIND HELP IN THIS GODFORSAKEN PLACE..."
PIECE OF JUNK! I COULD HAVE BEEN KILLED! STUPID BRAKES...
BLAST! I'M IN THE MIDDLE OF NOWHERE! AND TO MAKE MATTERS WORSE, IT'S GETTING DARK OUT! IF ONLY I KNEW HOW FAR THE NEAREST TOWN WAS...
ABOUT TWO MILES, MORE OR LESS...
WHO...?!
I DIDN'T MEAN TO SCARE YOU, SIR... I LIVE NEARBY...AND I WAS JUST TAKING A STROLL WHEN I HEARD THE CRASH... ARE YOU ALRIGHT?
SCARE ME? ON THE CONTRARY, MY BOY, YOU'RE MY SALVATION! YOU SAY YOU LIVE CLOSE BY? DO YOU THINK I WOULD BE ABLE TO SPEND THE NIGHT AT YOUR HOUSE?
YOU CAN STAY IF YOU WANT...BUT THERE IS NOTHING TO EAT...THE HOUSE IS KIND OF MESSY...
OH, MY BOY, YOU DON'T HAVE ANYTHING TO BE EMBARRASSED ABOUT. AS FOR FOOD, I HAVE SOME SNACKS I PACKED FOR THE TRIP, SO WE CAN EAT LIKE KINGS.
DON'T WORRY ABOUT ME, MISTER...I ALREADY ATE. FOLLOW ME, WE AREN'T FAR...

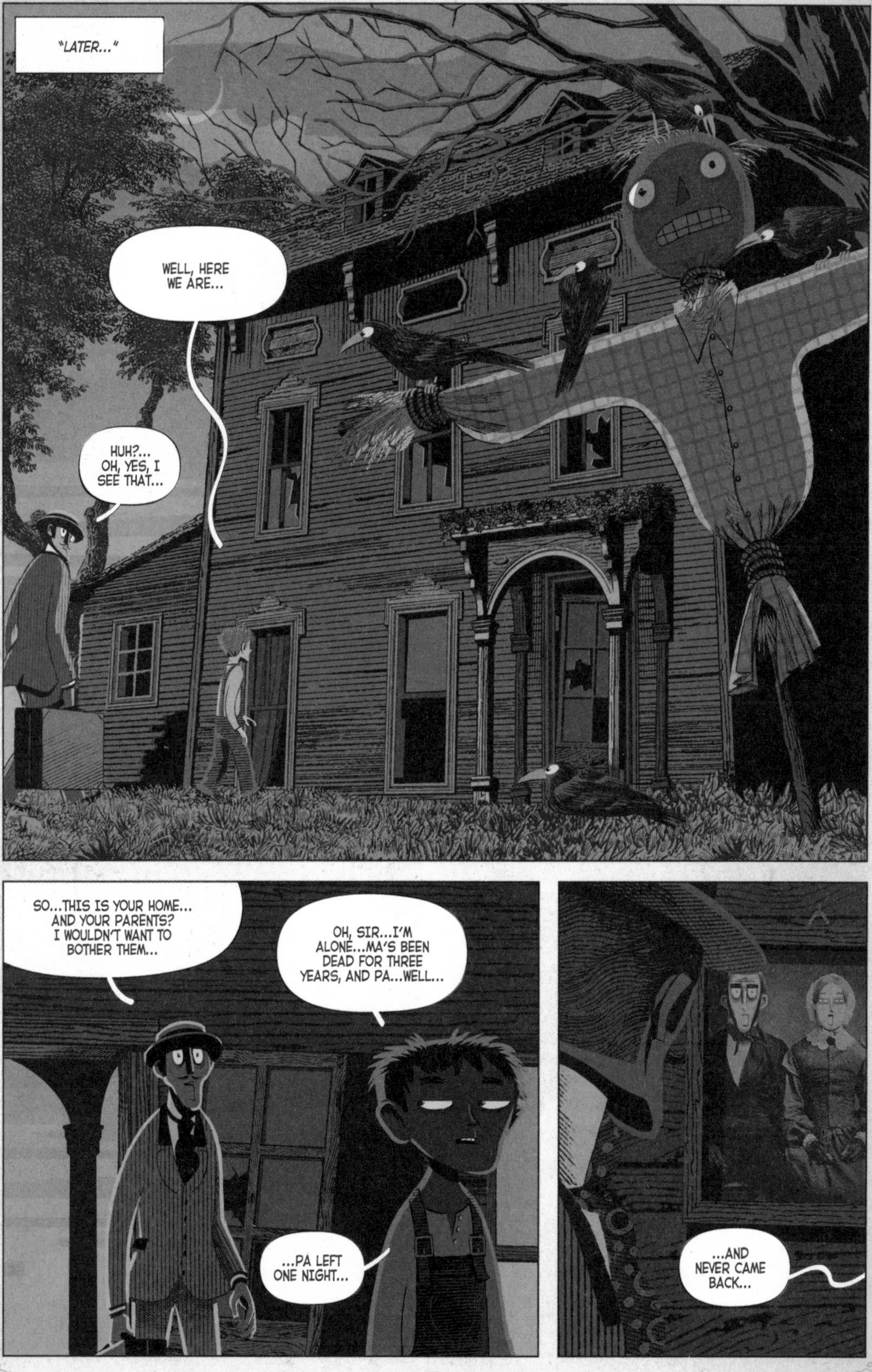
"LATER..."
WELL, HERE WE ARE...
HUH?... OH, YES, I SEE THAT...
SO...THIS IS YOUR HOME... AND YOUR PARENTS? I WOULDN'T WANT TO BOTHER THEM...
OH, SIR...I'M ALONE...MA'S BEEN DEAD FOR THREE YEARS, AND PA...WELL...
...PA LEFT ONE NIGHT...
...AND NEVER CAME BACK...

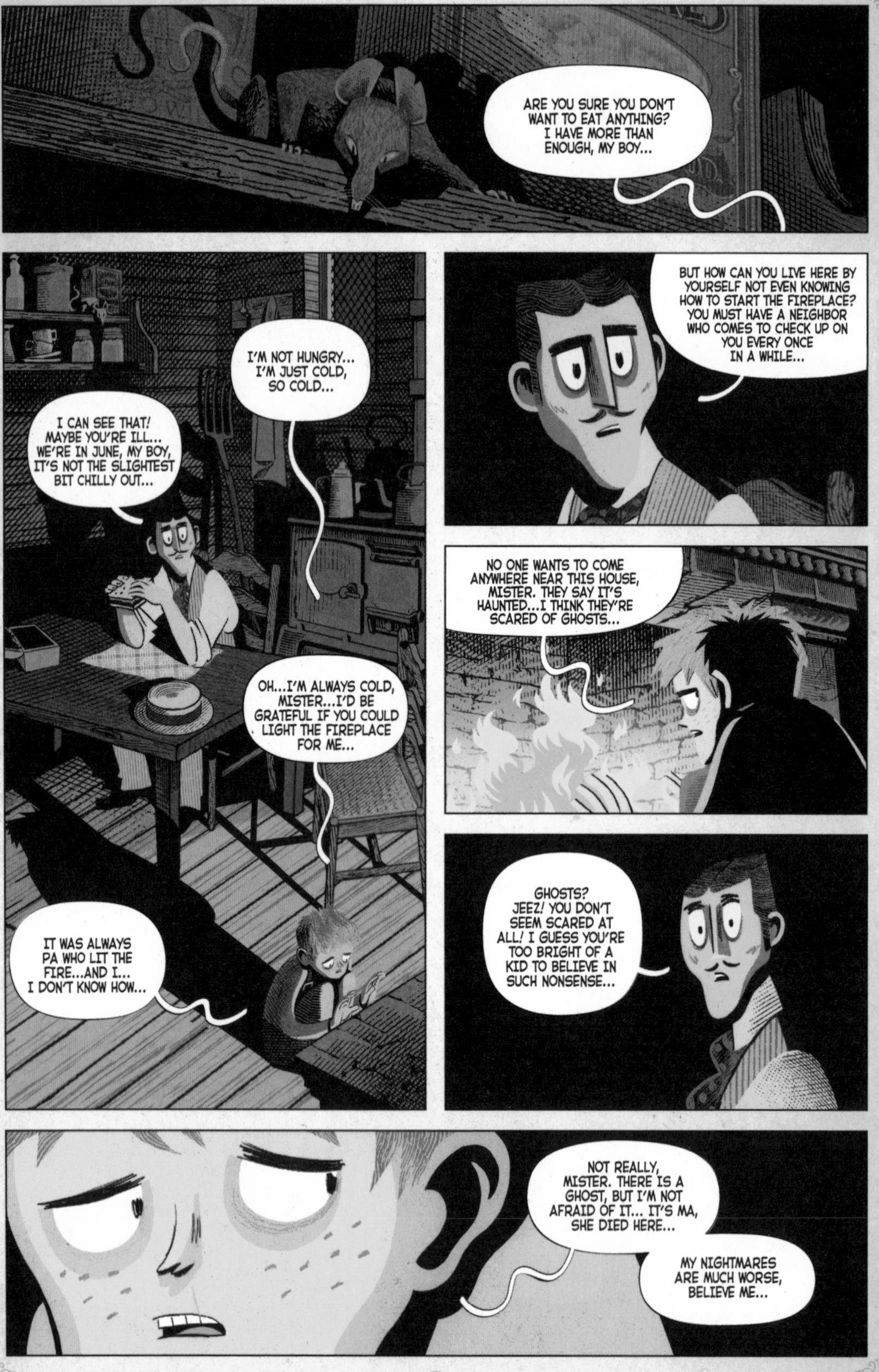
ARE YOU SURE YOU DON'T WANT TO EAT ANYTHING? I HAVE MORE THAN ENOUGH, MY BOY...
I'M NOT HUNGRY... I'M JUST COLD, SO COLD...
I CAN SEE THAT! MAYBE YOU'RE ILL... WE'RE IN JUNE, MY BOY, IT'S NOT THE SLIGHTEST BIT CHILLY OUT...
OH...I'M ALWAYS COLD, MISTER...I'D BE GRATEFUL IF YOU COULD LIGHT THE FIREPLACE FOR ME...
IT WAS ALWAYS PA WHO LIT THE FIRE...AND I... I DON'T KNOW HOW...
BUT HOW CAN YOU LIVE HERE BY YOURSELF NOT EVEN KNOWING HOW TO START THE FIREPLACE? YOU MUST HAVE A NEIGHBOR WHO COMES TO CHECK UP ON YOU EVERY ONCE IN A WHILE...
NO ONE WANTS TO COME ANYWHERE NEAR THIS HOUSE, MISTER. THEY SAY IT'S HAUNTED...I THINK THEY'RE SCARED OF GHOSTS...
GHOSTS? JEEZ! YOU DON'T SEEM SCARED AT ALL! I GUESS YOU'RE TOO BRIGHT OF A KID TO BELIEVE IN SUCH NONSENSE...
NOT REALLY, MISTER. THERE IS A GHOST, BUT I'M NOT AFRAID OF IT... IT'S MA, SHE DIED HERE...
MY NIGHTMARES ARE MUCH WORSE, BELIEVE ME...

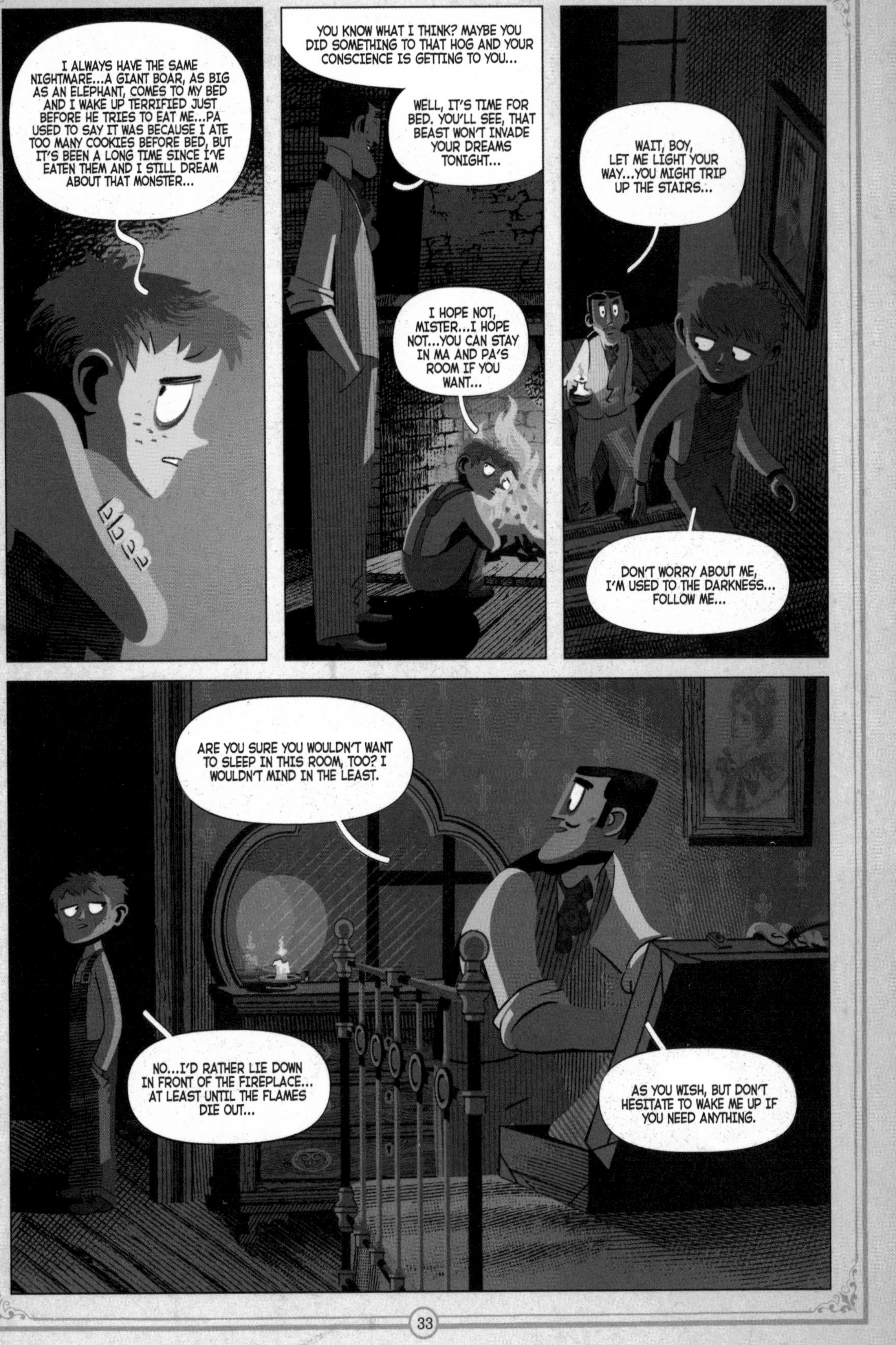
I ALWAYS HAVE THE SAME NIGHTMARE...A GIANT BOAR, AS BIG AS AN ELEPHANT, COMES TO MY BED AND I WAKE UP TERRIFIED JUST BEFORE HE TRIES TO EAT ME...PA USED TO SAY IT WAS BECAUSE I ATE TOO MANY COOKIES BEFORE BED, BUT IT'S BEEN A LONG TIME SINCE I'VE EATEN THEM AND I STILL DREAM ABOUT THAT MONSTER...
YOU KNOW WHAT I THINK? MAYBE YOU DID SOMETHING TO THAT HOG AND YOUR CONSCIENCE IS GETTING TO YOU...
WELL, IT'S TIME FOR BED. YOU'LL SEE, THAT BEAST WON'T INVADE YOUR DREAMS TONIGHT...
I HOPE NOT, MISTER...I HOPE NOT...YOU CAN STAY IN MA AND PA'S ROOM IF YOU WANT...
WAIT, BOY, LET ME LIGHT YOUR WAY...YOU MIGHT TRIP UP THE STAIRS...
DON'T WORRY ABOUT ME, I'M USED TO THE DARKNESS... FOLLOW ME...
ARE YOU SURE YOU WOULDN'T WANT TO SLEEP IN THIS ROOM, TOO? I WOULDN'T MIND IN THE LEAST.
NO...I'D RATHER LIE DOWN IN FRONT OF THE FIREPLACE... AT LEAST UNTIL THE FLAMES DIE OUT...
AS YOU WISH, BUT DON'T HESITATE TO WAKE ME UP IF YOU NEED ANYTHING.

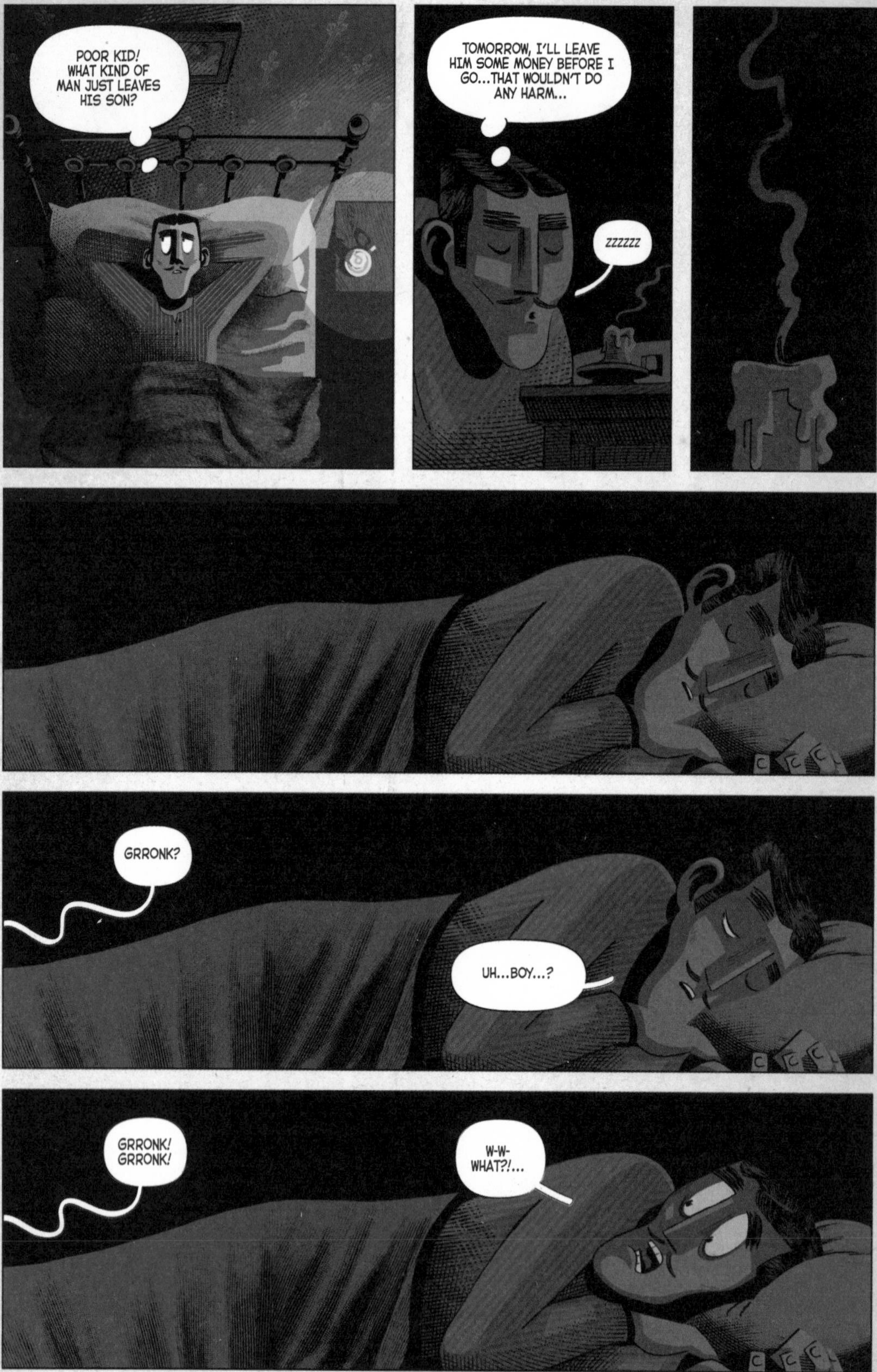
POOR KID! WHAT KIND OF MAN JUST LEAVES HIS SON?
TOMORROW, I'LL LEAVE HIM SOME MONEY BEFORE I GO...THAT WOULDN'T DO ANY HARM...
ZZZZZZ
GRRONK?
UH...BOY...?
GRRONK! GRRONK!
W-W-WHAT?!...

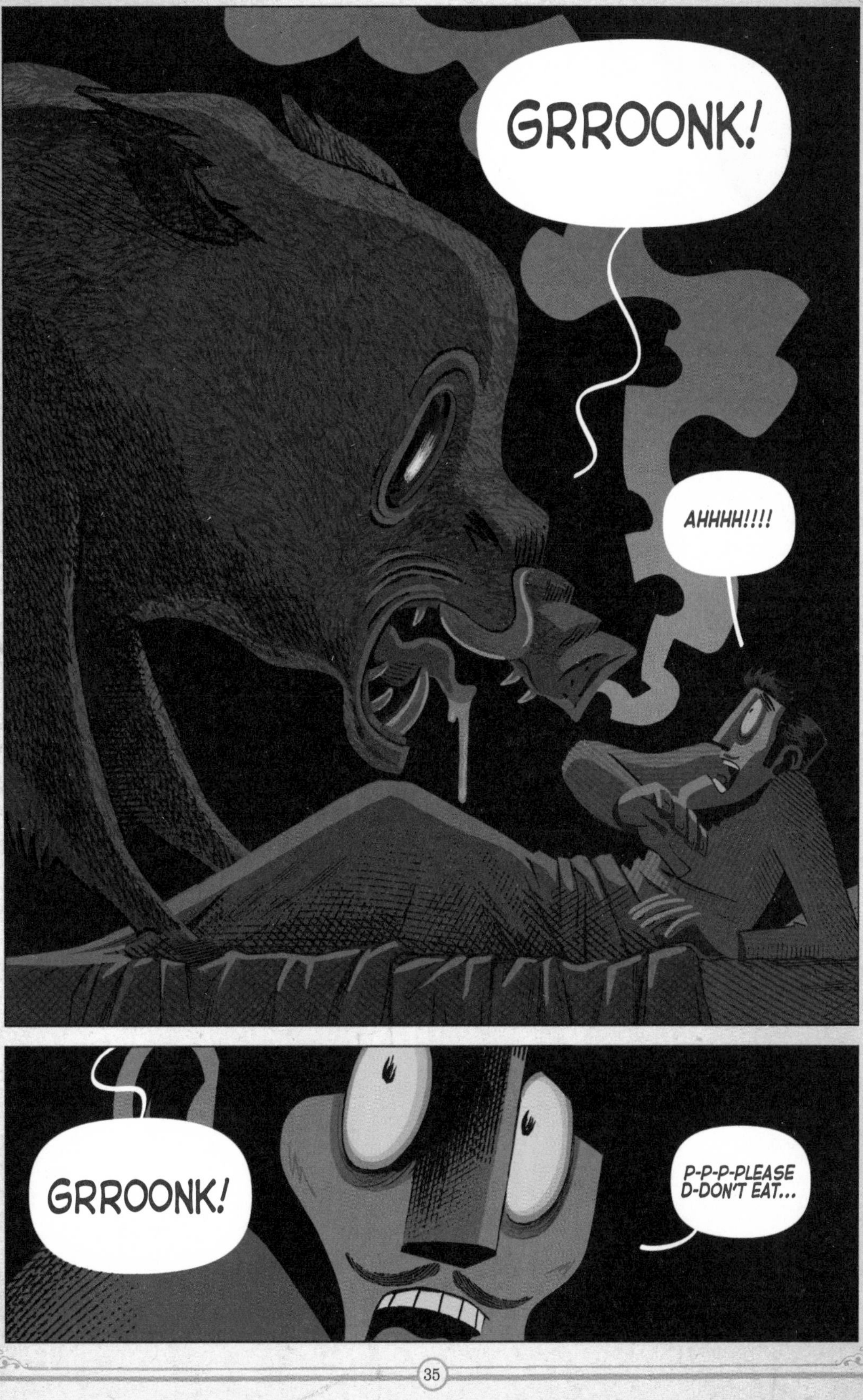
GRROONK!
AHHHH!!!!
GRROONK!
P-P-P-PLEASE D-DON'T EAT...

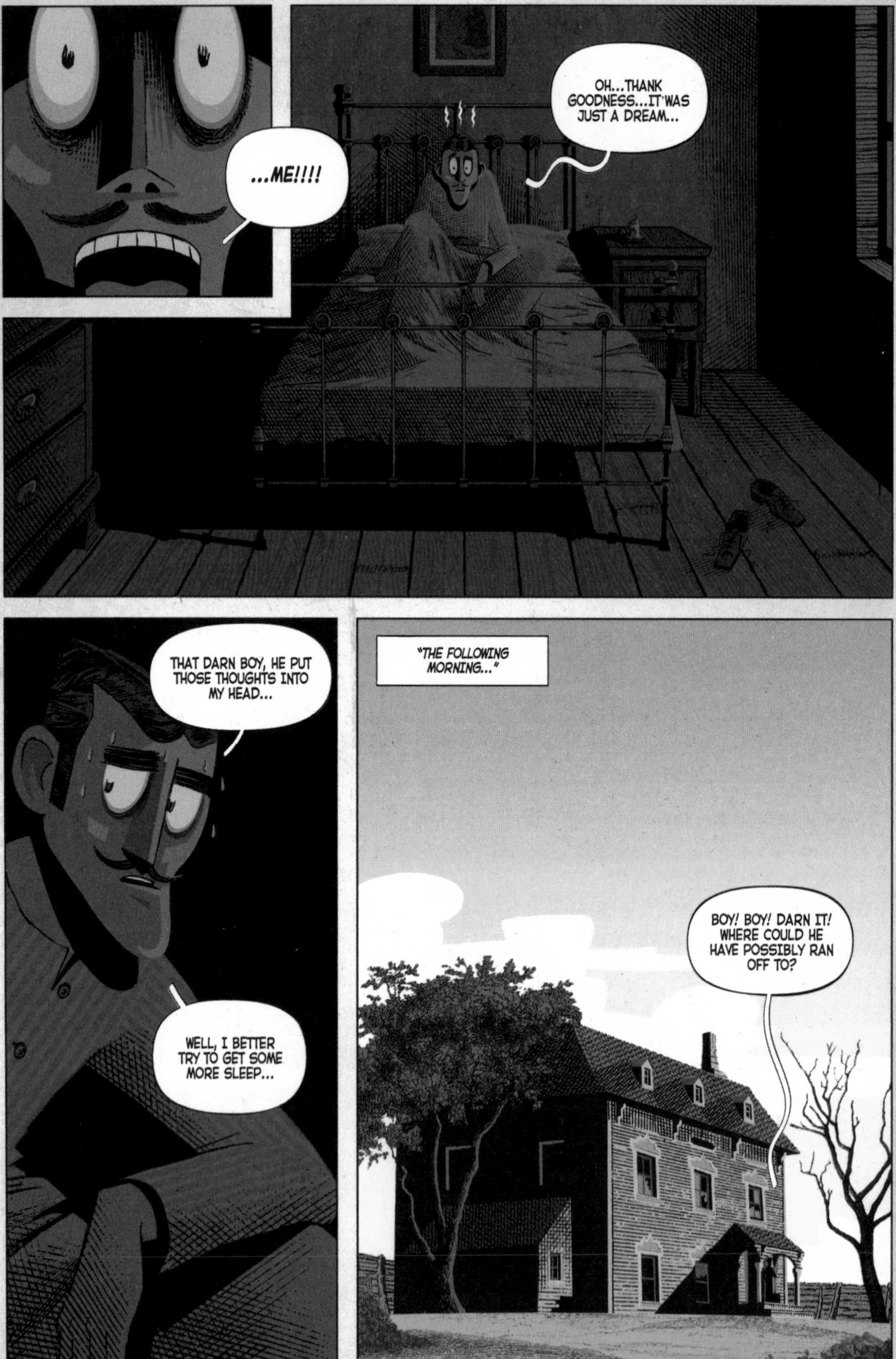
...ME!!!!
OH...THANK GOODNESS...IT WAS JUST A DREAM...
THAT DARN BOY, HE PUT THOSE THOUGHTS INTO MY HEAD...
WELL, I BETTER TRY TO GET SOME MORE SLEEP...
"THE FOLLOWING MORNING..."
BOY! BOY! DARN IT! WHERE COULD HE HAVE POSSIBLY RAN OFF TO?

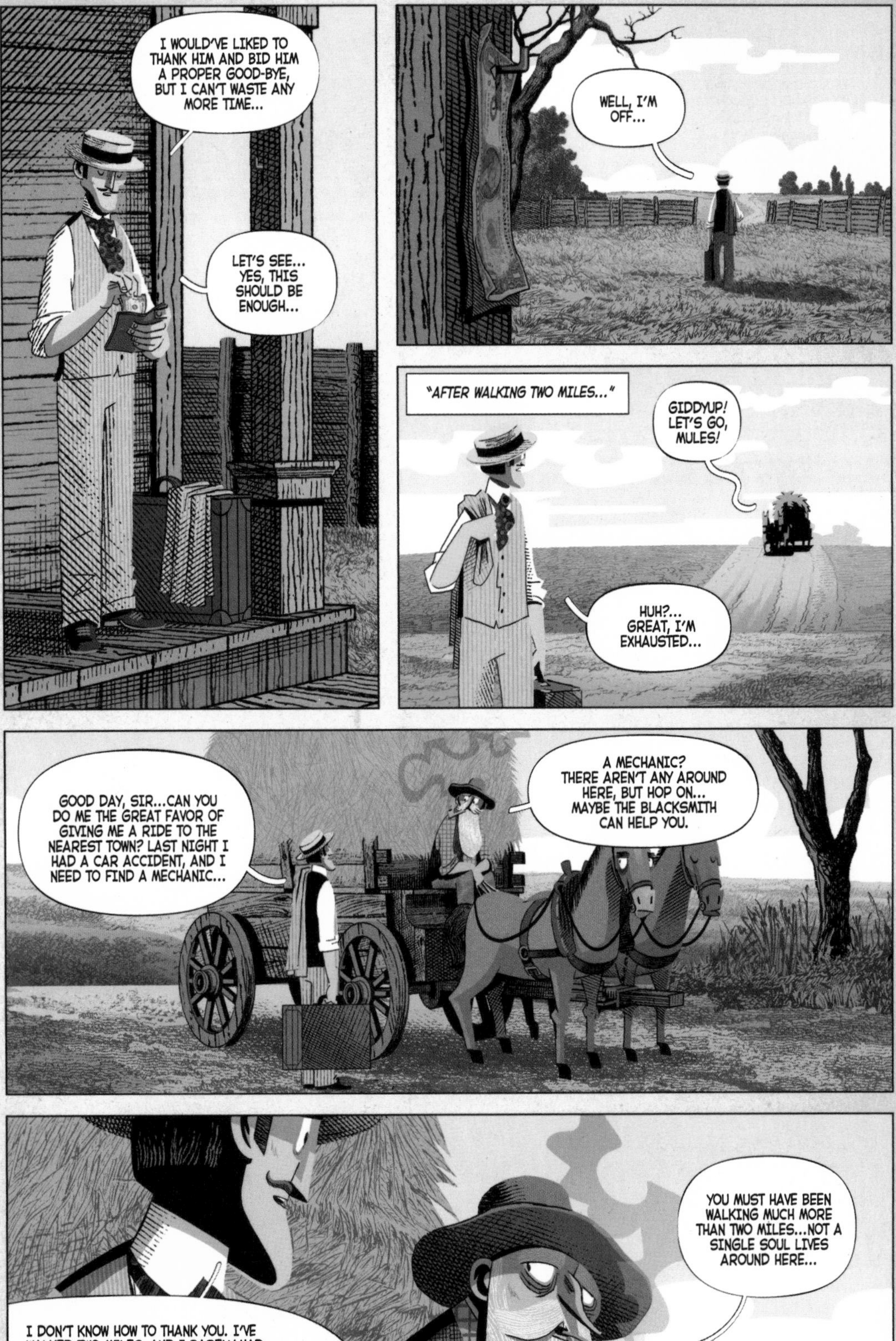
I WOULD'VE LIKED TO THANK HIM AND BID HIM A PROPER GOOD-BYE, BUT I CAN'T WASTE ANY MORE TIME...
LET'S SEE... YES, THIS SHOULD BE ENOUGH...
WELL, I'M OFF...
"AFTER WALKING TWO MILES..."
GIDDYUP! LET'S GO, MULES!
HUH?... GREAT, I'M EXHAUSTED...
GOOD DAY, SIR...CAN YOU DO ME THE GREAT FAVOR OF GIVING ME A RIDE TO THE NEAREST TOWN? LAST NIGHT I HAD A CAR ACCIDENT, AND I NEED TO FIND A MECHANIC...
A MECHANIC? THERE AREN'T ANY AROUND HERE, BUT HOP ON... MAYBE THE BLACKSMITH CAN HELP YOU.
I DON'T KNOW HOW TO THANK YOU. I'VE WALKED TWO MILES, AND I BARELY HAD ANY SLEEP LAST NIGHT...SOMETHING VERY STRANGE HAPPENED TO ME AT THAT HOUSE...
YOU MUST HAVE BEEN WALKING MUCH MORE THAN TWO MILES...NOT A SINGLE SOUL LIVES AROUND HERE...

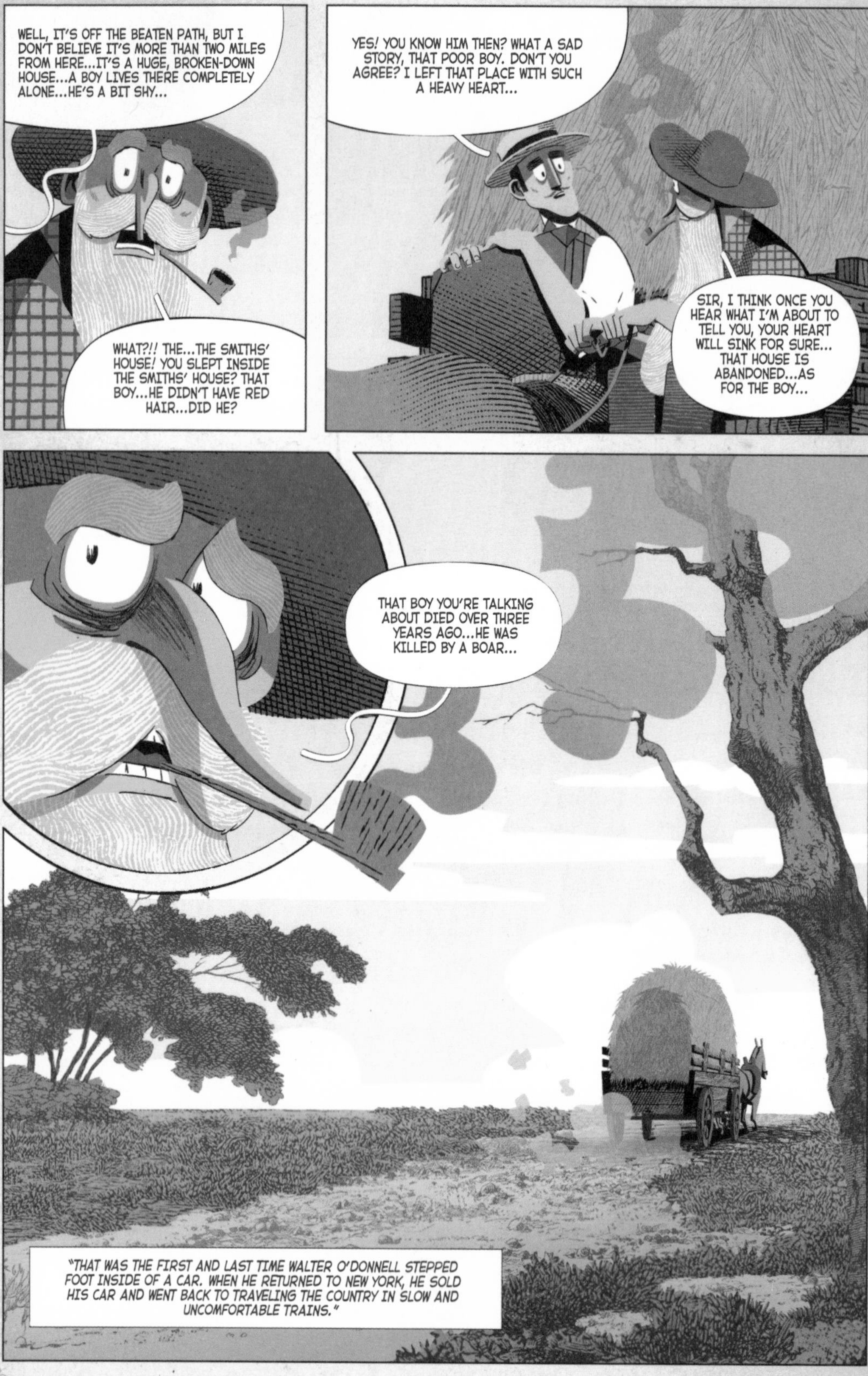
WELL, IT'S OFF THE BEATEN PATH, BUT I DON'T BELIEVE IT'S MORE THAN TWO MILES FROM HERE...IT'S A HUGE, BROKEN-DOWN HOUSE...A BOY LIVES THERE COMPLETELY ALONE...HE'S A BIT SHY...
WHAT?!! THE...THE SMITHS' HOUSE! YOU SLEPT INSIDE THE SMITHS' HOUSE? THAT BOY...HE DIDN'T HAVE RED HAIR...DID HE?
YES! YOU KNOW HIM THEN? WHAT A SAD STORY, THAT POOR BOY. DON'T YOU AGREE? I LEFT THAT PLACE WITH SUCH A HEAVY HEART...
SIR, I THINK ONCE YOU HEAR WHAT I'M ABOUT TO TELL YOU, YOUR HEART WILL SINK FOR SURE... THAT HOUSE IS ABANDONED...AS FOR THE BOY...
THAT BOY YOU'RE TALKING ABOUT DIED OVER THREE YEARS AGO...HE WAS KILLED BY A BOAR...
"THAT WAS THE FIRST AND LAST TIME WALTER O'DONNELL STEPPED FOOT INSIDE OF A CAR. WHEN HE RETURNED TO NEW YORK, HE SOLD HIS CAR AND WENT BACK TO TRAVELING THE COUNTRY IN SLOW AND UNCOMFORTABLE TRAINS."

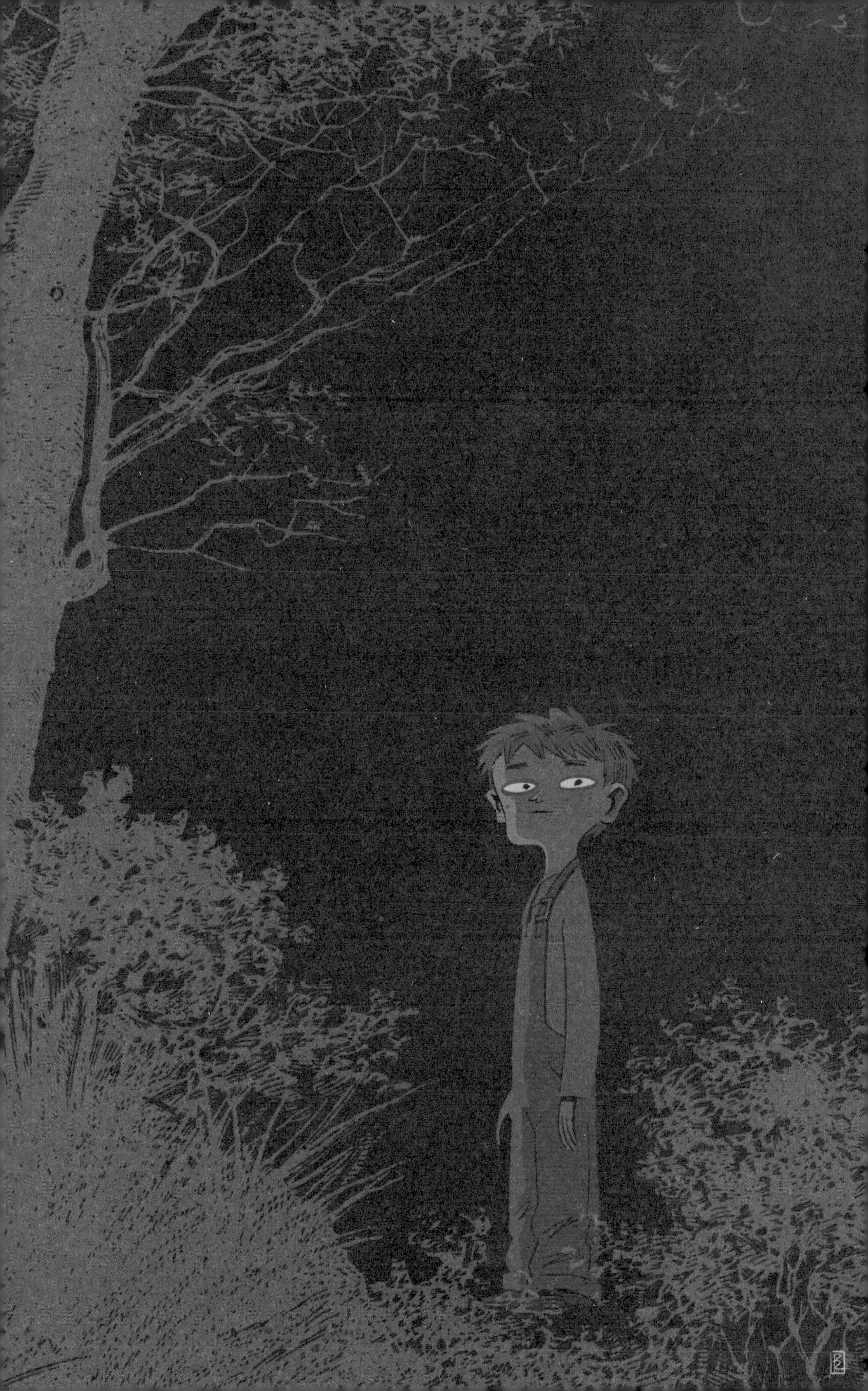

JOHN WILLIAM POLIDORI

THE VAMPIRE

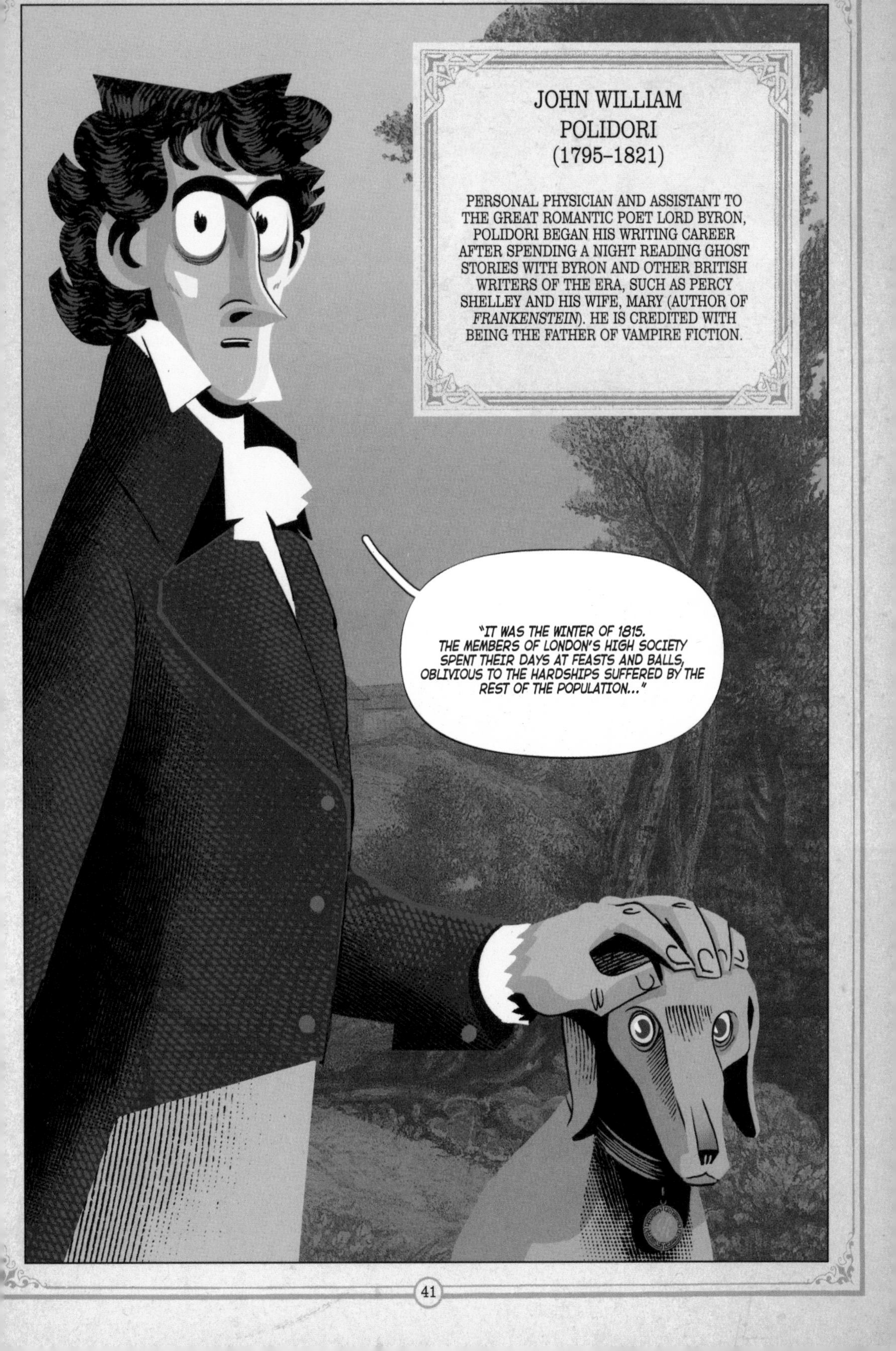
JOHN WILLIAM POLIDORI (1795–1821)
PERSONAL PHYSICIAN AND ASSISTANT TO THE GREAT ROMANTIC POET LORD BYRON, POLIDORI BEGAN HIS WRITING CAREER AFTER SPENDING A NIGHT READING GHOST STORIES WITH BYRON AND OTHER BRITISH WRITERS OF THE ERA, SUCH AS PERCY SHELLEY AND HIS WIFE, MARY (AUTHOR OF *FRANKENSTEIN*). HE IS CREDITED WITH BEING THE FATHER OF VAMPIRE FICTION.
"IT WAS THE WINTER OF 1815. THE MEMBERS OF LONDON'S HIGH SOCIETY SPENT THEIR DAYS AT FEASTS AND BALLS, OBLIVIOUS TO THE HARDSHIPS SUFFERED BY THE REST OF THE POPULATION..."

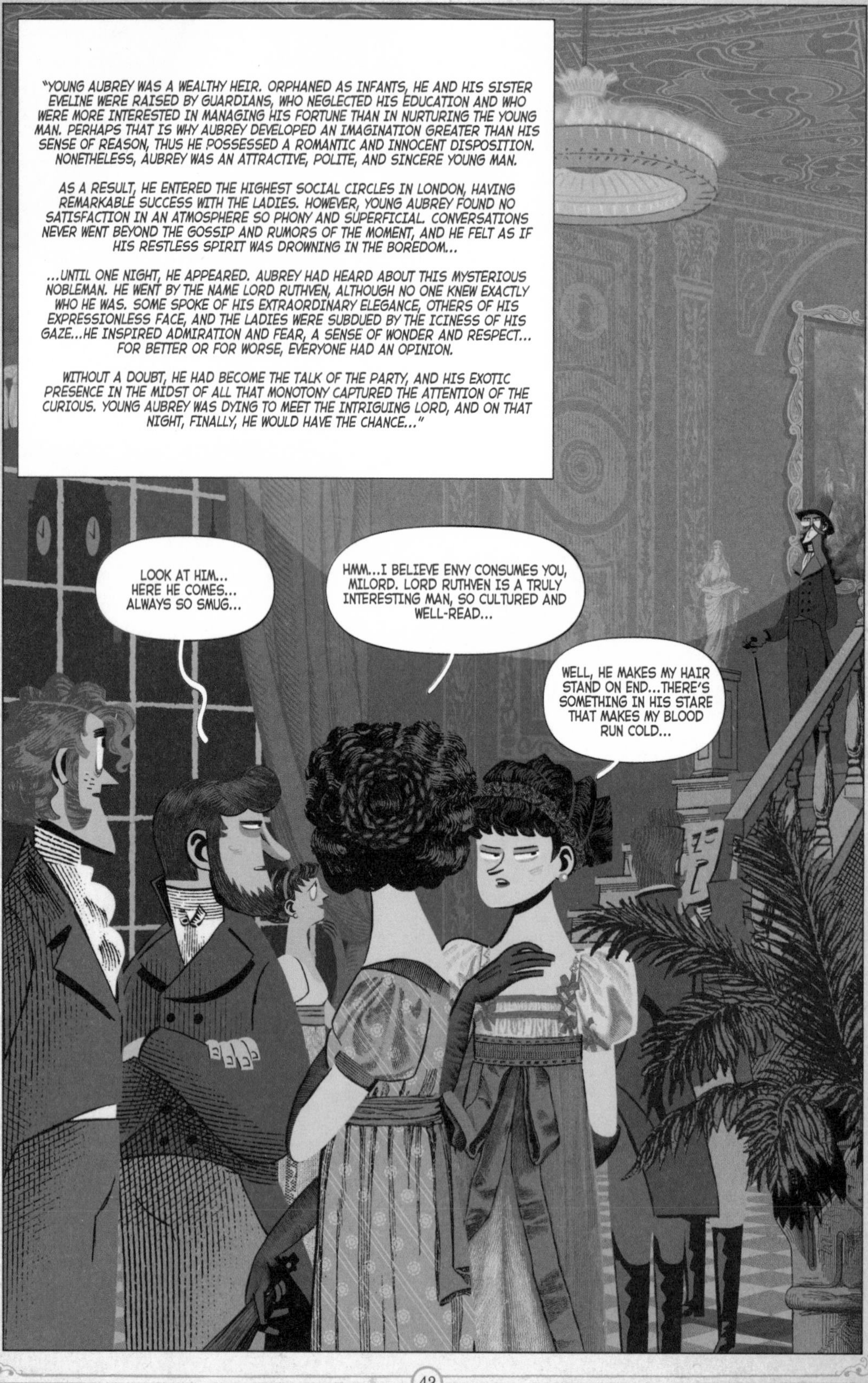
"YOUNG AUBREY WAS A WEALTHY HEIR. ORPHANED AS INFANTS, HE AND HIS SISTER EVELINE WERE RAISED BY GUARDIANS, WHO NEGLECTED HIS EDUCATION AND WHO WERE MORE INTERESTED IN MANAGING HIS FORTUNE THAN IN NURTURING THE YOUNG MAN. PERHAPS THAT IS WHY AUBREY DEVELOPED AN IMAGINATION GREATER THAN HIS SENSE OF REASON, THUS HE POSSESSED A ROMANTIC AND INNOCENT DISPOSITION. NONETHELESS, AUBREY WAS AN ATTRACTIVE, POLITE, AND SINCERE YOUNG MAN.
AS A RESULT, HE ENTERED THE HIGHEST SOCIAL CIRCLES IN LONDON, HAVING REMARKABLE SUCCESS WITH THE LADIES. HOWEVER, YOUNG AUBREY FOUND NO SATISFACTION IN AN ATMOSPHERE SO PHONY AND SUPERFICIAL. CONVERSATIONS NEVER WENT BEYOND THE GOSSIP AND RUMORS OF THE MOMENT, AND HE FELT AS IF HIS RESTLESS SPIRIT WAS DROWNING IN THE BOREDOM...
...UNTIL ONE NIGHT, HE APPEARED. AUBREY HAD HEARD ABOUT THIS MYSTERIOUS NOBLEMAN. HE WENT BY THE NAME LORD RUTHVEN, ALTHOUGH NO ONE KNEW EXACTLY WHO HE WAS. SOME SPOKE OF HIS EXTRAORDINARY ELEGANCE, OTHERS OF HIS EXPRESSIONLESS FACE, AND THE LADIES WERE SUBDUED BY THE ICINESS OF HIS GAZE...HE INSPIRED ADMIRATION AND FEAR, A SENSE OF WONDER AND RESPECT... FOR BETTER OR FOR WORSE, EVERYONE HAD AN OPINION.
WITHOUT A DOUBT, HE HAD BECOME THE TALK OF THE PARTY, AND HIS EXOTIC PRESENCE IN THE MIDST OF ALL THAT MONOTONY CAPTURED THE ATTENTION OF THE CURIOUS. YOUNG AUBREY WAS DYING TO MEET THE INTRIGUING LORD, AND ON THAT NIGHT, FINALLY, HE WOULD HAVE THE CHANCE..."
LOOK AT HIM... HERE HE COMES... ALWAYS SO SMUG...
HMM...I BELIEVE ENVY CONSUMES YOU, MILORD. LORD RUTHVEN IS A TRULY INTERESTING MAN, SO CULTURED AND WELL-READ...
WELL, HE MAKES MY HAIR STAND ON END...THERE'S SOMETHING IN HIS STARE THAT MAKES MY BLOOD RUN COLD...

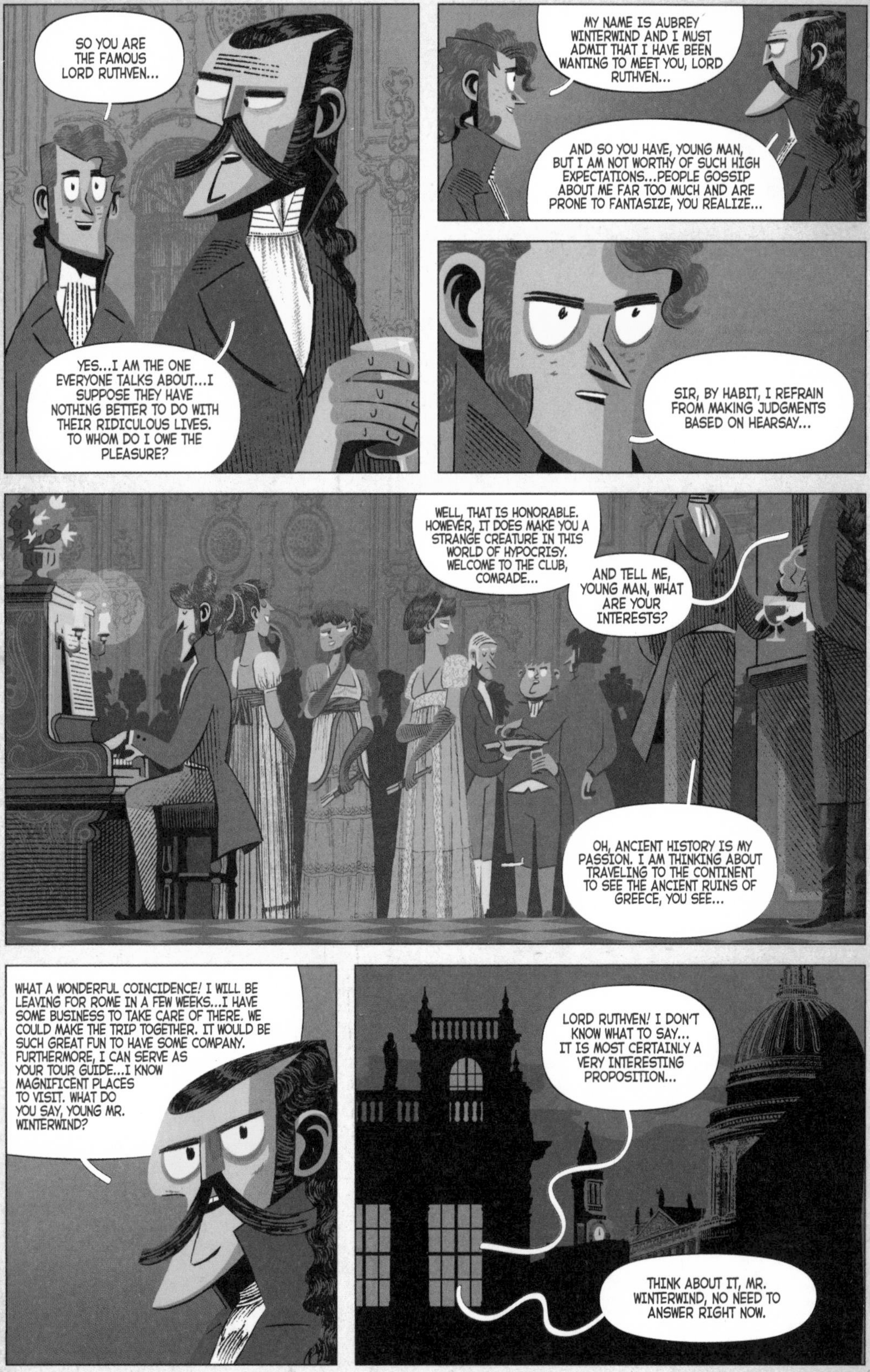

SO YOU ARE THE FAMOUS LORD RUTHVEN...
YES...I AM THE ONE EVERYONE TALKS ABOUT...I SUPPOSE THEY HAVE NOTHING BETTER TO DO WITH THEIR RIDICULOUS LIVES. TO WHOM DO I OWE THE PLEASURE?
MY NAME IS AUBREY WINTERWIND AND I MUST ADMIT THAT I HAVE BEEN WANTING TO MEET YOU, LORD RUTHVEN...
AND SO YOU HAVE, YOUNG MAN, BUT I AM NOT WORTHY OF SUCH HIGH EXPECTATIONS...PEOPLE GOSSIP ABOUT ME FAR TOO MUCH AND ARE PRONE TO FANTASIZE, YOU REALIZE...
SIR, BY HABIT, I REFRAIN FROM MAKING JUDGMENTS BASED ON HEARSAY...
WELL, THAT IS HONORABLE. HOWEVER, IT DOES MAKE YOU A STRANGE CREATURE IN THIS WORLD OF HYPOCRISY. WELCOME TO THE CLUB, COMRADE...
AND TELL ME, YOUNG MAN, WHAT ARE YOUR INTERESTS?
OH, ANCIENT HISTORY IS MY PASSION. I AM THINKING ABOUT TRAVELING TO THE CONTINENT TO SEE THE ANCIENT RUINS OF GREECE, YOU SEE...
WHAT A WONDERFUL COINCIDENCE! I WILL BE LEAVING FOR ROME IN A FEW WEEKS...I HAVE SOME BUSINESS TO TAKE CARE OF THERE. WE COULD MAKE THE TRIP TOGETHER. IT WOULD BE SUCH GREAT FUN TO HAVE SOME COMPANY. FURTHERMORE, I CAN SERVE AS YOUR TOUR GUIDE...I KNOW MAGNIFICENT PLACES TO VISIT. WHAT DO YOU SAY, YOUNG MR. WINTERWIND?
LORD RUTHVEN! I DON'T KNOW WHAT TO SAY... IT IS MOST CERTAINLY A VERY INTERESTING PROPOSITION...
THINK ABOUT IT, MR. WINTERWIND, NO NEED TO ANSWER RIGHT NOW.

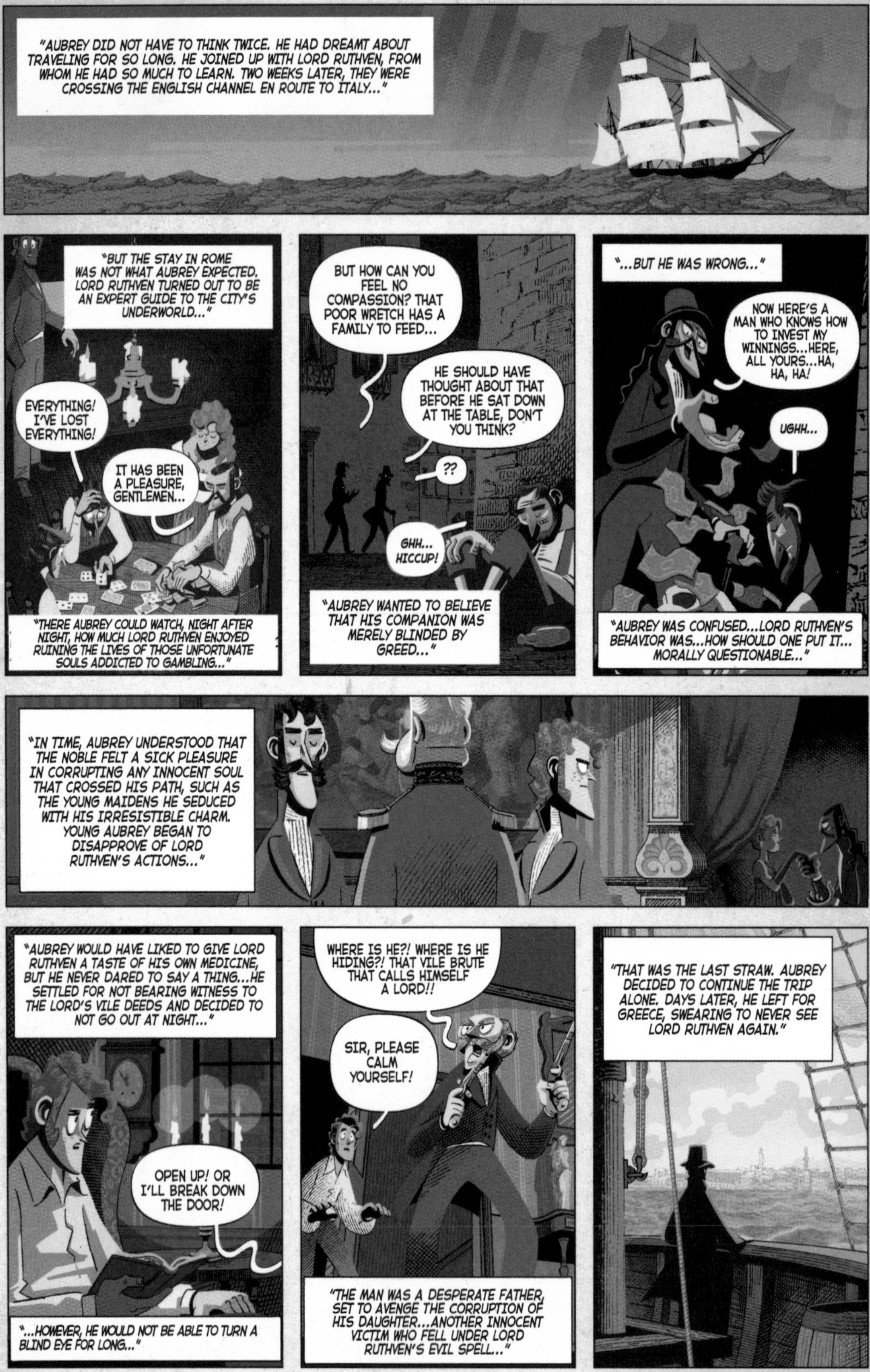
"AUBREY DID NOT HAVE TO THINK TWICE. HE HAD DREAMT ABOUT TRAVELING FOR SO LONG. HE JOINED UP WITH LORD RUTHVEN, FROM WHOM HE HAD SO MUCH TO LEARN. TWO WEEKS LATER, THEY WERE CROSSING THE ENGLISH CHANNEL EN ROUTE TO ITALY..."
"BUT THE STAY IN ROME WAS NOT WHAT AUBREY EXPECTED. LORD RUTHVEN TURNED OUT TO BE AN EXPERT GUIDE TO THE CITY'S UNDERWORLD..."
EVERYTHING! I'VE LOST EVERYTHING!
IT HAS BEEN A PLEASURE, GENTLEMEN...
"THERE AUBREY COULD WATCH, NIGHT AFTER NIGHT, HOW MUCH LORD RUTHVEN ENJOYED RUINING THE LIVES OF THOSE UNFORTUNATE SOULS ADDICTED TO GAMBLING..."
BUT HOW CAN YOU FEEL NO COMPASSION? THAT POOR WRETCH HAS A FAMILY TO FEED...
HE SHOULD HAVE THOUGHT ABOUT THAT BEFORE HE SAT DOWN AT THE TABLE, DON'T YOU THINK?
??
GHH... HICCUP!
"AUBREY WANTED TO BELIEVE THAT HIS COMPANION WAS MERELY BLINDED BY GREED..."
"...BUT HE WAS WRONG..."
NOW HERE'S A MAN WHO KNOWS HOW TO INVEST MY WINNINGS...HERE, ALL YOURS...HA, HA, HA!
UGHH...
"AUBREY WAS CONFUSED...LORD RUTHVEN'S BEHAVIOR WAS...HOW SHOULD ONE PUT IT... MORALLY QUESTIONABLE..."
"IN TIME, AUBREY UNDERSTOOD THAT THE NOBLE FELT A SICK PLEASURE IN CORRUPTING ANY INNOCENT SOUL THAT CROSSED HIS PATH, SUCH AS THE YOUNG MAIDENS HE SEDUCED WITH HIS IRRESISTIBLE CHARM. YOUNG AUBREY BEGAN TO DISAPPROVE OF LORD RUTHVEN'S ACTIONS..."
"AUBREY WOULD HAVE LIKED TO GIVE LORD RUTHVEN A TASTE OF HIS OWN MEDICINE, BUT HE NEVER DARED TO SAY A THING...HE SETTLED FOR NOT BEARING WITNESS TO THE LORD'S VILE DEEDS AND DECIDED TO NOT GO OUT AT NIGHT..."
OPEN UP! OR I'LL BREAK DOWN THE DOOR!
"...HOWEVER, HE WOULD NOT BE ABLE TO TURN A BLIND EYE FOR LONG..."
WHERE IS HE?! WHERE IS HE HIDING?! THAT VILE BRUTE THAT CALLS HIMSELF A LORD!!
SIR, PLEASE CALM YOURSELF!
"THE MAN WAS A DESPERATE FATHER, SET TO AVENGE THE CORRUPTION OF HIS DAUGHTER...ANOTHER INNOCENT VICTIM WHO FELL UNDER LORD RUTHVEN'S EVIL SPELL..."
"THAT WAS THE LAST STRAW. AUBREY DECIDED TO CONTINUE THE TRIP ALONE. DAYS LATER, HE LEFT FOR GREECE, SWEARING TO NEVER SEE LORD RUTHVEN AGAIN."

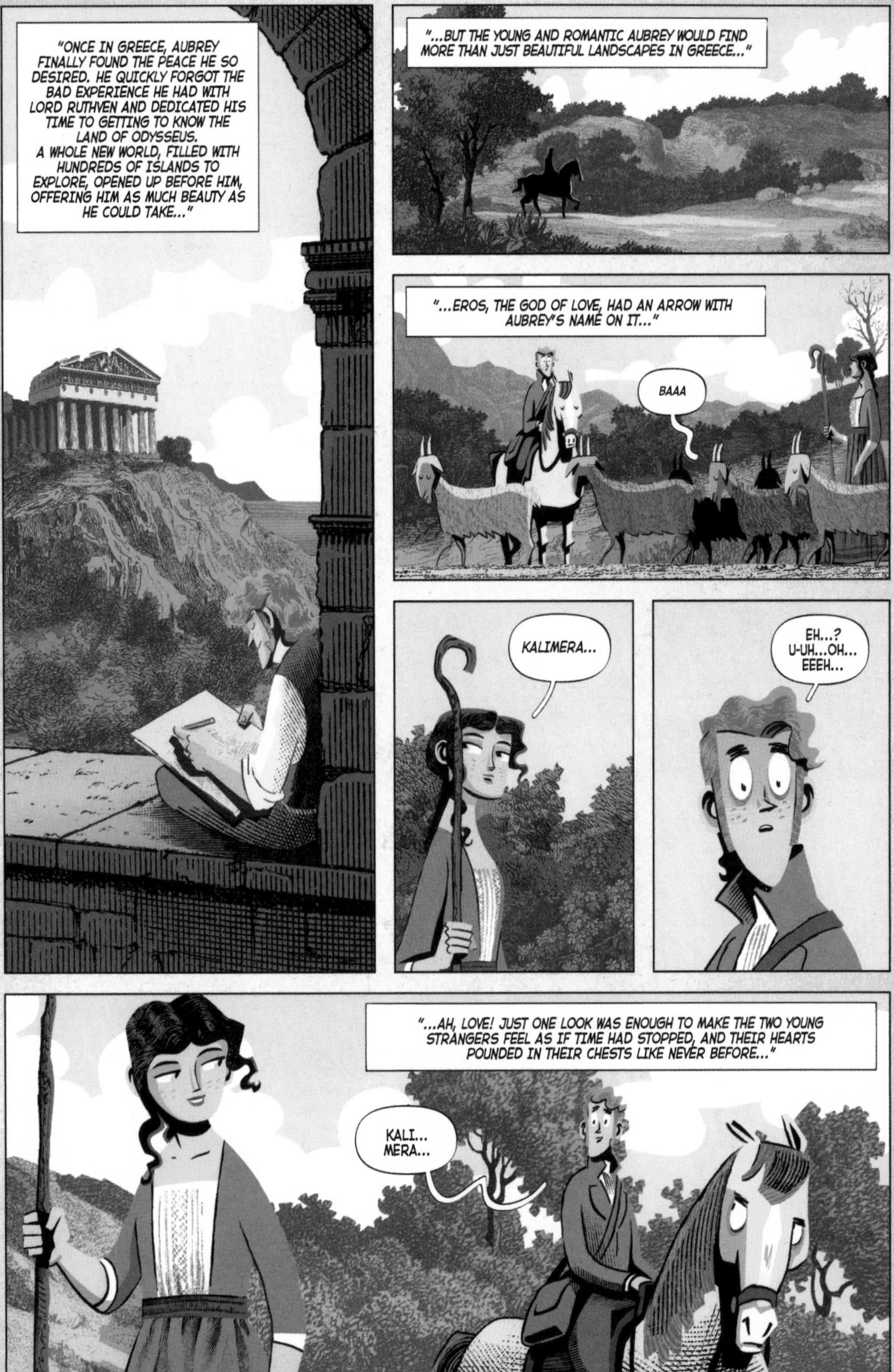
"ONCE IN GREECE, AUBREY FINALLY FOUND THE PEACE HE SO DESIRED. HE QUICKLY FORGOT THE BAD EXPERIENCE HE HAD WITH LORD RUTHVEN AND DEDICATED HIS TIME TO GETTING TO KNOW THE LAND OF ODYSSEUS.
A WHOLE NEW WORLD, FILLED WITH HUNDREDS OF ISLANDS TO EXPLORE, OPENED UP BEFORE HIM, OFFERING HIM AS MUCH BEAUTY AS HE COULD TAKE..."
"...BUT THE YOUNG AND ROMANTIC AUBREY WOULD FIND MORE THAN JUST BEAUTIFUL LANDSCAPES IN GREECE..."
"...EROS, THE GOD OF LOVE, HAD AN ARROW WITH AUBREY'S NAME ON IT..."
BAAA
KALIMERA...
EH...? U-UH...OH... EEEH...
"...AH, LOVE! JUST ONE LOOK WAS ENOUGH TO MAKE THE TWO YOUNG STRANGERS FEEL AS IF TIME HAD STOPPED, AND THEIR HEARTS POUNDED IN THEIR CHESTS LIKE NEVER BEFORE..."
KALI... MERA...

KALIMERA: "GOOD DAY," IN GREEK.

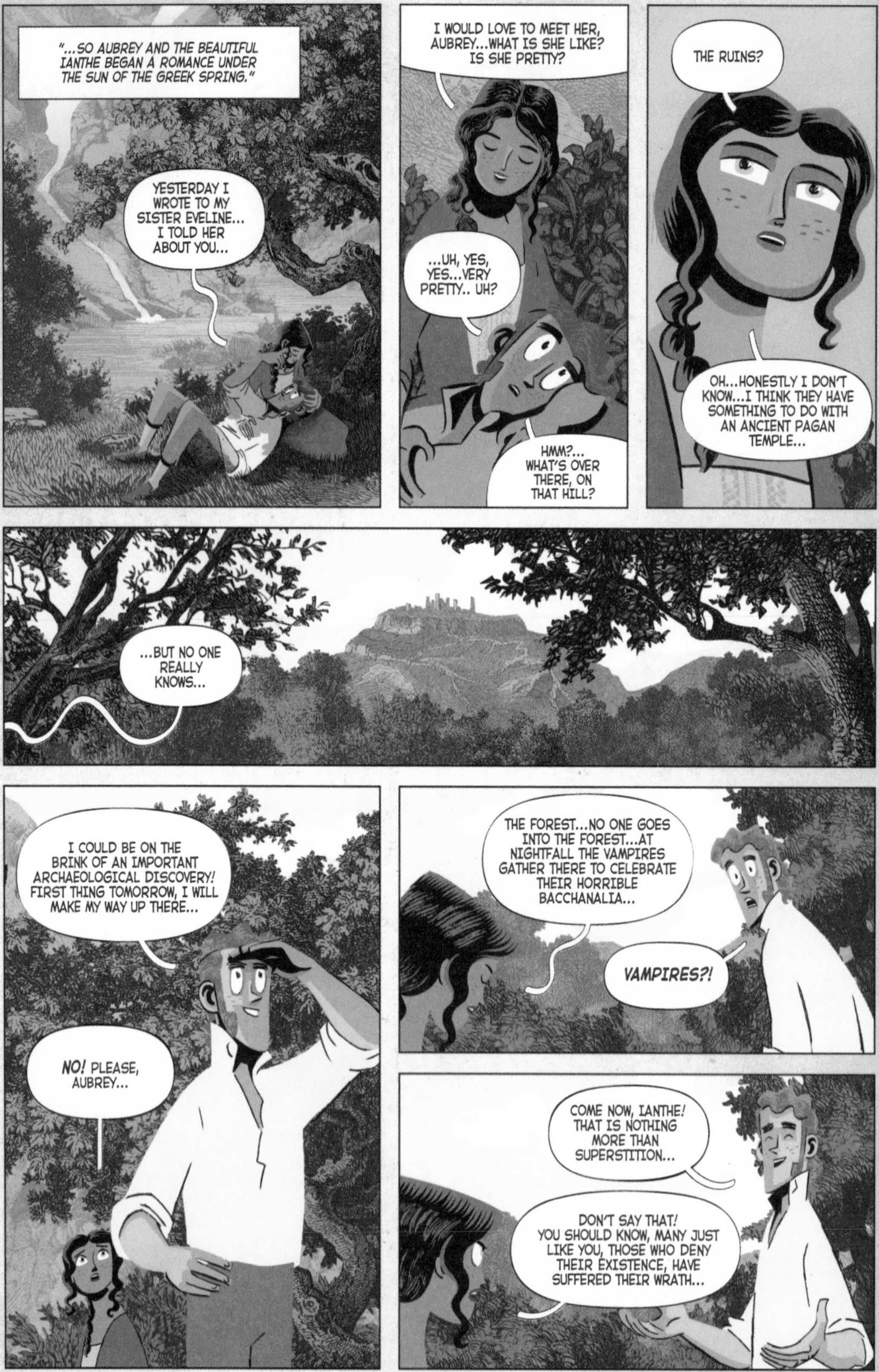
"...SO AUBREY AND THE BEAUTIFUL IANTHE BEGAN A ROMANCE UNDER THE SUN OF THE GREEK SPRING."
YESTERDAY I WROTE TO MY SISTER EVELINE... I TOLD HER ABOUT YOU...
I WOULD LOVE TO MEET HER, AUBREY...WHAT IS SHE LIKE? IS SHE PRETTY?
...UH, YES, YES...VERY PRETTY.. UH?
HMM?... WHAT'S OVER THERE, ON THAT HILL?
THE RUINS?
OH...HONESTLY I DON'T KNOW...I THINK THEY HAVE SOMETHING TO DO WITH AN ANCIENT PAGAN TEMPLE...
...BUT NO ONE REALLY KNOWS...
I COULD BE ON THE BRINK OF AN IMPORTANT ARCHAEOLOGICAL DISCOVERY! FIRST THING TOMORROW, I WILL MAKE MY WAY UP THERE...
NO! PLEASE, AUBREY...
THE FOREST...NO ONE GOES INTO THE FOREST...AT NIGHTFALL THE VAMPIRES GATHER THERE TO CELEBRATE THEIR HORRIBLE BACCHANALIA...
VAMPIRES?!
COME NOW, IANTHE! THAT IS NOTHING MORE THAN SUPERSTITION...
DON'T SAY THAT! YOU SHOULD KNOW, MANY JUST LIKE YOU, THOSE WHO DENY THEIR EXISTENCE, HAVE SUFFERED THEIR WRATH...

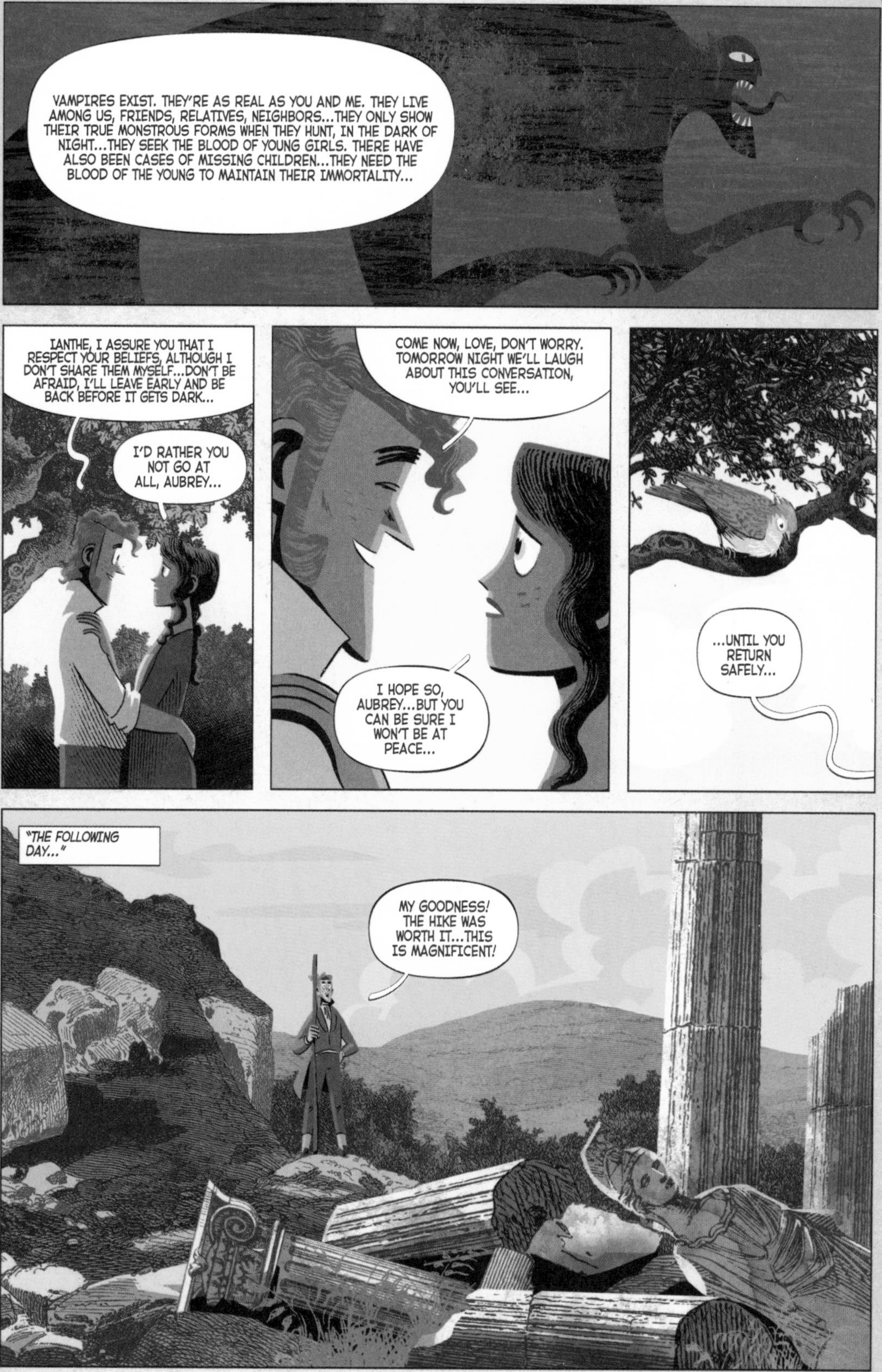
VAMPIRES EXIST. THEY'RE AS REAL AS YOU AND ME. THEY LIVE AMONG US, FRIENDS, RELATIVES, NEIGHBORS...THEY ONLY SHOW THEIR TRUE MONSTROUS FORMS WHEN THEY HUNT, IN THE DARK OF NIGHT...THEY SEEK THE BLOOD OF YOUNG GIRLS. THERE HAVE ALSO BEEN CASES OF MISSING CHILDREN...THEY NEED THE BLOOD OF THE YOUNG TO MAINTAIN THEIR IMMORTALITY...
IANTHE, I ASSURE YOU THAT I RESPECT YOUR BELIEFS, ALTHOUGH I DON'T SHARE THEM MYSELF...DON'T BE AFRAID, I'LL LEAVE EARLY AND BE BACK BEFORE IT GETS DARK...
I'D RATHER YOU NOT GO AT ALL, AUBREY...
COME NOW, LOVE, DON'T WORRY. TOMORROW NIGHT WE'LL LAUGH ABOUT THIS CONVERSATION, YOU'LL SEE...
I HOPE SO, AUBREY...BUT YOU CAN BE SURE I WON'T BE AT PEACE...
...UNTIL YOU RETURN SAFELY...
"THE FOLLOWING DAY..."
MY GOODNESS! THE HIKE WAS WORTH IT...THIS IS MAGNIFICENT!

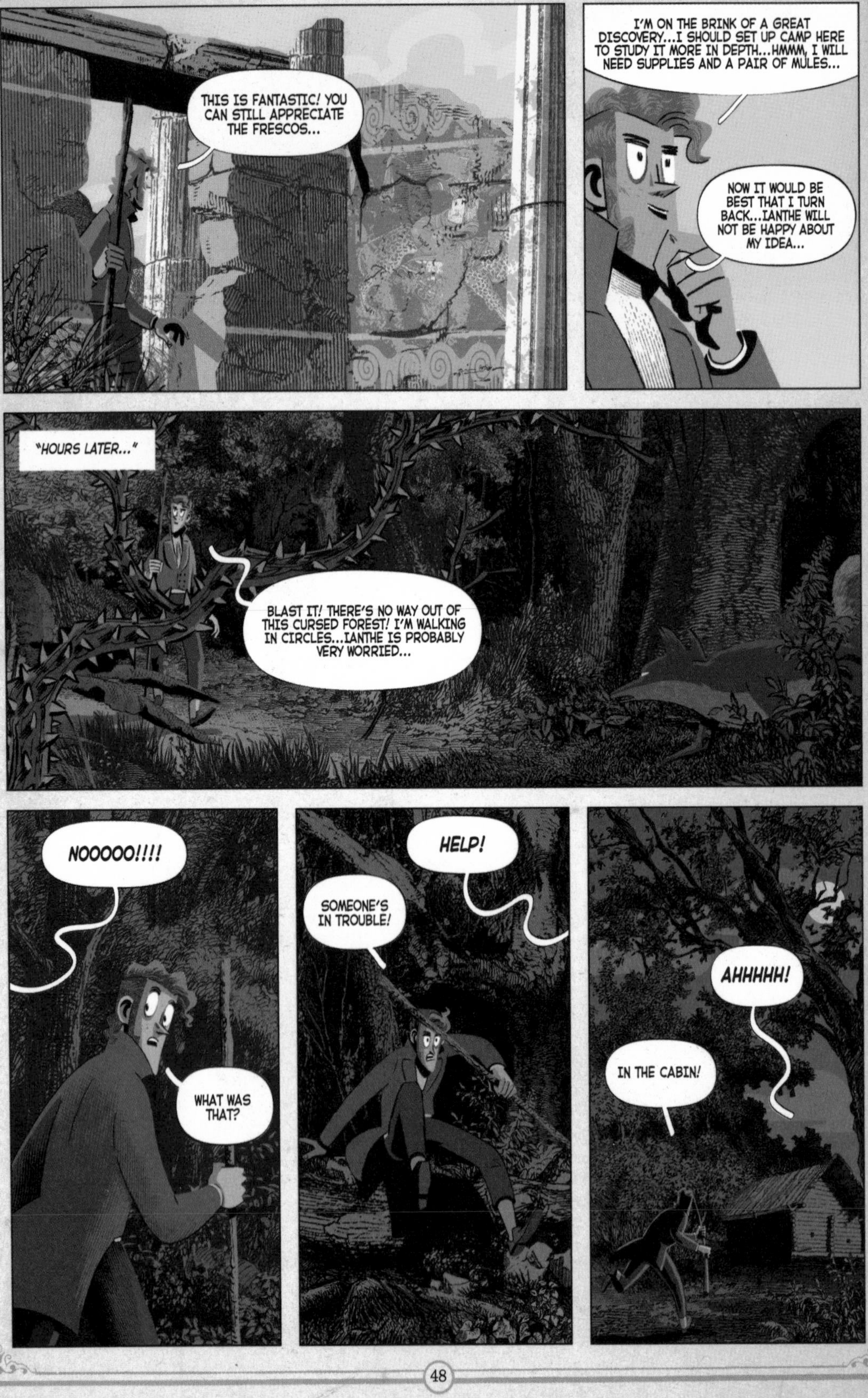
THIS IS FANTASTIC! YOU CAN STILL APPRECIATE THE FRESCOS...
I'M ON THE BRINK OF A GREAT DISCOVERY...I SHOULD SET UP CAMP HERE TO STUDY IT MORE IN DEPTH...HMMM, I WILL NEED SUPPLIES AND A PAIR OF MULES...
NOW IT WOULD BE BEST THAT I TURN BACK...IANTHE WILL NOT BE HAPPY ABOUT MY IDEA...
"HOURS LATER..."
BLAST IT! THERE'S NO WAY OUT OF THIS CURSED FOREST! I'M WALKING IN CIRCLES...IANTHE IS PROBABLY VERY WORRIED...
NOOOOO!!!!
WHAT WAS THAT?
HELP!
SOMEONE'S IN TROUBLE!
AHHHHH!
IN THE CABIN!

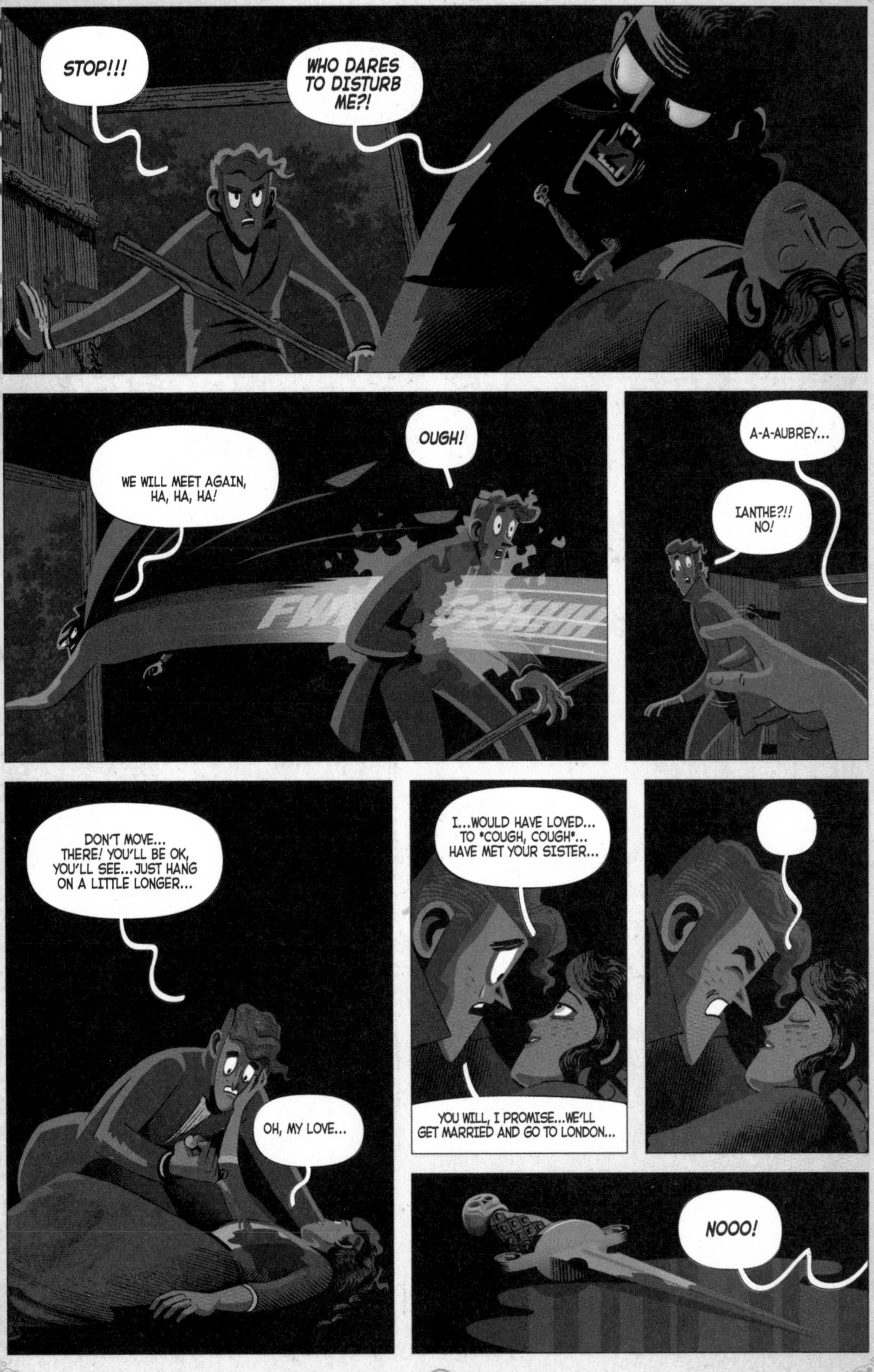
STOP!!!
WHO DARES TO DISTURB ME?!
WE WILL MEET AGAIN, HA, HA, HA!
OUGH!
A-A-AUBREY...
IANTHE?!! NO!
DON'T MOVE... THERE! YOU'LL BE OK, YOU'LL SEE...JUST HANG ON A LITTLE LONGER...
OH, MY LOVE...
I...WOULD HAVE LOVED... TO *COUGH, COUGH*... HAVE MET YOUR SISTER...
YOU WILL, I PROMISE...WE'LL GET MARRIED AND GO TO LONDON...
NOOO!

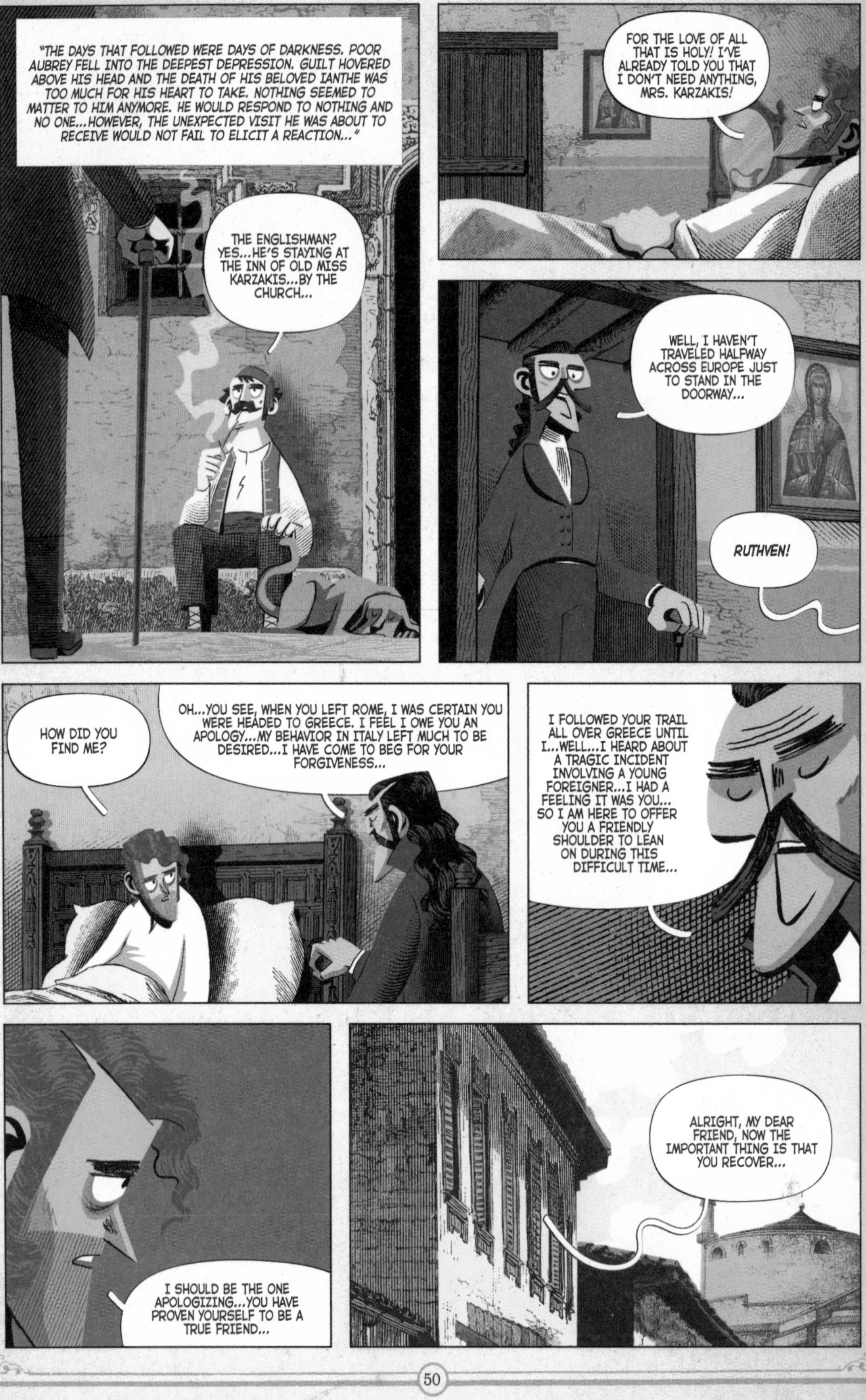
"THE DAYS THAT FOLLOWED WERE DAYS OF DARKNESS. POOR AUBREY FELL INTO THE DEEPEST DEPRESSION. GUILT HOVERED ABOVE HIS HEAD AND THE DEATH OF HIS BELOVED IANTHE WAS TOO MUCH FOR HIS HEART TO TAKE. NOTHING SEEMED TO MATTER TO HIM ANYMORE. HE WOULD RESPOND TO NOTHING AND NO ONE...HOWEVER, THE UNEXPECTED VISIT HE WAS ABOUT TO RECEIVE WOULD NOT FAIL TO ELICIT A REACTION..."
THE ENGLISHMAN? YES...HE'S STAYING AT THE INN OF OLD MISS KARZAKIS...BY THE CHURCH...
FOR THE LOVE OF ALL THAT IS HOLY! I'VE ALREADY TOLD YOU THAT I DON'T NEED ANYTHING, MRS. KARZAKIS!
WELL, I HAVEN'T TRAVELED HALFWAY ACROSS EUROPE JUST TO STAND IN THE DOORWAY...
RUTHVEN!
HOW DID YOU FIND ME?
OH...YOU SEE, WHEN YOU LEFT ROME, I WAS CERTAIN YOU WERE HEADED TO GREECE. I FEEL I OWE YOU AN APOLOGY...MY BEHAVIOR IN ITALY LEFT MUCH TO BE DESIRED...I HAVE COME TO BEG FOR YOUR FORGIVENESS...
I FOLLOWED YOUR TRAIL ALL OVER GREECE UNTIL I...WELL...I HEARD ABOUT A TRAGIC INCIDENT INVOLVING A YOUNG FOREIGNER...I HAD A FEELING IT WAS YOU... SO I AM HERE TO OFFER YOU A FRIENDLY SHOULDER TO LEAN ON DURING THIS DIFFICULT TIME...
I SHOULD BE THE ONE APOLOGIZING...YOU HAVE PROVEN YOURSELF TO BE A TRUE FRIEND...
ALRIGHT, MY DEAR FRIEND, NOW THE IMPORTANT THING IS THAT YOU RECOVER...

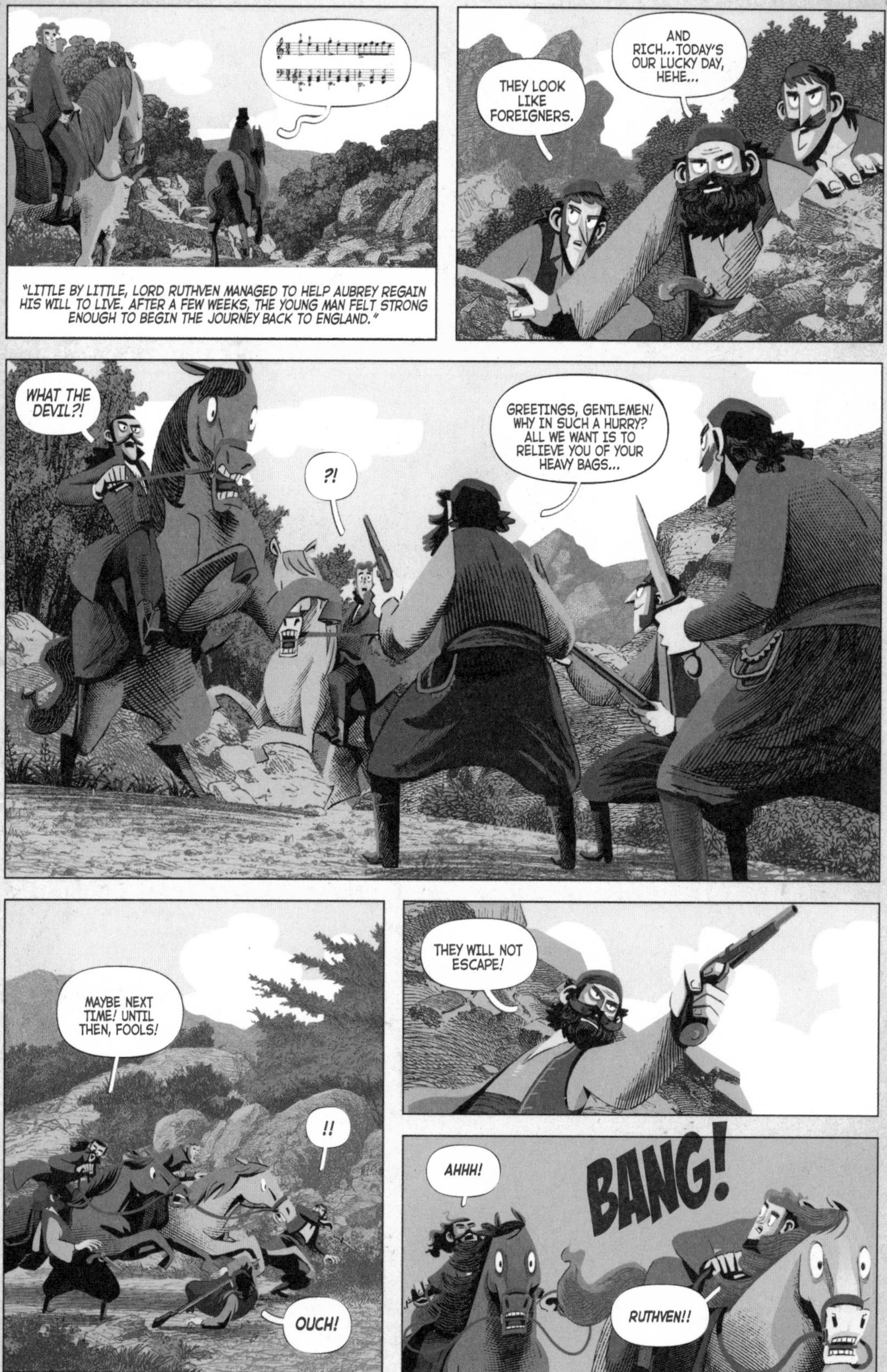
"LITTLE BY LITTLE, LORD RUTHVEN MANAGED TO HELP AUBREY REGAIN HIS WILL TO LIVE. AFTER A FEW WEEKS, THE YOUNG MAN FELT STRONG ENOUGH TO BEGIN THE JOURNEY BACK TO ENGLAND."
THEY LOOK LIKE FOREIGNERS.
AND RICH... TODAY'S OUR LUCKY DAY, HEHE...
WHAT THE DEVIL?!
?!
GREETINGS, GENTLEMEN! WHY IN SUCH A HURRY? ALL WE WANT IS TO RELIEVE YOU OF YOUR HEAVY BAGS...
MAYBE NEXT TIME! UNTIL THEN, FOOLS!
!!
OUCH!
THEY WILL NOT ESCAPE!
AHHH!
BANG!
RUTHVEN!!

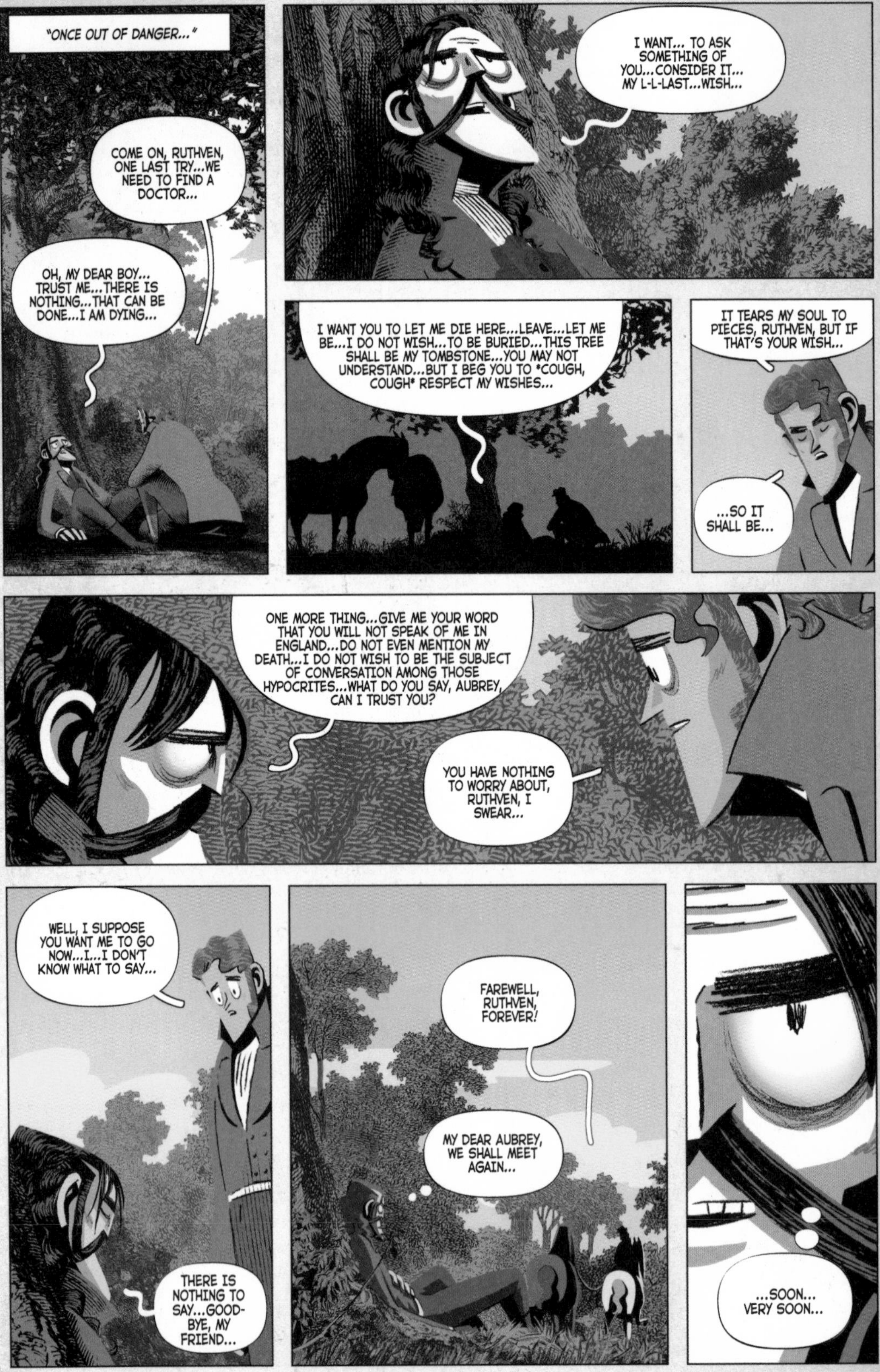
"ONCE OUT OF DANGER..."
COME ON, RUTHVEN, ONE LAST TRY...WE NEED TO FIND A DOCTOR...
OH, MY DEAR BOY... TRUST ME...THERE IS NOTHING...THAT CAN BE DONE...I AM DYING...
I WANT... TO ASK SOMETHING OF YOU...CONSIDER IT... MY L-L-LAST...WISH...
I WANT YOU TO LET ME DIE HERE...LEAVE...LET ME BE...I DO NOT WISH...TO BE BURIED...THIS TREE SHALL BE MY TOMBSTONE...YOU MAY NOT UNDERSTAND...BUT I BEG YOU TO *COUGH, COUGH* RESPECT MY WISHES...
IT TEARS MY SOUL TO PIECES, RUTHVEN, BUT IF THAT'S YOUR WISH...
...SO IT SHALL BE...
ONE MORE THING...GIVE ME YOUR WORD THAT YOU WILL NOT SPEAK OF ME IN ENGLAND...DO NOT EVEN MENTION MY DEATH...I DO NOT WISH TO BE THE SUBJECT OF CONVERSATION AMONG THOSE HYPOCRITES...WHAT DO YOU SAY, AUBREY, CAN I TRUST YOU?
YOU HAVE NOTHING TO WORRY ABOUT, RUTHVEN, I SWEAR...
WELL, I SUPPOSE YOU WANT ME TO GO NOW...I...I DON'T KNOW WHAT TO SAY...
THERE IS NOTHING TO SAY...GOOD-BYE, MY FRIEND...
FAREWELL, RUTHVEN, FOREVER!
MY DEAR AUBREY, WE SHALL MEET AGAIN...
...SOON... VERY SOON...

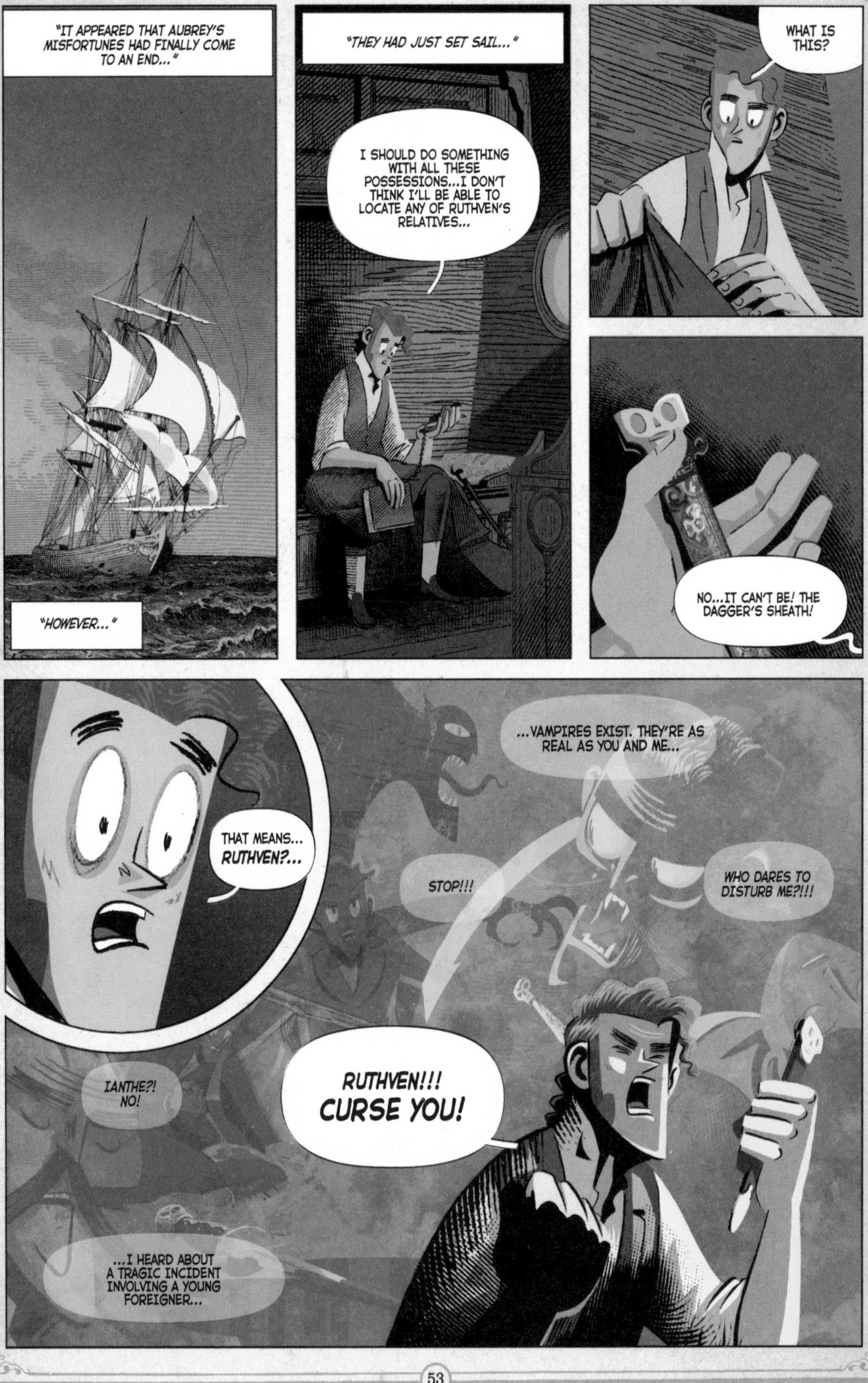
"IT APPEARED THAT AUBREY'S MISFORTUNES HAD FINALLY COME TO AN END..."
"HOWEVER..."
"THEY HAD JUST SET SAIL..."
I SHOULD DO SOMETHING WITH ALL THESE POSSESSIONS...I DON'T THINK I'LL BE ABLE TO LOCATE ANY OF RUTHVEN'S RELATIVES...
WHAT IS THIS?
NO...IT CAN'T BE! THE DAGGER'S SHEATH!
THAT MEANS... RUTHVEN?...
...VAMPIRES EXIST. THEY'RE AS REAL AS YOU AND ME...
STOP!!!
WHO DARES TO DISTURB ME?!!!
IANTHE?! NO!
RUTHVEN!!! CURSE YOU!
...I HEARD ABOUT A TRAGIC INCIDENT INVOLVING A YOUNG FOREIGNER...

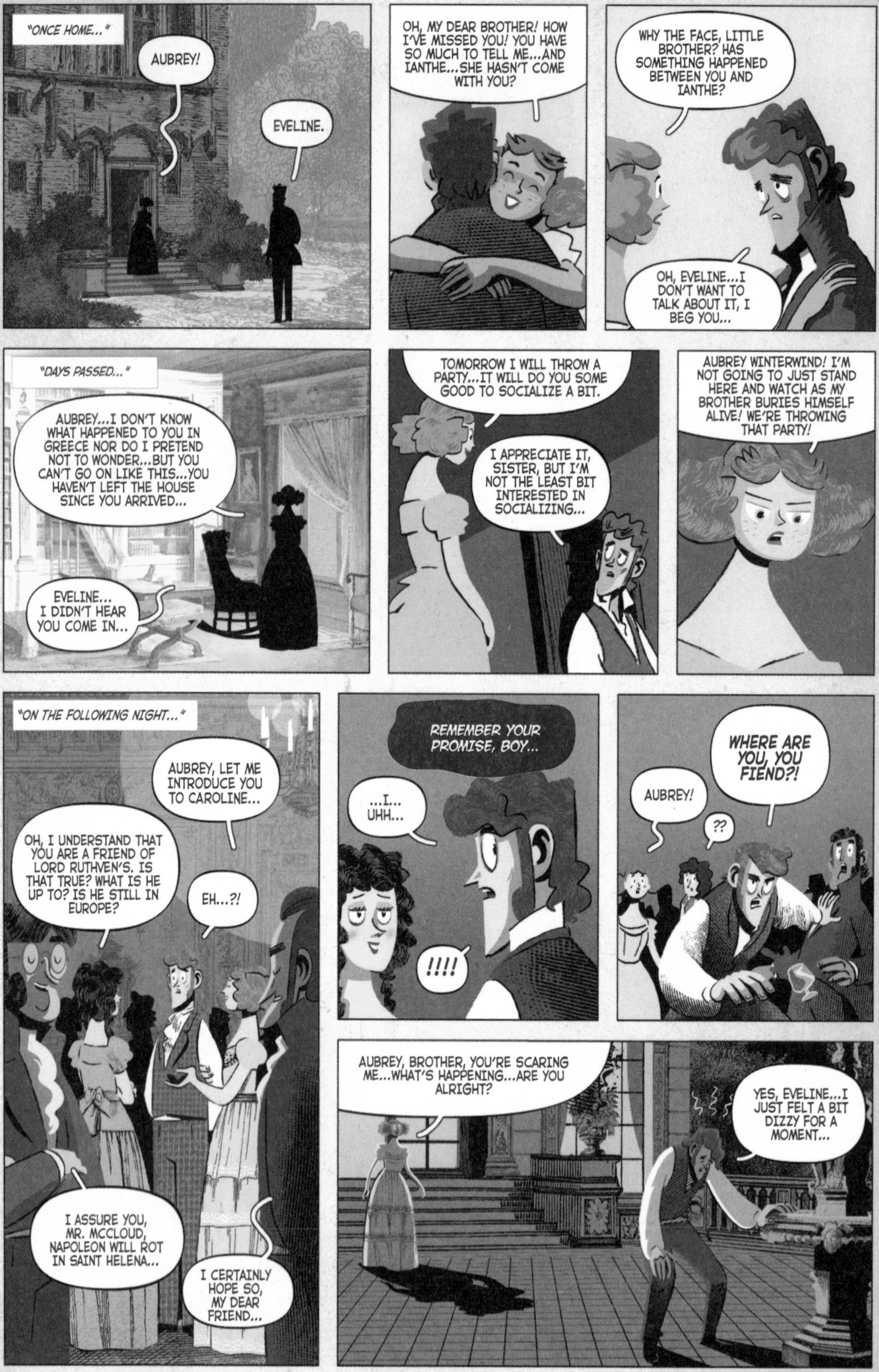
"ONCE HOME..."
AUBREY!
EVELINE.
OH, MY DEAR BROTHER! HOW I'VE MISSED YOU! YOU HAVE SO MUCH TO TELL ME...AND IANTHE...SHE HASN'T COME WITH YOU?
WHY THE FACE, LITTLE BROTHER? HAS SOMETHING HAPPENED BETWEEN YOU AND IANTHE?
OH, EVELINE...I DON'T WANT TO TALK ABOUT IT, I BEG YOU...
"DAYS PASSED..."
AUBREY...I DON'T KNOW WHAT HAPPENED TO YOU IN GREECE NOR DO I PRETEND NOT TO WONDER...BUT YOU CAN'T GO ON LIKE THIS...YOU HAVEN'T LEFT THE HOUSE SINCE YOU ARRIVED...
EVELINE... I DIDN'T HEAR YOU COME IN...
TOMORROW I WILL THROW A PARTY...IT WILL DO YOU SOME GOOD TO SOCIALIZE A BIT.
I APPRECIATE IT, SISTER, BUT I'M NOT THE LEAST BIT INTERESTED IN SOCIALIZING...
AUBREY WINTERWIND! I'M NOT GOING TO JUST STAND HERE AND WATCH AS MY BROTHER BURIES HIMSELF ALIVE! WE'RE THROWING THAT PARTY!
"ON THE FOLLOWING NIGHT..."
AUBREY, LET ME INTRODUCE YOU TO CAROLINE...
OH, I UNDERSTAND THAT YOU ARE A FRIEND OF LORD RUTHVEN'S. IS THAT TRUE? WHAT IS HE UP TO? IS HE STILL IN EUROPE?
EH...?!
I ASSURE YOU, MR. MCCLOUD, NAPOLEON WILL ROT IN SAINT HELENA...
I CERTAINLY HOPE SO, MY DEAR FRIEND...
REMEMBER YOUR PROMISE, BOY...
...I... UHH...
!!!!
AUBREY!
WHERE ARE YOU, YOU FIEND?!
??
AUBREY, BROTHER, YOU'RE SCARING ME...WHAT'S HAPPENING...ARE YOU ALRIGHT?
YES, EVELINE...I JUST FELT A BIT DIZZY FOR A MOMENT...

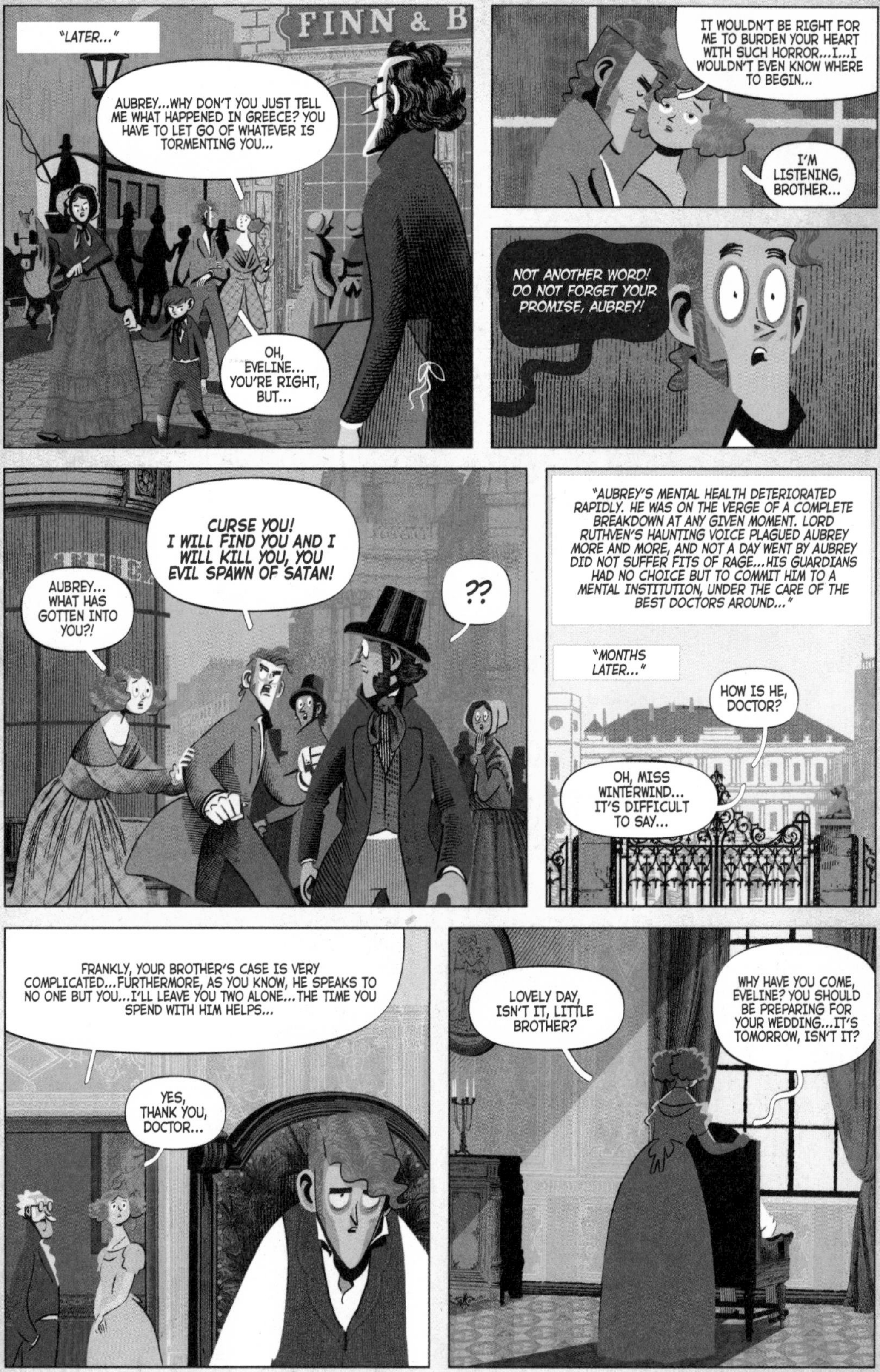
"LATER..."
FINN & B
AUBREY...WHY DON'T YOU JUST TELL ME WHAT HAPPENED IN GREECE? YOU HAVE TO LET GO OF WHATEVER IS TORMENTING YOU...
OH, EVELINE... YOU'RE RIGHT, BUT...
IT WOULDN'T BE RIGHT FOR ME TO BURDEN YOUR HEART WITH SUCH HORROR...I...I WOULDN'T EVEN KNOW WHERE TO BEGIN...
I'M LISTENING, BROTHER...
NOT ANOTHER WORD! DO NOT FORGET YOUR PROMISE, AUBREY!
CURSE YOU! I WILL FIND YOU AND I WILL KILL YOU, YOU EVIL SPAWN OF SATAN!
AUBREY... WHAT HAS GOTTEN INTO YOU?!
??
"AUBREY'S MENTAL HEALTH DETERIORATED RAPIDLY. HE WAS ON THE VERGE OF A COMPLETE BREAKDOWN AT ANY GIVEN MOMENT. LORD RUTHVEN'S HAUNTING VOICE PLAGUED AUBREY MORE AND MORE, AND NOT A DAY WENT BY AUBREY DID NOT SUFFER FITS OF RAGE...HIS GUARDIANS HAD NO CHOICE BUT TO COMMIT HIM TO A MENTAL INSTITUTION, UNDER THE CARE OF THE BEST DOCTORS AROUND..."
"MONTHS LATER..."
HOW IS HE, DOCTOR?
OH, MISS WINTERWIND... IT'S DIFFICULT TO SAY...
FRANKLY, YOUR BROTHER'S CASE IS VERY COMPLICATED...FURTHERMORE, AS YOU KNOW, HE SPEAKS TO NO ONE BUT YOU...I'LL LEAVE YOU TWO ALONE...THE TIME YOU SPEND WITH HIM HELPS...
YES, THANK YOU, DOCTOR...
LOVELY DAY, ISN'T IT, LITTLE BROTHER?
WHY HAVE YOU COME, EVELINE? YOU SHOULD BE PREPARING FOR YOUR WEDDING...IT'S TOMORROW, ISN'T IT?

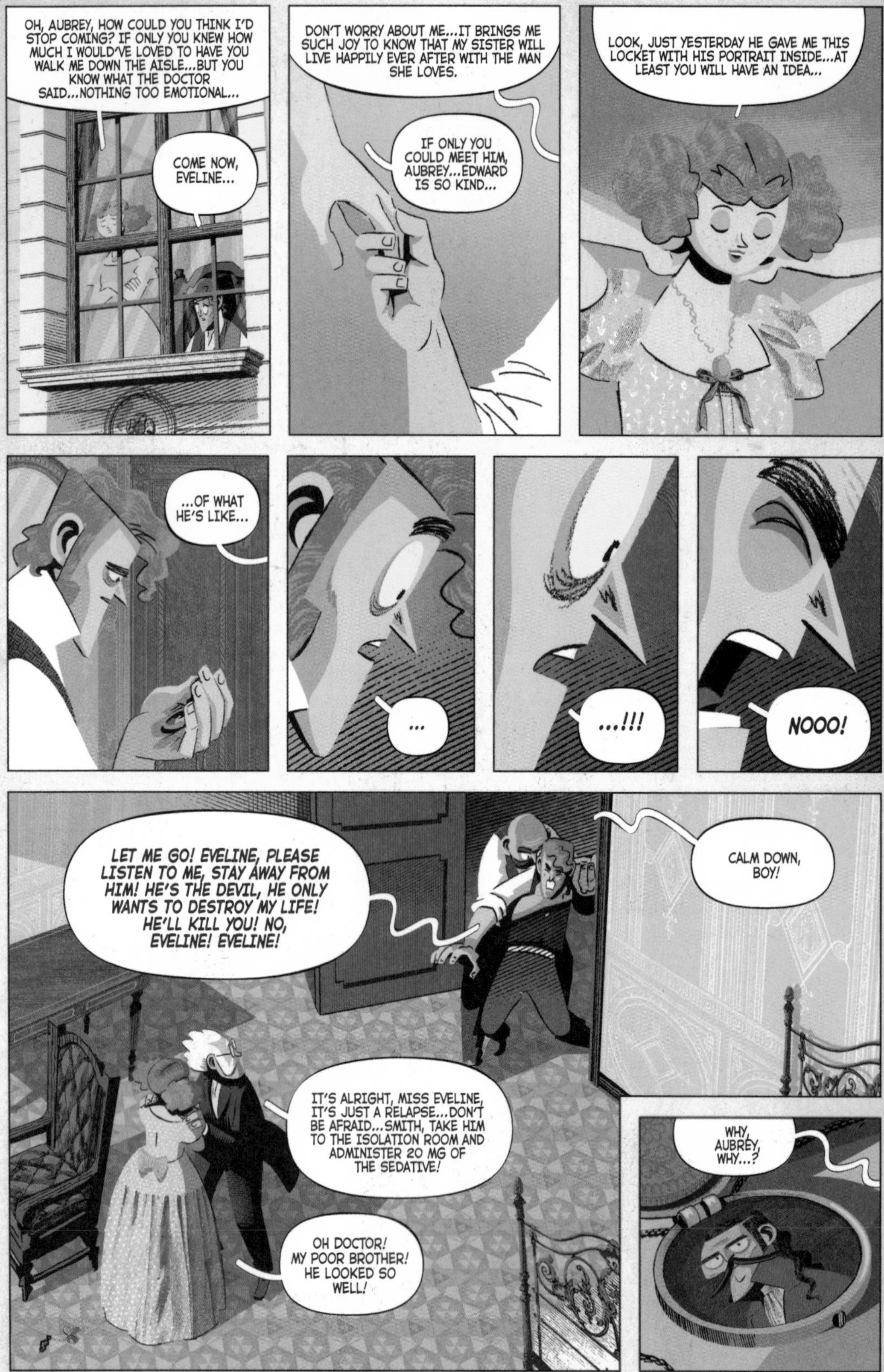
OH, AUBREY, HOW COULD YOU THINK I'D STOP COMING? IF ONLY YOU KNEW HOW MUCH I WOULD'VE LOVED TO HAVE YOU WALK ME DOWN THE AISLE...BUT YOU KNOW WHAT THE DOCTOR SAID...NOTHING TOO EMOTIONAL...
COME NOW, EVELINE...
DON'T WORRY ABOUT ME...IT BRINGS ME SUCH JOY TO KNOW THAT MY SISTER WILL LIVE HAPPILY EVER AFTER WITH THE MAN SHE LOVES.
IF ONLY YOU COULD MEET HIM, AUBREY...EDWARD IS SO KIND...
LOOK, JUST YESTERDAY HE GAVE ME THIS LOCKET WITH HIS PORTRAIT INSIDE...AT LEAST YOU WILL HAVE AN IDEA...
...OF WHAT HE'S LIKE...
...
...!!!
NOOO!
LET ME GO! EVELINE, PLEASE LISTEN TO ME, STAY AWAY FROM HIM! HE'S THE DEVIL, HE ONLY WANTS TO DESTROY MY LIFE! HE'LL KILL YOU! NO, EVELINE! EVELINE!
CALM DOWN, BOY!
IT'S ALRIGHT, MISS EVELINE, IT'S JUST A RELAPSE...DON'T BE AFRAID...SMITH, TAKE HIM TO THE ISOLATION ROOM AND ADMINISTER 20 MG OF THE SEDATIVE!
OH DOCTOR! MY POOR BROTHER! HE LOOKED SO WELL!
WHY, AUBREY, WHY...?

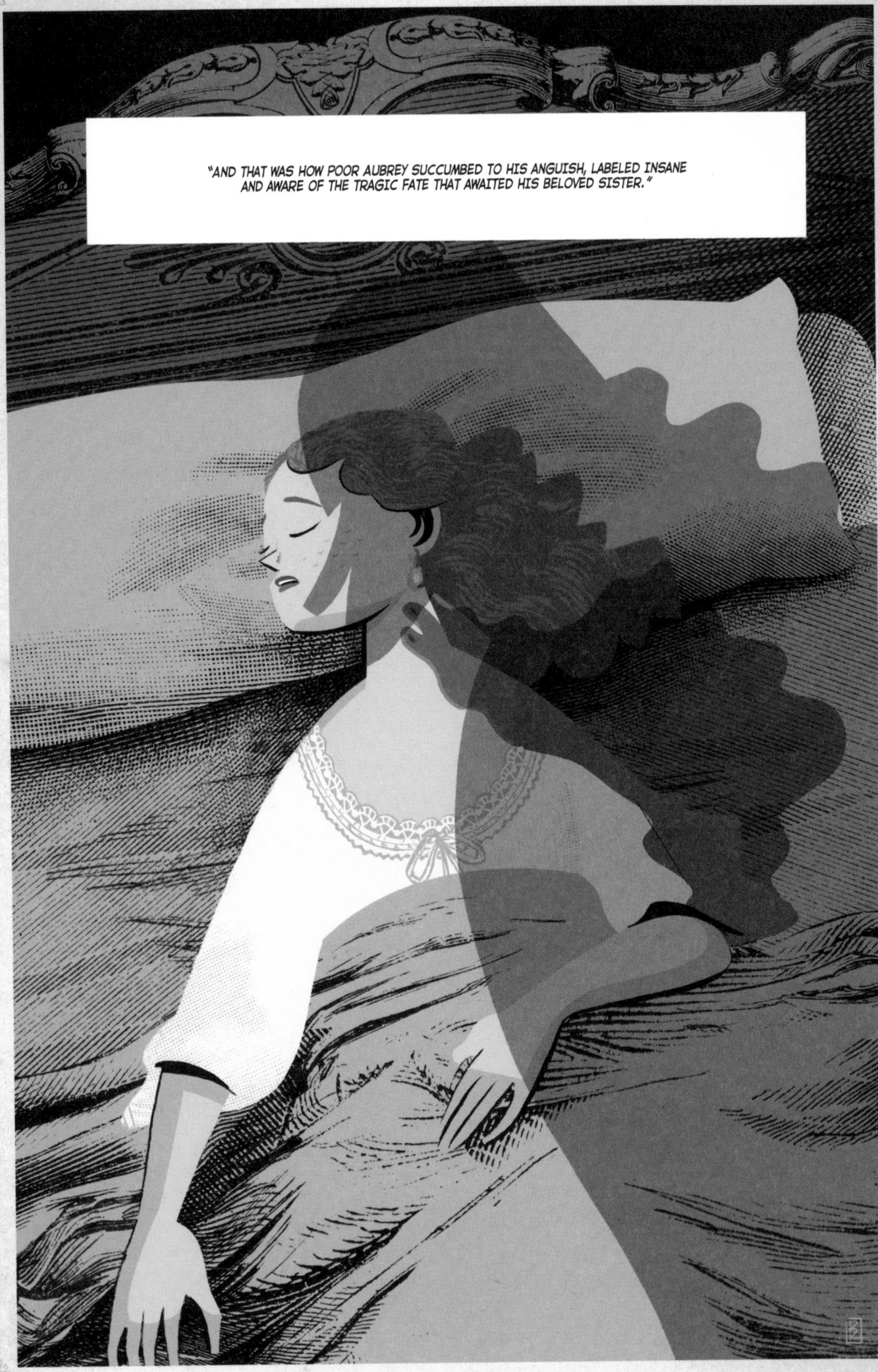
"AND THAT WAS HOW POOR AUBREY SUCCUMBED TO HIS ANGUISH, LABELED INSANE AND AWARE OF THE TRAGIC FATE THAT AWAITED HIS BELOVED SISTER."

HOUSE B...
ON CAMDEN HILL

CATHERINE CROWE
(1800–1876)

BORN IN KENT, ENGLAND, SHE SPENT HER LIFE IN EDINBURGH, SCOTLAND. THERE, SHE SPLIT HER TIME BETWEEN DEFENDING WOMEN'S EDUCATIONAL RIGHTS AND HER WRITING CAREER. IN ADDITION TO DRAMAS, NOVELS, AND CHILDREN'S BOOKS, SHE ALSO WROTE ABOUT THE OCCULT. THE MAJORITY OF HER STORIES ABOUT APPARITIONS AND GHOSTS WERE BASED ON TRUE EVENTS. SHE LIVED TO BE 76.

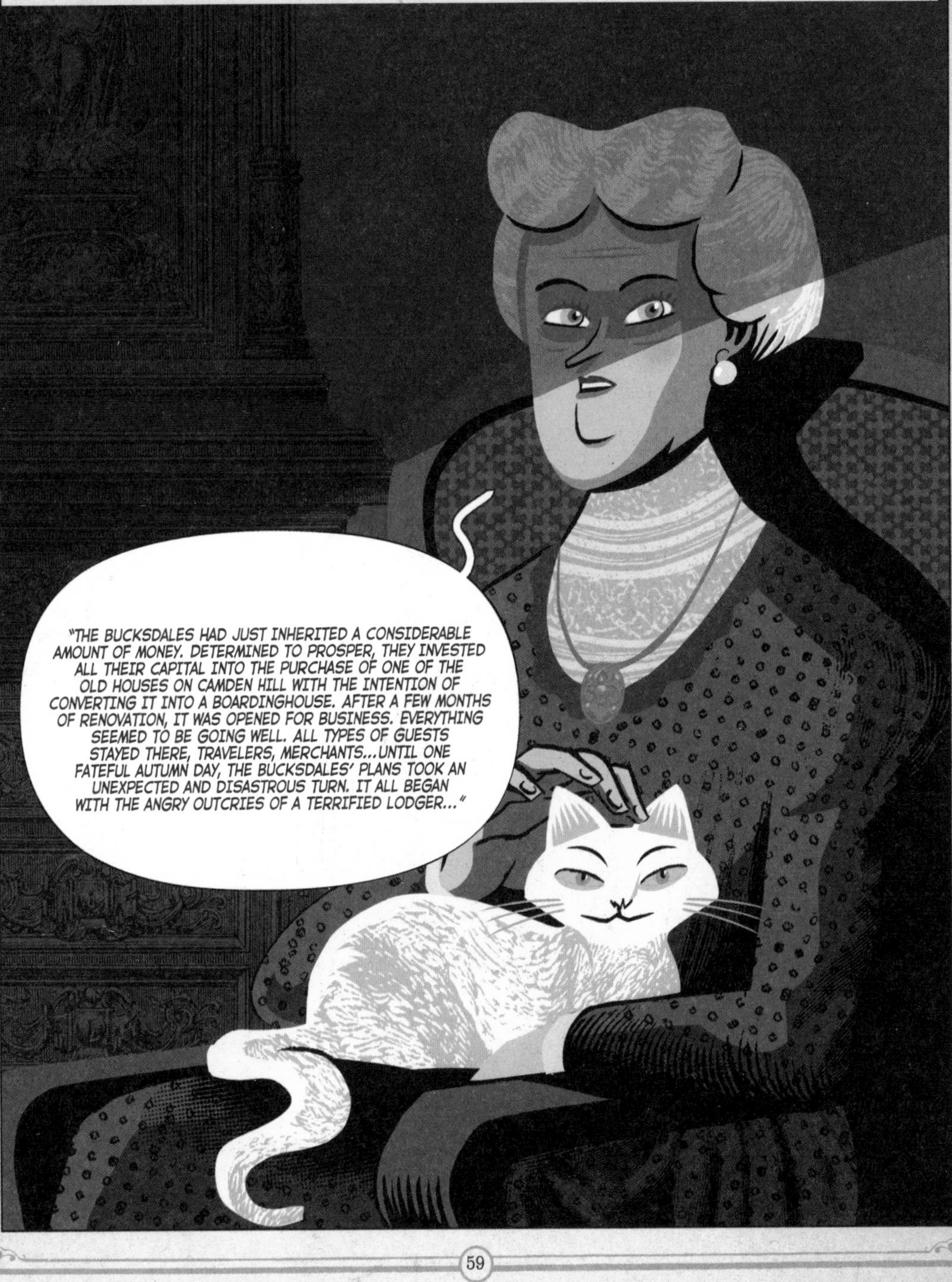
"THE BUCKSDALES HAD JUST INHERITED A CONSIDERABLE AMOUNT OF MONEY. DETERMINED TO PROSPER, THEY INVESTED ALL THEIR CAPITAL INTO THE PURCHASE OF ONE OF THE OLD HOUSES ON CAMDEN HILL WITH THE INTENTION OF CONVERTING IT INTO A BOARDINGHOUSE. AFTER A FEW MONTHS OF RENOVATION, IT WAS OPENED FOR BUSINESS. EVERYTHING SEEMED TO BE GOING WELL. ALL TYPES OF GUESTS STAYED THERE, TRAVELERS, MERCHANTS...UNTIL ONE FATEFUL AUTUMN DAY, THE BUCKSDALES' PLANS TOOK AN UNEXPECTED AND DISASTROUS TURN. IT ALL BEGAN WITH THE ANGRY OUTCRIES OF A TERRIFIED LODGER..."

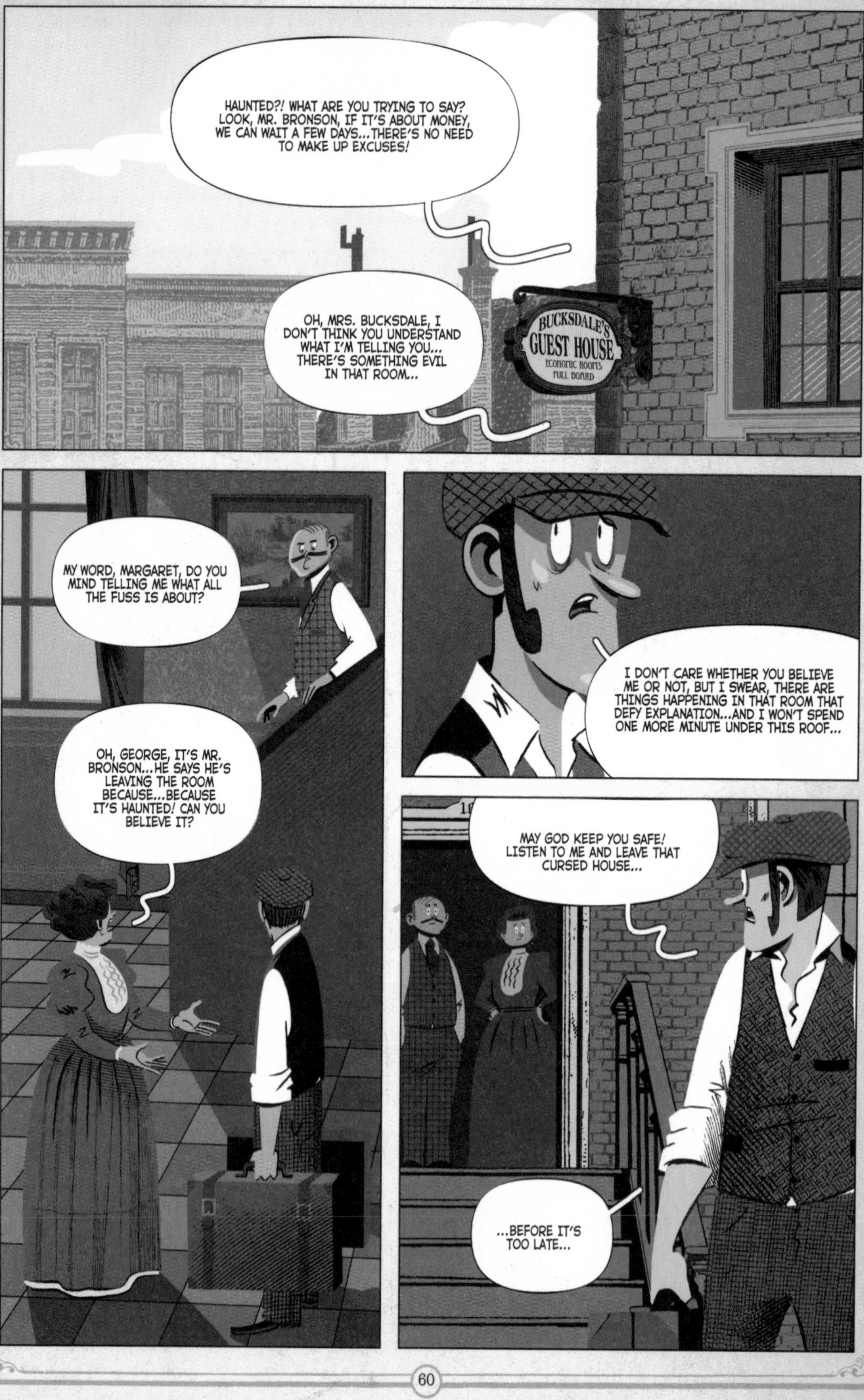
HAUNTED?! WHAT ARE YOU TRYING TO SAY? LOOK, MR. BRONSON, IF IT'S ABOUT MONEY, WE CAN WAIT A FEW DAYS...THERE'S NO NEED TO MAKE UP EXCUSES!
OH, MRS. BUCKSDALE, I DON'T THINK YOU UNDERSTAND WHAT I'M TELLING YOU... THERE'S SOMETHING EVIL IN THAT ROOM...
BUCKSDALE'S GUEST HOUSE
ECONOMIC ROOMS FULL BOARD
MY WORD, MARGARET, DO YOU MIND TELLING ME WHAT ALL THE FUSS IS ABOUT?
OH, GEORGE, IT'S MR. BRONSON...HE SAYS HE'S LEAVING THE ROOM BECAUSE...BECAUSE IT'S HAUNTED! CAN YOU BELIEVE IT?
I DON'T CARE WHETHER YOU BELIEVE ME OR NOT, BUT I SWEAR, THERE ARE THINGS HAPPENING IN THAT ROOM THAT DEFY EXPLANATION...AND I WON'T SPEND ONE MORE MINUTE UNDER THIS ROOF...
MAY GOD KEEP YOU SAFE! LISTEN TO ME AND LEAVE THAT CURSED HOUSE...
...BEFORE IT'S TOO LATE...

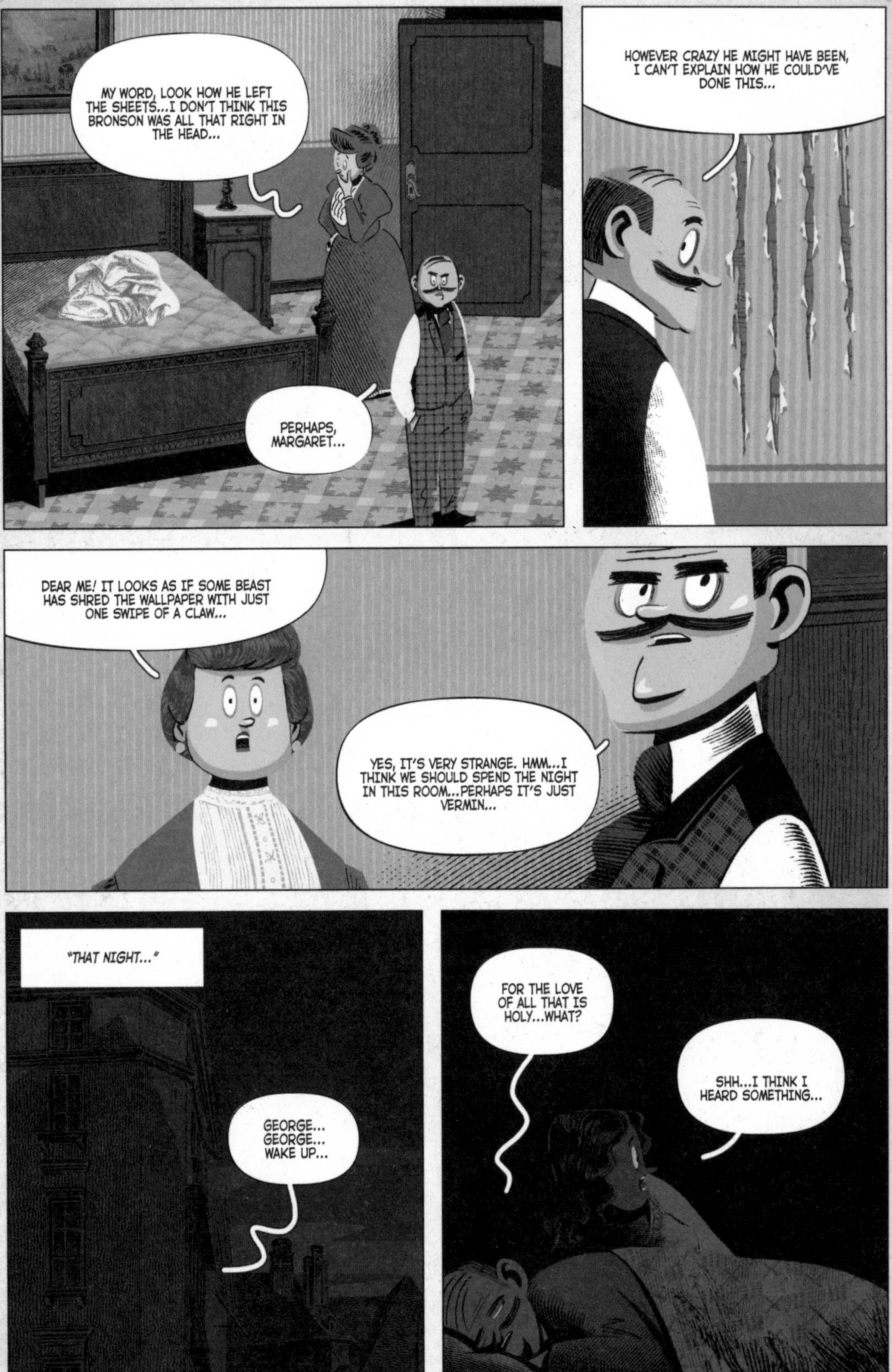
MY WORD, LOOK HOW HE LEFT THE SHEETS...I DON'T THINK THIS BRONSON WAS ALL THAT RIGHT IN THE HEAD...
PERHAPS, MARGARET...
HOWEVER CRAZY HE MIGHT HAVE BEEN, I CAN'T EXPLAIN HOW HE COULD'VE DONE THIS...
DEAR ME! IT LOOKS AS IF SOME BEAST HAS SHRED THE WALLPAPER WITH JUST ONE SWIPE OF A CLAW...
YES, IT'S VERY STRANGE. HMM...I THINK WE SHOULD SPEND THE NIGHT IN THIS ROOM...PERHAPS IT'S JUST VERMIN...
"THAT NIGHT..."
GEORGE... GEORGE... WAKE UP...
FOR THE LOVE OF ALL THAT IS HOLY...WHAT?
SHH...I THINK I HEARD SOMETHING...

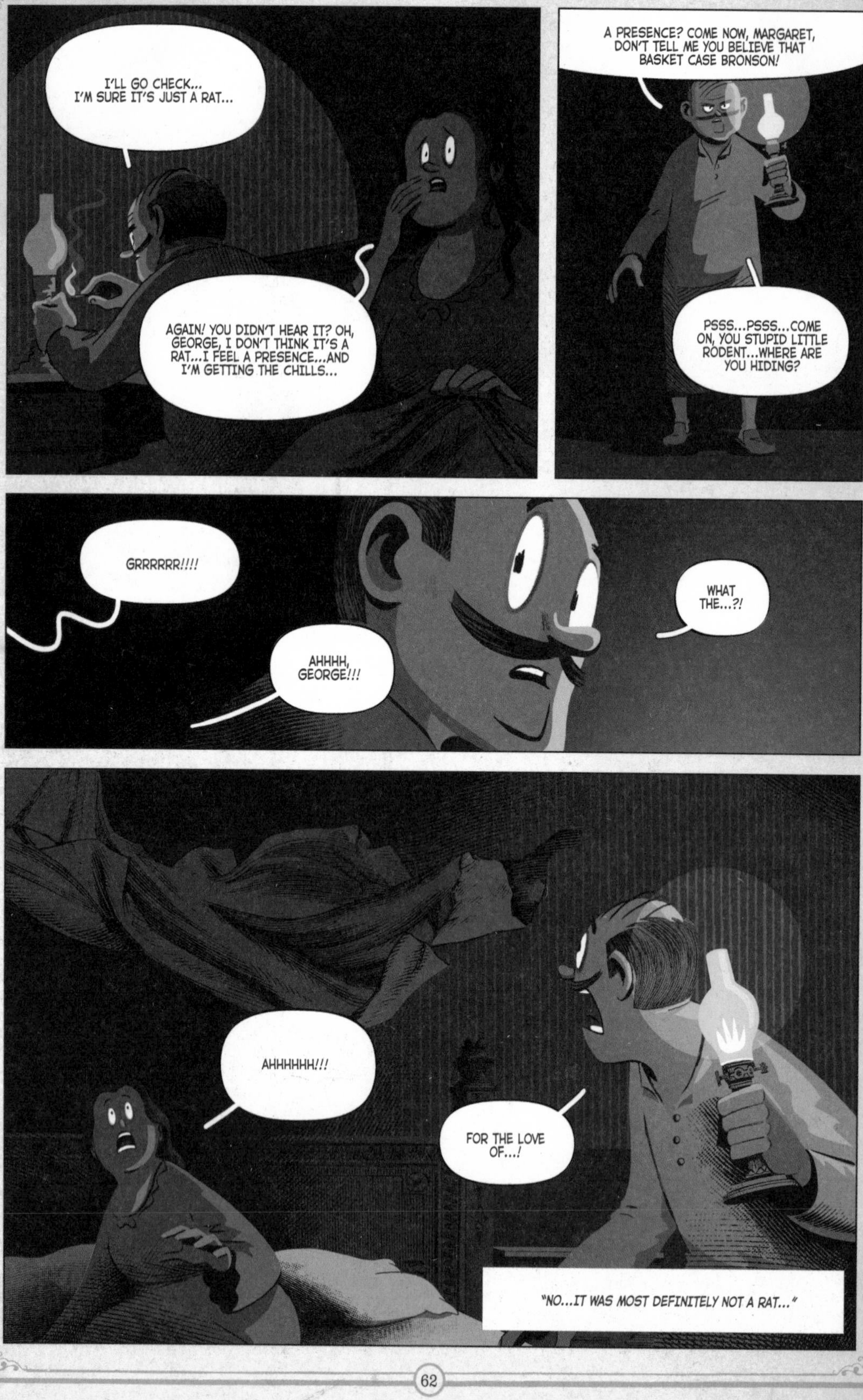
I'LL GO CHECK... I'M SURE IT'S JUST A RAT...
AGAIN! YOU DIDN'T HEAR IT? OH, GEORGE, I DON'T THINK IT'S A RAT...I FEEL A PRESENCE...AND I'M GETTING THE CHILLS...
A PRESENCE? COME NOW, MARGARET, DON'T TELL ME YOU BELIEVE THAT BASKET CASE BRONSON!
PSSS...PSSS...COME ON, YOU STUPID LITTLE RODENT...WHERE ARE YOU HIDING?
GRRRRRR!!!!
AHHHH, GEORGE!!!
WHAT THE...?!
AHHHHHH!!!
FOR THE LOVE OF...!
"NO...IT WAS MOST DEFINITELY NOT A RAT..."

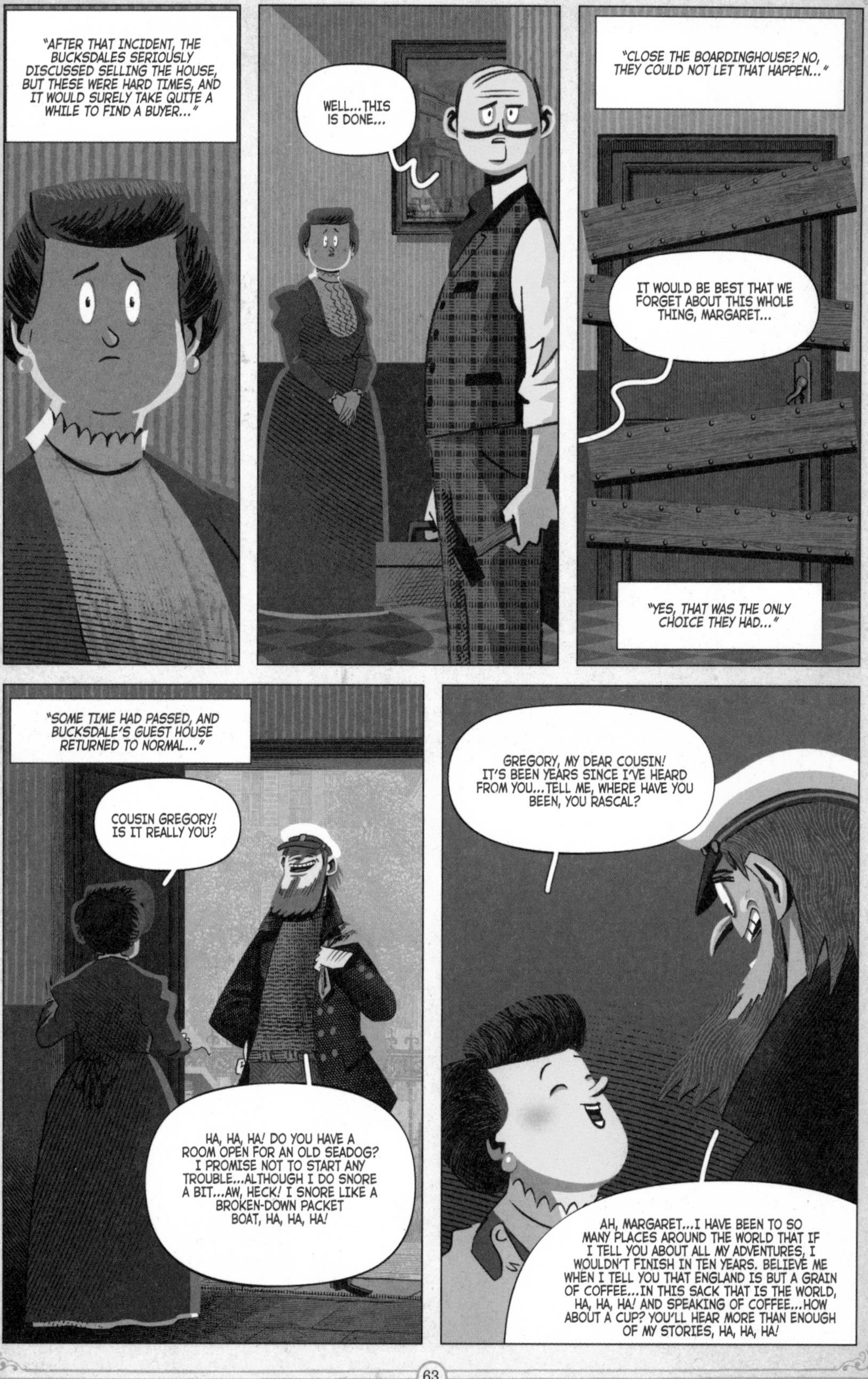
"AFTER THAT INCIDENT, THE BUCKSDALES SERIOUSLY DISCUSSED SELLING THE HOUSE, BUT THESE WERE HARD TIMES, AND IT WOULD SURELY TAKE QUITE A WHILE TO FIND A BUYER..."
WELL...THIS IS DONE...
"CLOSE THE BOARDINGHOUSE? NO, THEY COULD NOT LET THAT HAPPEN..."
IT WOULD BE BEST THAT WE FORGET ABOUT THIS WHOLE THING, MARGARET...
"YES, THAT WAS THE ONLY CHOICE THEY HAD..."
"SOME TIME HAD PASSED, AND BUCKSDALE'S GUEST HOUSE RETURNED TO NORMAL..."
COUSIN GREGORY! IS IT REALLY YOU?
HA, HA, HA! DO YOU HAVE A ROOM OPEN FOR AN OLD SEADOG? I PROMISE NOT TO START ANY TROUBLE...ALTHOUGH I DO SNORE A BIT...AW, HECK! I SNORE LIKE A BROKEN-DOWN PACKET BOAT, HA, HA, HA!
GREGORY, MY DEAR COUSIN! IT'S BEEN YEARS SINCE I'VE HEARD FROM YOU...TELL ME, WHERE HAVE YOU BEEN, YOU RASCAL?
AH, MARGARET...I HAVE BEEN TO SO MANY PLACES AROUND THE WORLD THAT IF I TELL YOU ABOUT ALL MY ADVENTURES, I WOULDN'T FINISH IN TEN YEARS. BELIEVE ME WHEN I TELL YOU THAT ENGLAND IS BUT A GRAIN OF COFFEE...IN THIS SACK THAT IS THE WORLD, HA, HA, HA! AND SPEAKING OF COFFEE...HOW ABOUT A CUP? YOU'LL HEAR MORE THAN ENOUGH OF MY STORIES, HA, HA, HA!

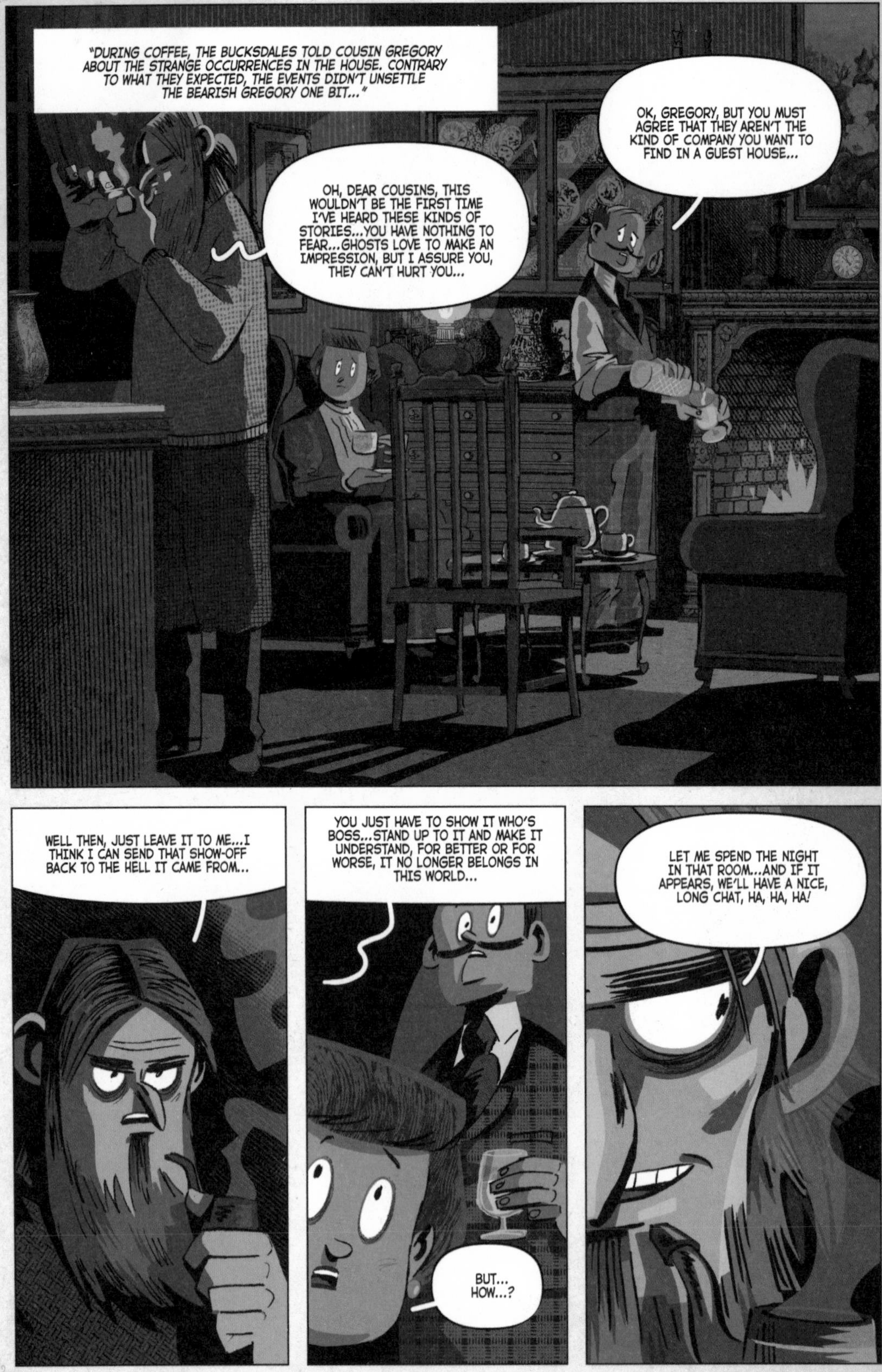
"DURING COFFEE, THE BUCKSDALES TOLD COUSIN GREGORY ABOUT THE STRANGE OCCURRENCES IN THE HOUSE. CONTRARY TO WHAT THEY EXPECTED, THE EVENTS DIDN'T UNSETTLE THE BEARISH GREGORY ONE BIT..."
OH, DEAR COUSINS, THIS WOULDN'T BE THE FIRST TIME I'VE HEARD THESE KINDS OF STORIES...YOU HAVE NOTHING TO FEAR...GHOSTS LOVE TO MAKE AN IMPRESSION, BUT I ASSURE YOU, THEY CAN'T HURT YOU...
OK, GREGORY, BUT YOU MUST AGREE THAT THEY AREN'T THE KIND OF COMPANY YOU WANT TO FIND IN A GUEST HOUSE...
WELL THEN, JUST LEAVE IT TO ME...I THINK I CAN SEND THAT SHOW-OFF BACK TO THE HELL IT CAME FROM...
YOU JUST HAVE TO SHOW IT WHO'S BOSS...STAND UP TO IT AND MAKE IT UNDERSTAND, FOR BETTER OR FOR WORSE, IT NO LONGER BELONGS IN THIS WORLD...
BUT... HOW...?
LET ME SPEND THE NIGHT IN THAT ROOM...AND IF IT APPEARS, WE'LL HAVE A NICE, LONG CHAT, HA, HA, HA!

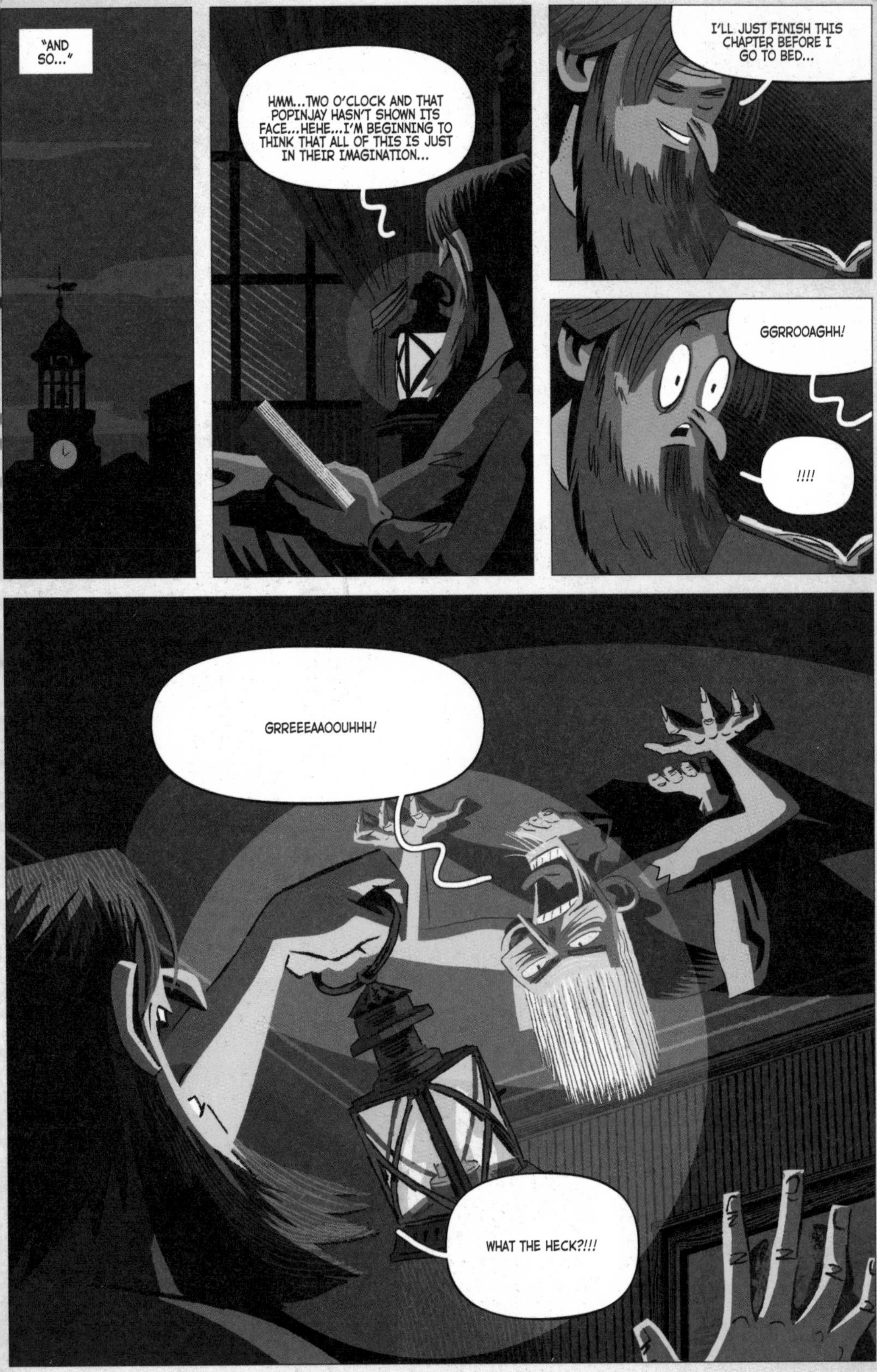
"AND SO..."
HMM...TWO O'CLOCK AND THAT POPINJAY HASN'T SHOWN ITS FACE...HEHE...I'M BEGINNING TO THINK THAT ALL OF THIS IS JUST IN THEIR IMAGINATION...
I'LL JUST FINISH THIS CHAPTER BEFORE I GO TO BED...
GGRROOAGHH!
!!!!
GRREEEAAOOUHHH!
WHAT THE HECK?!!!

WICKED MONSTER!

HIIIA!

GRAAAH!

I'M NOT AFRAID OF YOU, DEMON!

I'LL SEND YOU RIGHT BACK TO HELL!

??

FSHHH!

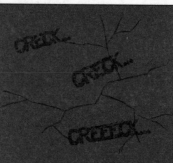

CREICK...

CREICK...

CREEECK...

CREEECK...!

WHAT THE DEVIL...

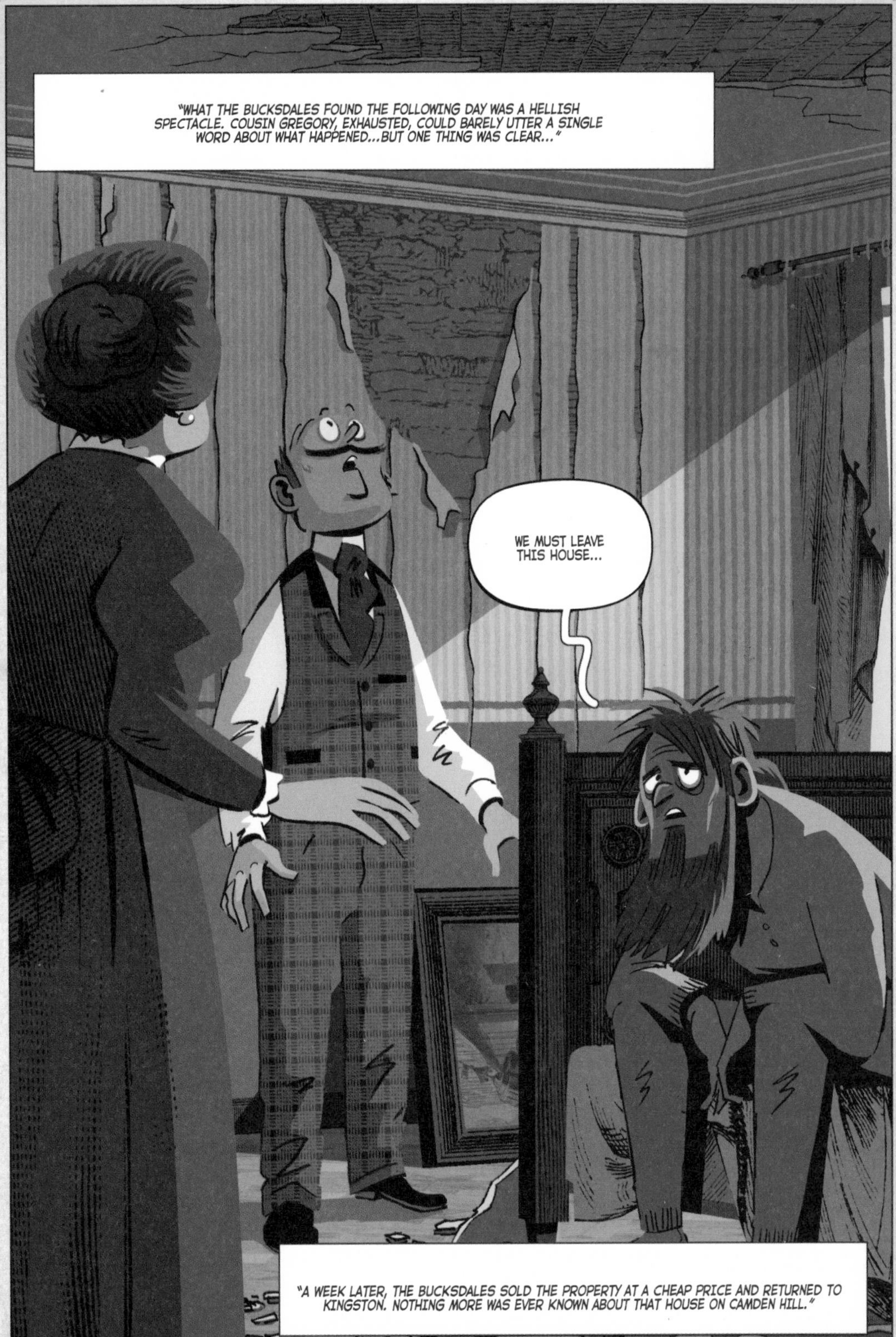
"WHAT THE BUCKSDALES FOUND THE FOLLOWING DAY WAS A HELLISH SPECTACLE. COUSIN GREGORY, EXHAUSTED, COULD BARELY UTTER A SINGLE WORD ABOUT WHAT HAPPENED...BUT ONE THING WAS CLEAR..."
WE MUST LEAVE THIS HOUSE...
"A WEEK LATER, THE BUCKSDALES SOLD THE PROPERTY AT A CHEAP PRICE AND RETURNED TO KINGSTON. NOTHING MORE WAS EVER KNOWN ABOUT THAT HOUSE ON CAMDEN HILL."

Robert Louis Stevenson

THE BODY SNATCHER

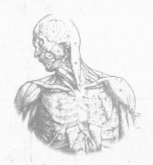

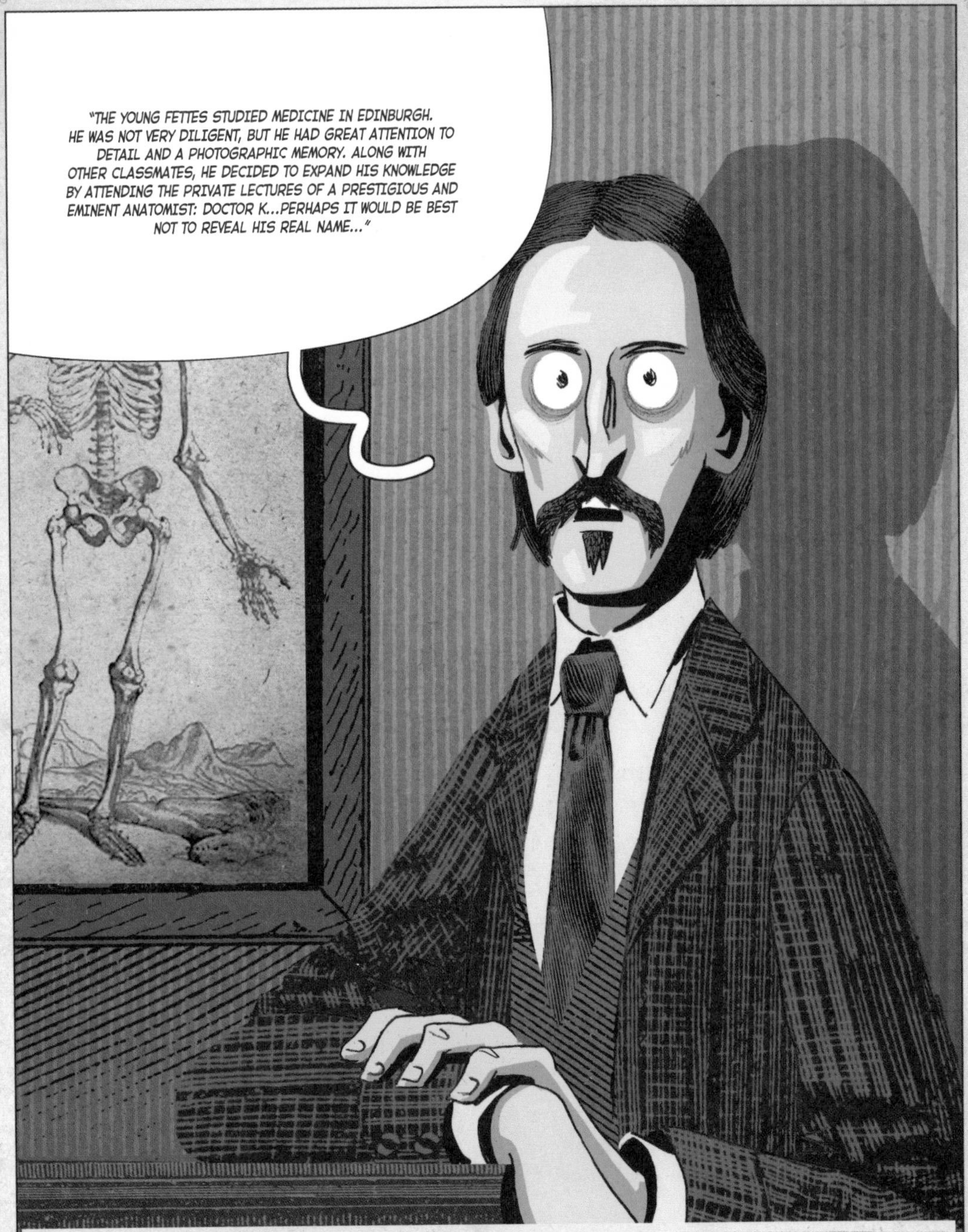
"THE YOUNG FETTES STUDIED MEDICINE IN EDINBURGH. HE WAS NOT VERY DILIGENT, BUT HE HAD GREAT ATTENTION TO DETAIL AND A PHOTOGRAPHIC MEMORY. ALONG WITH OTHER CLASSMATES, HE DECIDED TO EXPAND HIS KNOWLEDGE BY ATTENDING THE PRIVATE LECTURES OF A PRESTIGIOUS AND EMINENT ANATOMIST: DOCTOR K...PERHAPS IT WOULD BE BEST NOT TO REVEAL HIS REAL NAME..."

ROBERT LOUIS STEVENSON
(1850–1894)

PLAGUED BY ILLNESS SINCE CHILDHOOD, THIS SCOTTISH AUTHOR DECIDED TO DEDICATE HIS LIFE TO LITERATURE AT THE AGE OF 25. HE DIED AT HOME FROM A CEREBRAL HEMORRHAGE AT 44, BUT IN ADDITION TO POEMS AND SHORT STORIES, HIS LEGACY INCLUDES SUCH IMPORTANT WORKS AS *TREASURE ISLAND* AND *THE STRANGE CASE OF DR. JEKYLL AND MR. HYDE.*

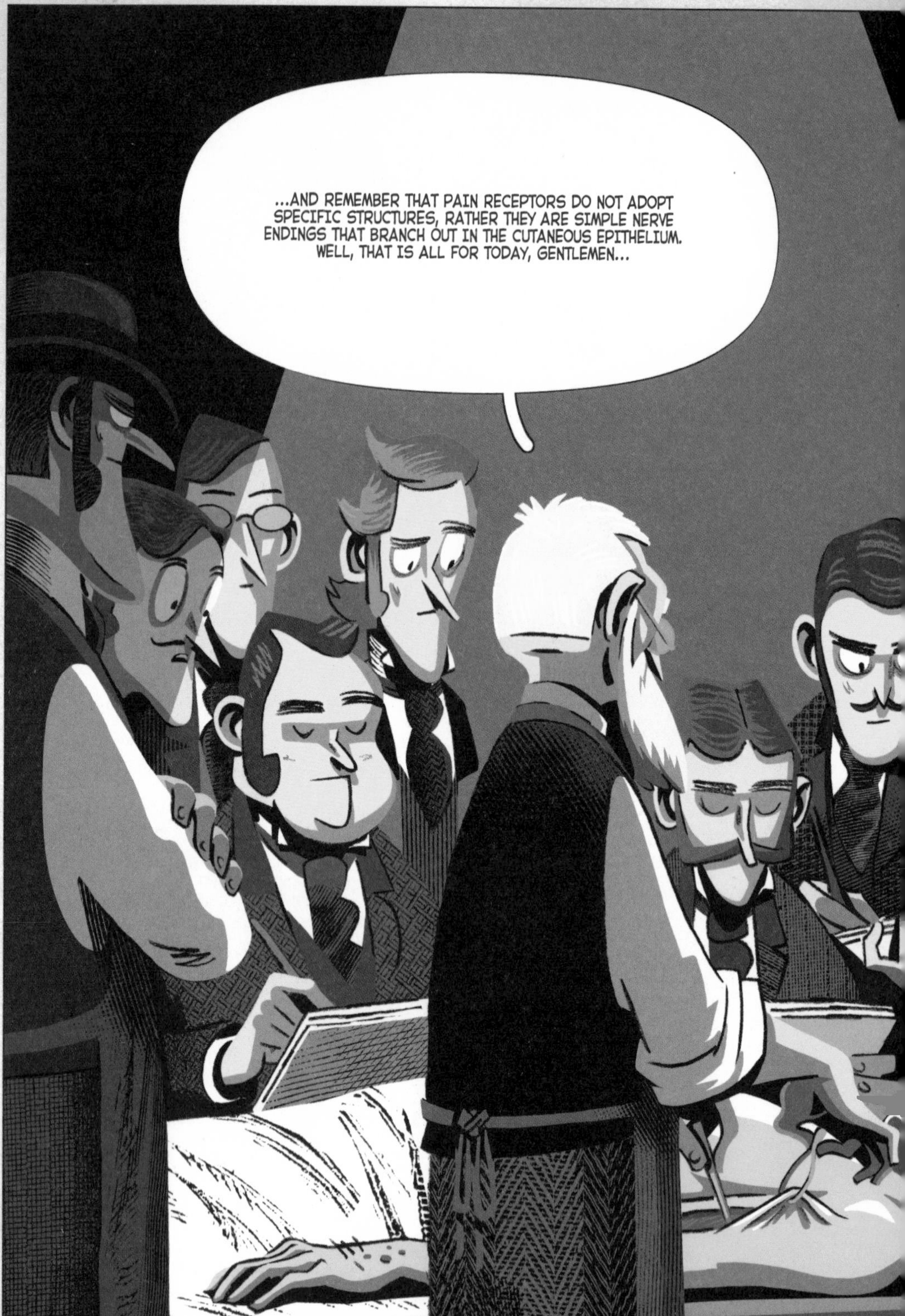
...AND REMEMBER THAT PAIN RECEPTORS DO NOT ADOPT SPECIFIC STRUCTURES, RATHER THEY ARE SIMPLE NERVE ENDINGS THAT BRANCH OUT IN THE CUTANEOUS EPITHELIUM. WELL, THAT IS ALL FOR TODAY, GENTLEMEN...

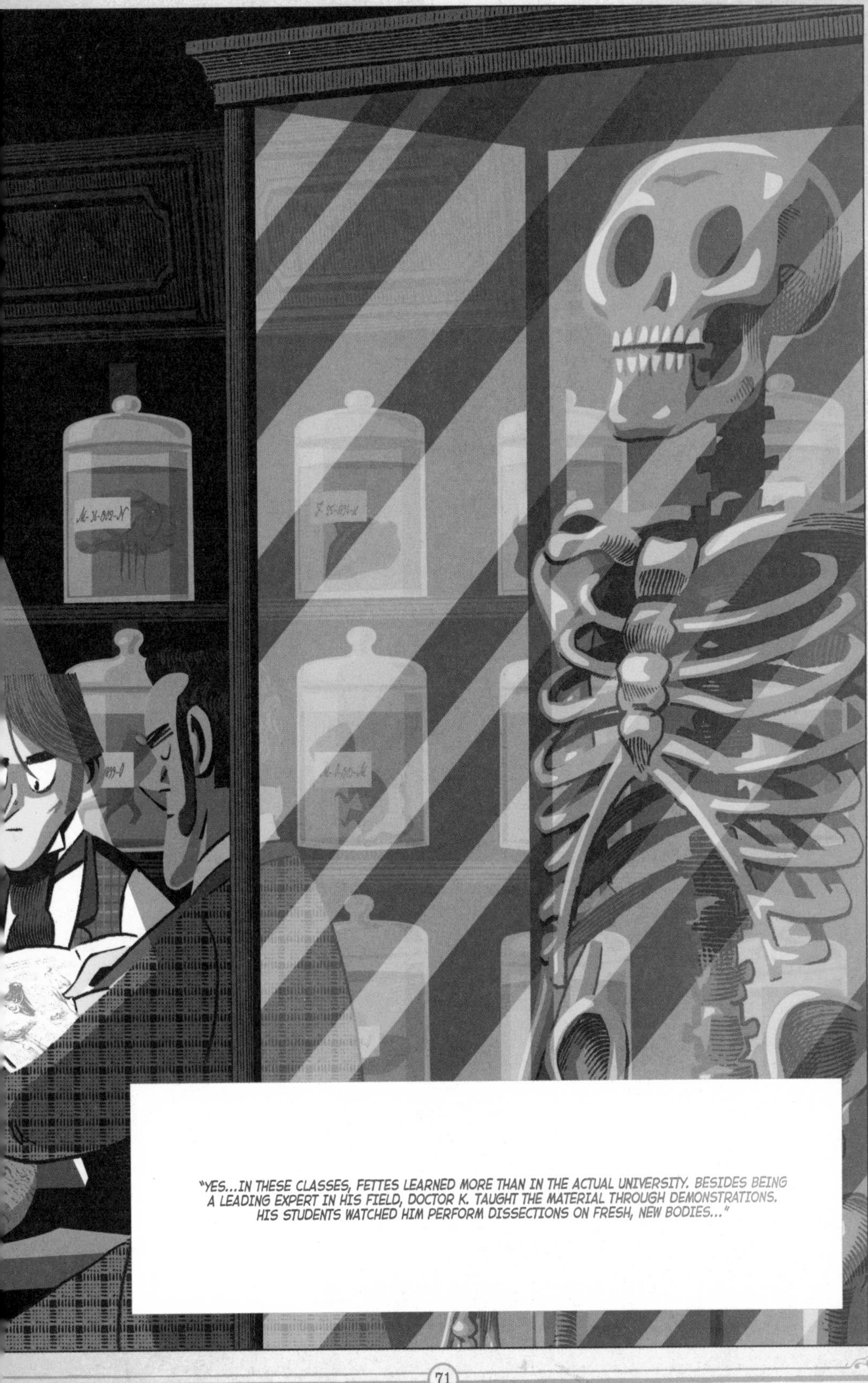
"YES...IN THESE CLASSES, FETTES LEARNED MORE THAN IN THE ACTUAL UNIVERSITY. BESIDES BEING A LEADING EXPERT IN HIS FIELD, DOCTOR K. TAUGHT THE MATERIAL THROUGH DEMONSTRATIONS. HIS STUDENTS WATCHED HIM PERFORM DISSECTIONS ON FRESH, NEW BODIES..."

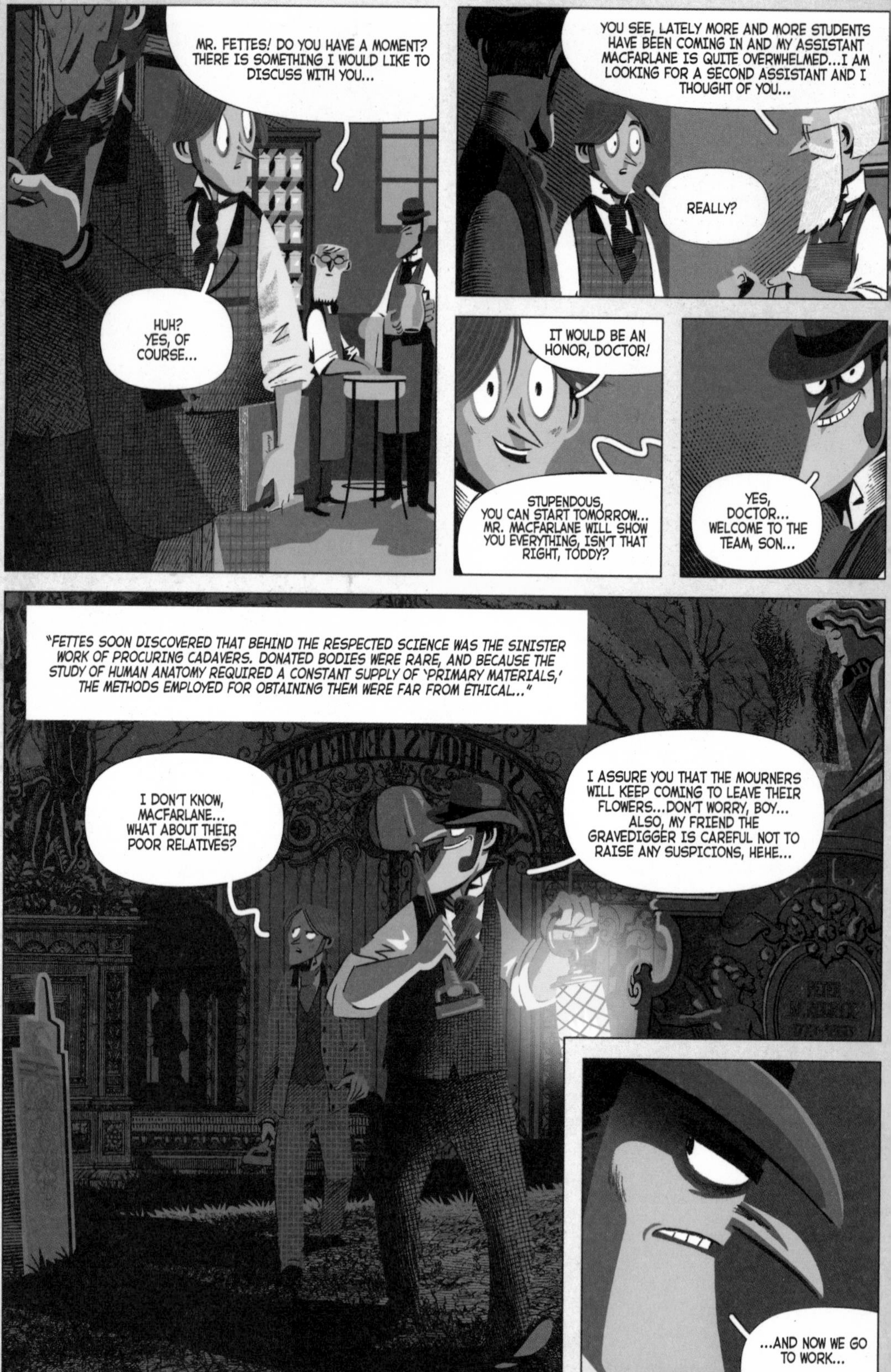
MR. FETTES! DO YOU HAVE A MOMENT? THERE IS SOMETHING I WOULD LIKE TO DISCUSS WITH YOU...
HUH? YES, OF COURSE...
YOU SEE, LATELY MORE AND MORE STUDENTS HAVE BEEN COMING IN AND MY ASSISTANT MACFARLANE IS QUITE OVERWHELMED...I AM LOOKING FOR A SECOND ASSISTANT AND I THOUGHT OF YOU...
REALLY?
IT WOULD BE AN HONOR, DOCTOR!
STUPENDOUS, YOU CAN START TOMORROW... MR. MACFARLANE WILL SHOW YOU EVERYTHING, ISN'T THAT RIGHT, TODDY?
YES, DOCTOR... WELCOME TO THE TEAM, SON...
"FETTES SOON DISCOVERED THAT BEHIND THE RESPECTED SCIENCE WAS THE SINISTER WORK OF PROCURING CADAVERS. DONATED BODIES WERE RARE, AND BECAUSE THE STUDY OF HUMAN ANATOMY REQUIRED A CONSTANT SUPPLY OF 'PRIMARY MATERIALS,' THE METHODS EMPLOYED FOR OBTAINING THEM WERE FAR FROM ETHICAL..."
I DON'T KNOW, MACFARLANE... WHAT ABOUT THEIR POOR RELATIVES?
I ASSURE YOU THAT THE MOURNERS WILL KEEP COMING TO LEAVE THEIR FLOWERS...DON'T WORRY, BOY... ALSO, MY FRIEND THE GRAVEDIGGER IS CAREFUL NOT TO RAISE ANY SUSPICIONS, HEHE...
...AND NOW WE GO TO WORK...

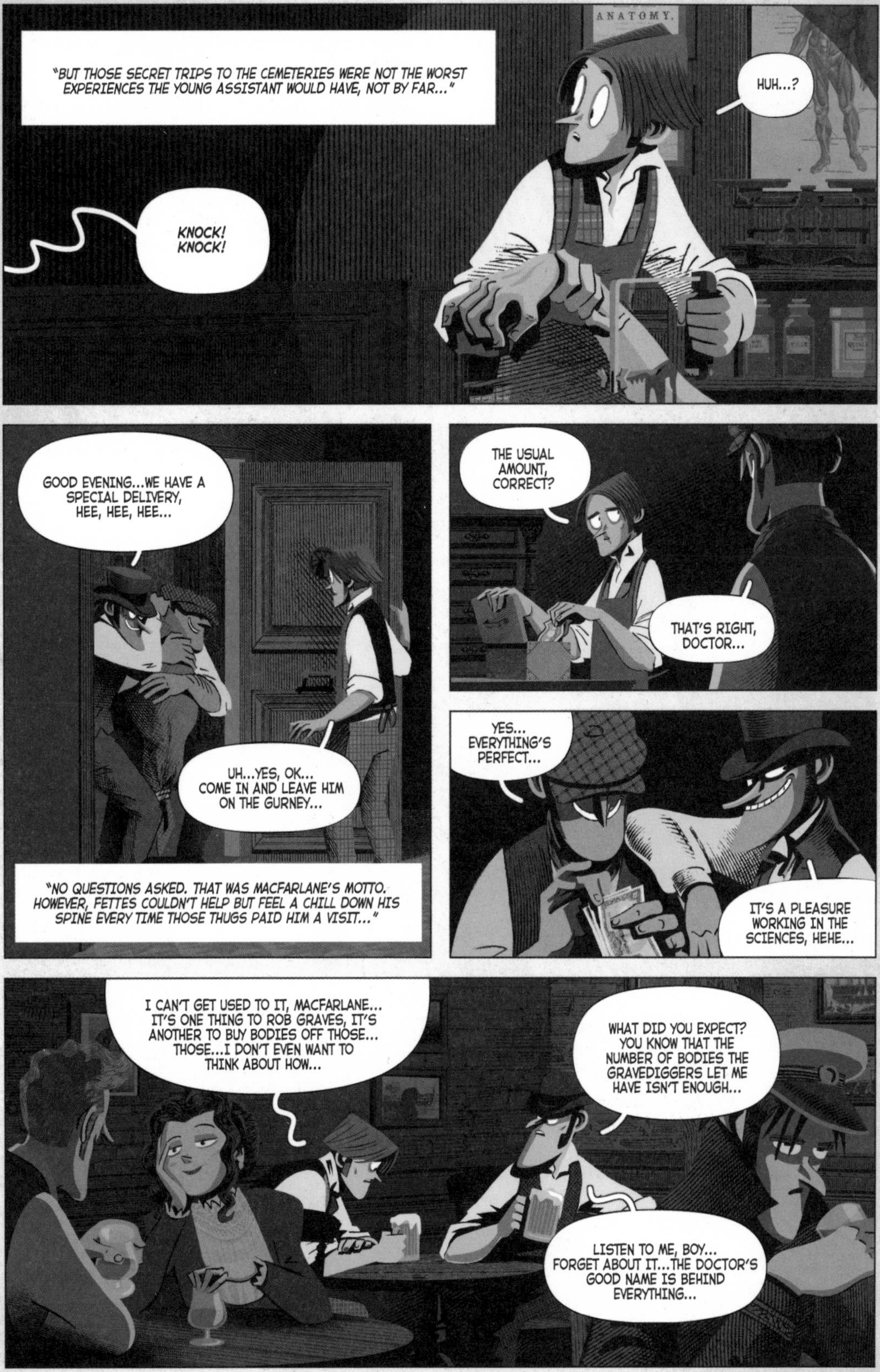
"BUT THOSE SECRET TRIPS TO THE CEMETERIES WERE NOT THE WORST EXPERIENCES THE YOUNG ASSISTANT WOULD HAVE, NOT BY FAR..."
ANATOMY.
HUH...?
KNOCK! KNOCK!
GOOD EVENING...WE HAVE A SPECIAL DELIVERY, HEE, HEE, HEE...
UH...YES, OK... COME IN AND LEAVE HIM ON THE GURNEY...
"NO QUESTIONS ASKED. THAT WAS MACFARLANE'S MOTTO. HOWEVER, FETTES COULDN'T HELP BUT FEEL A CHILL DOWN HIS SPINE EVERY TIME THOSE THUGS PAID HIM A VISIT..."
THE USUAL AMOUNT, CORRECT?
THAT'S RIGHT, DOCTOR...
YES... EVERYTHING'S PERFECT...
IT'S A PLEASURE WORKING IN THE SCIENCES, HEHE...
I CAN'T GET USED TO IT, MACFARLANE... IT'S ONE THING TO ROB GRAVES, IT'S ANOTHER TO BUY BODIES OFF THOSE... THOSE...I DON'T EVEN WANT TO THINK ABOUT HOW...
WHAT DID YOU EXPECT? YOU KNOW THAT THE NUMBER OF BODIES THE GRAVEDIGGERS LET ME HAVE ISN'T ENOUGH...
LISTEN TO ME, BOY... FORGET ABOUT IT...THE DOCTOR'S GOOD NAME IS BEHIND EVERYTHING...

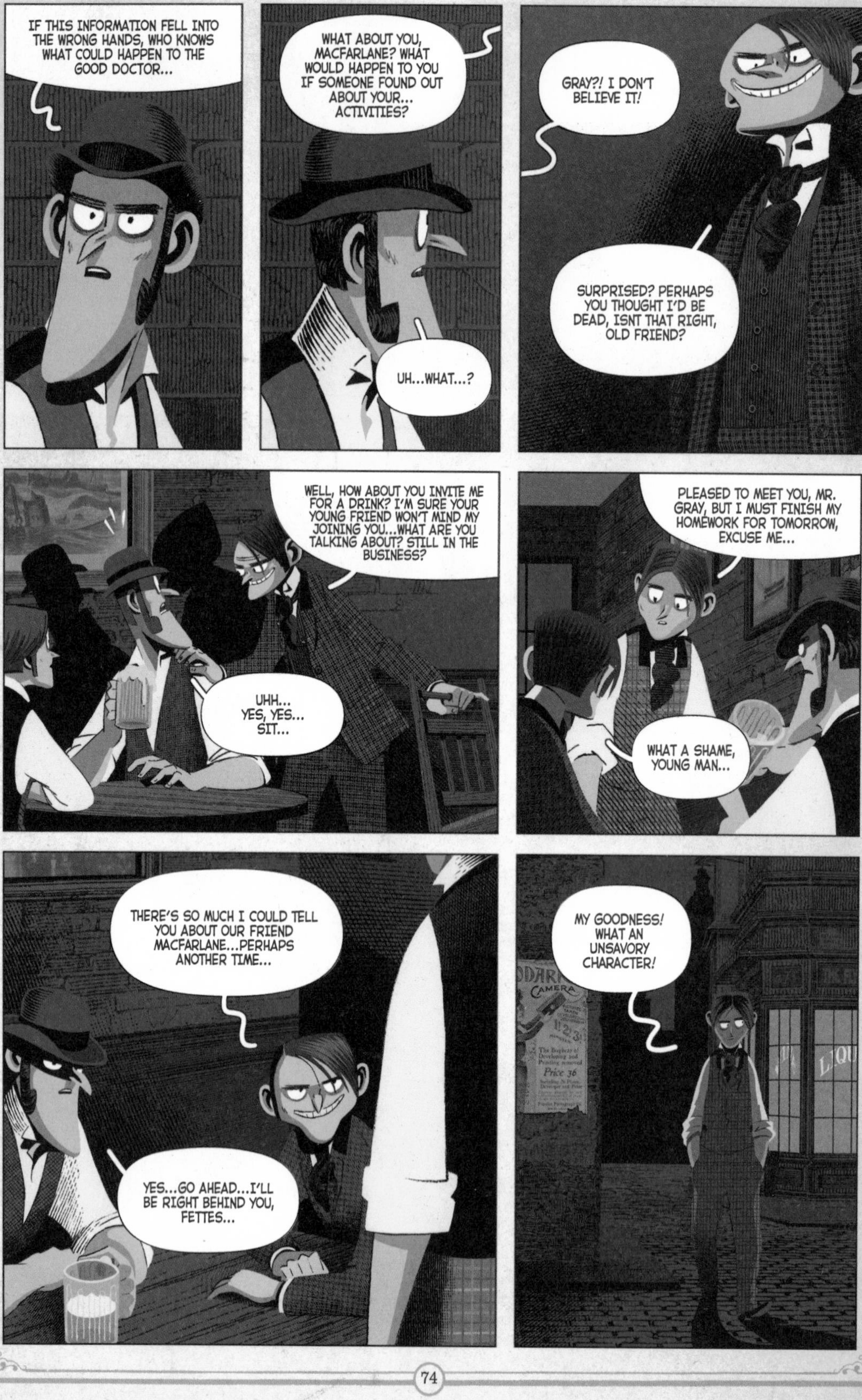
IF THIS INFORMATION FELL INTO THE WRONG HANDS, WHO KNOWS WHAT COULD HAPPEN TO THE GOOD DOCTOR...
WHAT ABOUT YOU, MACFARLANE? WHAT WOULD HAPPEN TO YOU IF SOMEONE FOUND OUT ABOUT YOUR... ACTIVITIES?
UH...WHAT...?
GRAY?! I DON'T BELIEVE IT!
SURPRISED? PERHAPS YOU THOUGHT I'D BE DEAD, ISNT THAT RIGHT, OLD FRIEND?
WELL, HOW ABOUT YOU INVITE ME FOR A DRINK? I'M SURE YOUR YOUNG FRIEND WON'T MIND MY JOINING YOU...WHAT ARE YOU TALKING ABOUT? STILL IN THE BUSINESS?
UHH... YES, YES... SIT...
PLEASED TO MEET YOU, MR. GRAY, BUT I MUST FINISH MY HOMEWORK FOR TOMORROW, EXCUSE ME...
WHAT A SHAME, YOUNG MAN...
THERE'S SO MUCH I COULD TELL YOU ABOUT OUR FRIEND MACFARLANE...PERHAPS ANOTHER TIME...
YES...GO AHEAD...I'LL BE RIGHT BEHIND YOU, FETTES...
MY GOODNESS! WHAT AN UNSAVORY CHARACTER!

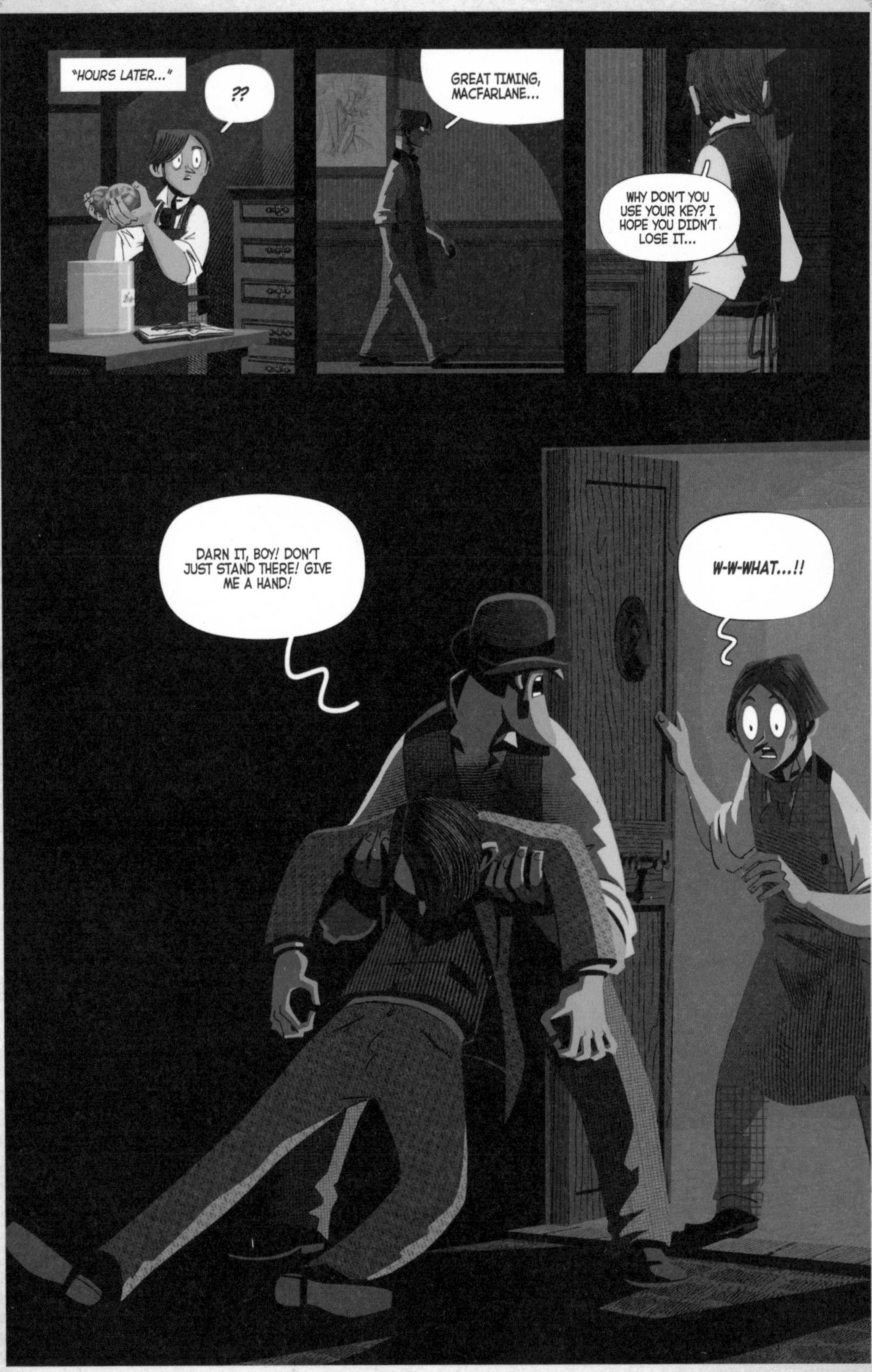
"HOURS LATER..."
??
GREAT TIMING, MACFARLANE...
WHY DON'T YOU USE YOUR KEY? I HOPE YOU DIDN'T LOSE IT...
DARN IT, BOY! DON'T JUST STAND THERE! GIVE ME A HAND!
W-W-WHAT...!!

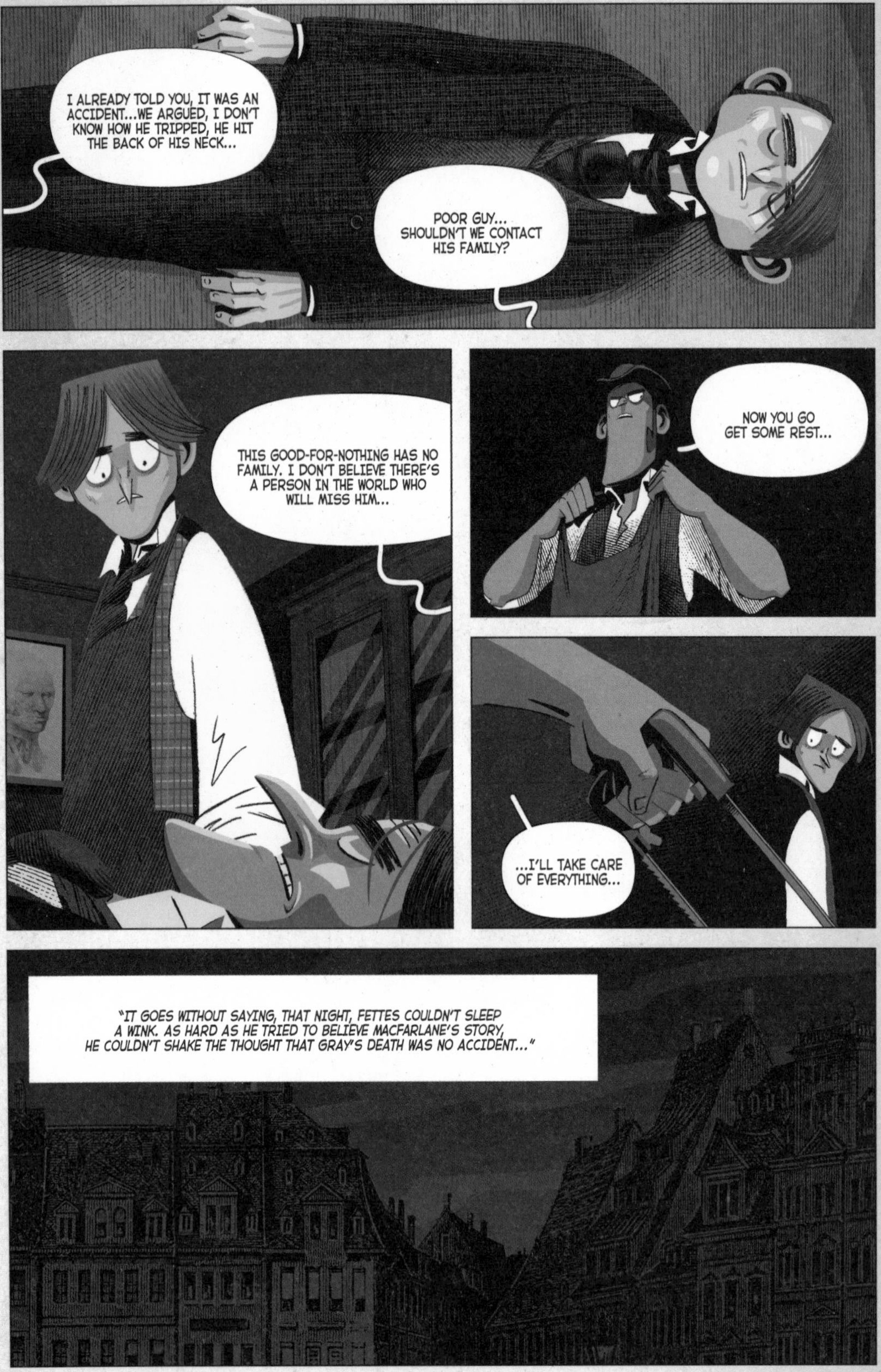
I ALREADY TOLD YOU, IT WAS AN ACCIDENT...WE ARGUED, I DON'T KNOW HOW HE TRIPPED, HE HIT THE BACK OF HIS NECK...
POOR GUY... SHOULDN'T WE CONTACT HIS FAMILY?
THIS GOOD-FOR-NOTHING HAS NO FAMILY. I DON'T BELIEVE THERE'S A PERSON IN THE WORLD WHO WILL MISS HIM...
NOW YOU GO GET SOME REST...
...I'LL TAKE CARE OF EVERYTHING...
"IT GOES WITHOUT SAYING, THAT NIGHT, FETTES COULDN'T SLEEP A WINK. AS HARD AS HE TRIED TO BELIEVE MACFARLANE'S STORY, HE COULDN'T SHAKE THE THOUGHT THAT GRAY'S DEATH WAS NO ACCIDENT..."

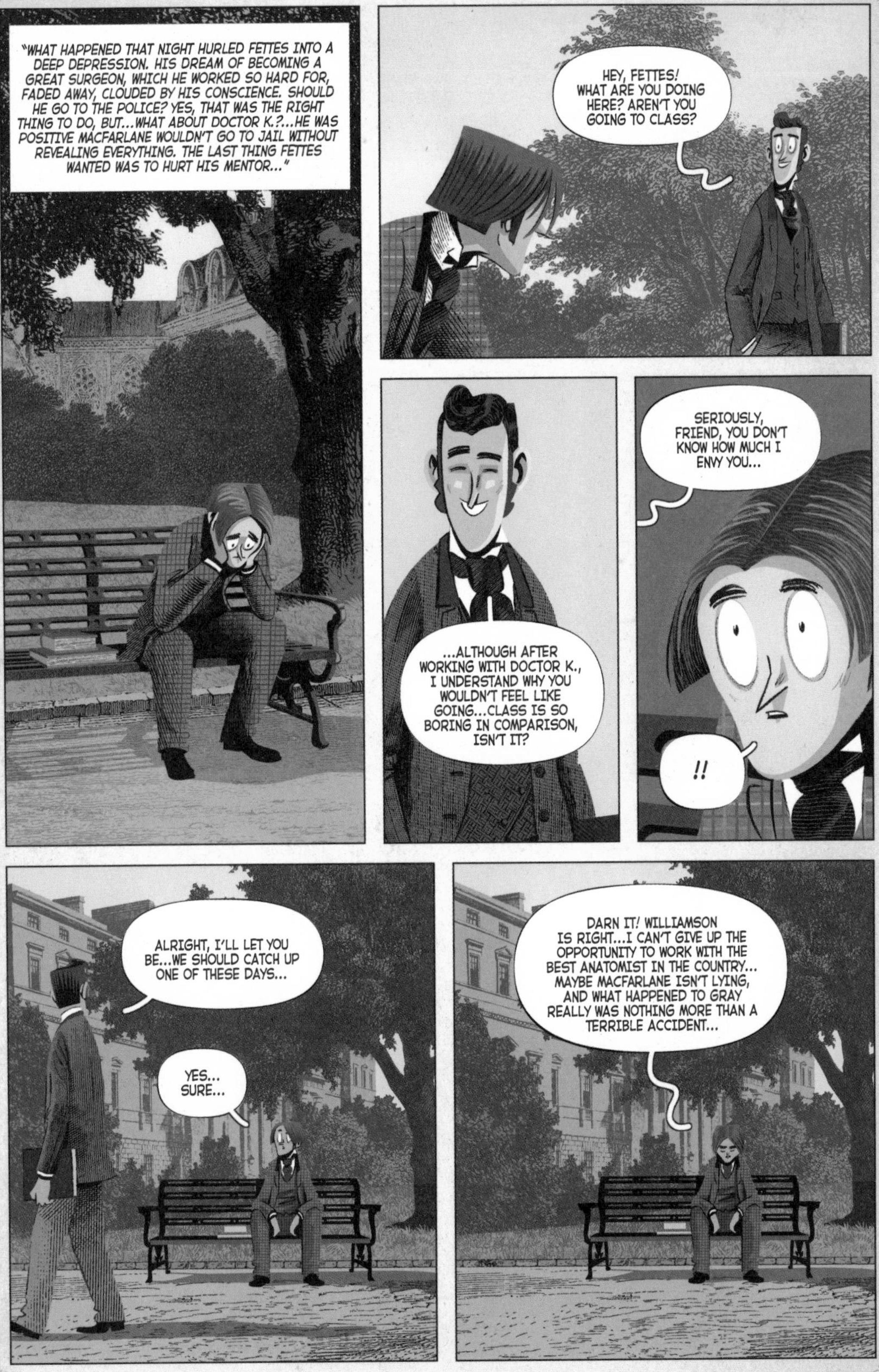
"WHAT HAPPENED THAT NIGHT HURLED FETTES INTO A DEEP DEPRESSION. HIS DREAM OF BECOMING A GREAT SURGEON, WHICH HE WORKED SO HARD FOR, FADED AWAY, CLOUDED BY HIS CONSCIENCE. SHOULD HE GO TO THE POLICE? YES, THAT WAS THE RIGHT THING TO DO, BUT...WHAT ABOUT DOCTOR K.?...HE WAS POSITIVE MACFARLANE WOULDN'T GO TO JAIL WITHOUT REVEALING EVERYTHING. THE LAST THING FETTES WANTED WAS TO HURT HIS MENTOR..."
HEY, FETTES! WHAT ARE YOU DOING HERE? AREN'T YOU GOING TO CLASS?
...ALTHOUGH AFTER WORKING WITH DOCTOR K., I UNDERSTAND WHY YOU WOULDN'T FEEL LIKE GOING...CLASS IS SO BORING IN COMPARISON, ISN'T IT?
SERIOUSLY, FRIEND, YOU DON'T KNOW HOW MUCH I ENVY YOU...
!!
ALRIGHT, I'LL LET YOU BE...WE SHOULD CATCH UP ONE OF THESE DAYS...
YES... SURE...
DARN IT! WILLIAMSON IS RIGHT...I CAN'T GIVE UP THE OPPORTUNITY TO WORK WITH THE BEST ANATOMIST IN THE COUNTRY... MAYBE MACFARLANE ISN'T LYING, AND WHAT HAPPENED TO GRAY REALLY WAS NOTHING MORE THAN A TERRIBLE ACCIDENT...

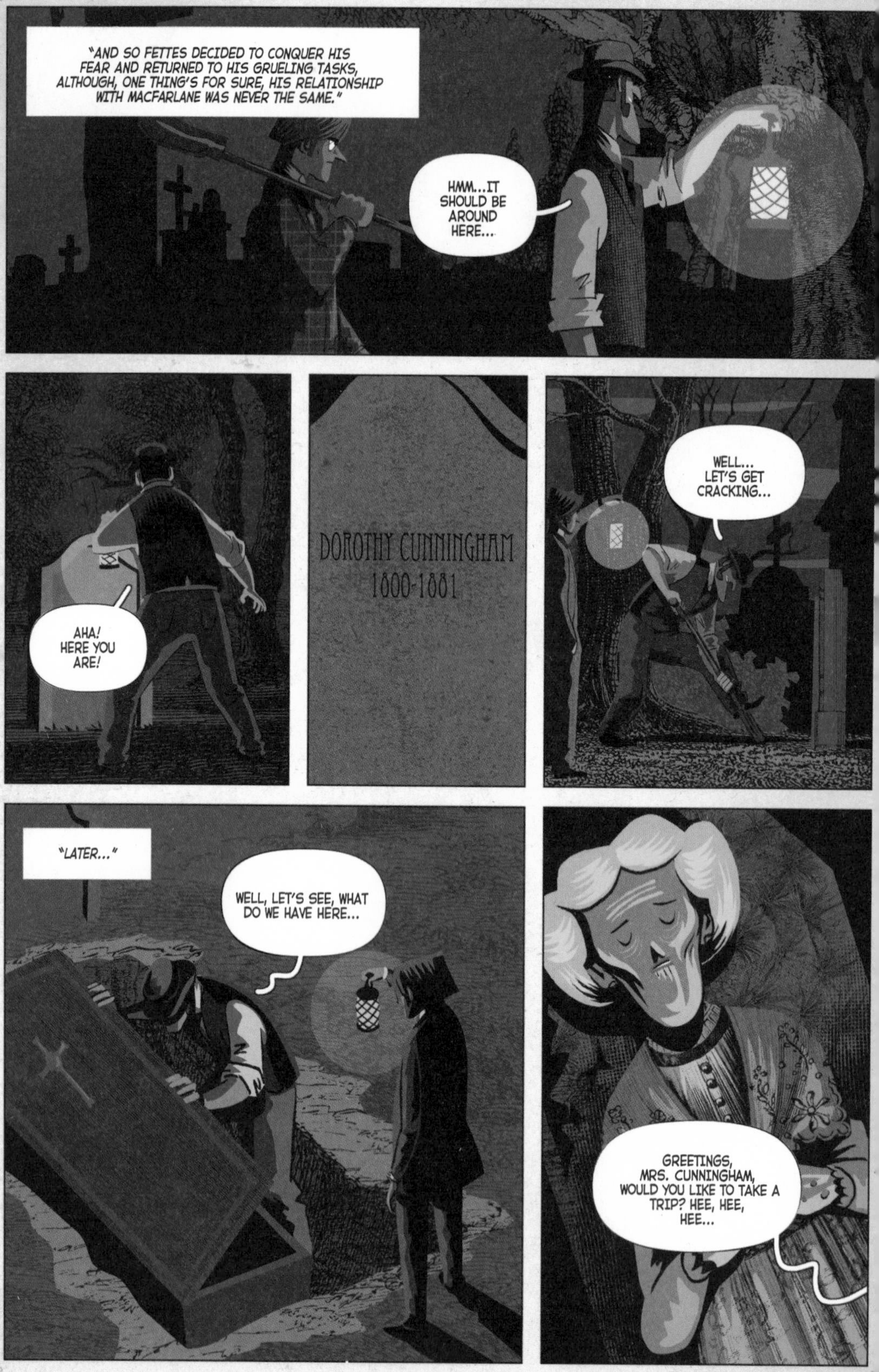
"AND SO FETTES DECIDED TO CONQUER HIS FEAR AND RETURNED TO HIS GRUELING TASKS, ALTHOUGH, ONE THING'S FOR SURE, HIS RELATIONSHIP WITH MACFARLANE WAS NEVER THE SAME."
HMM...IT SHOULD BE AROUND HERE...
AHA! HERE YOU ARE!
DOROTHY CUNNINGHAM
1800-1881
WELL... LET'S GET CRACKING...
"LATER..."
WELL, LET'S SEE, WHAT DO WE HAVE HERE...
GREETINGS, MRS. CUNNINGHAM, WOULD YOU LIKE TO TAKE A TRIP? HEE, HEE, HEE...

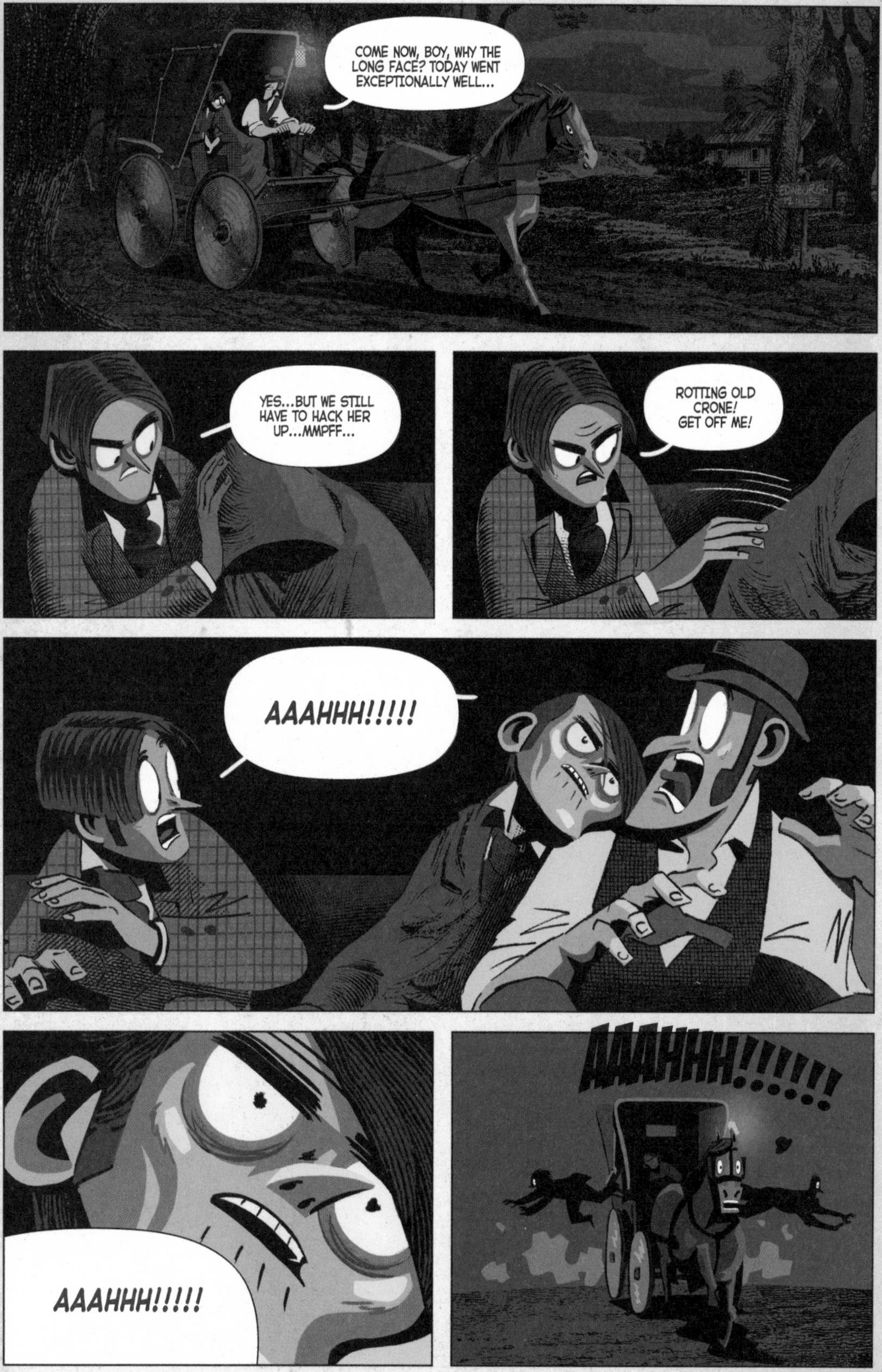
COME NOW, BOY, WHY THE LONG FACE? TODAY WENT EXCEPTIONALLY WELL...
EDINBURGH
YES...BUT WE STILL HAVE TO HACK HER UP...MMPFF...
ROTTING OLD CRONE! GET OFF ME!
AAAHHH!!!!!
AAAHHH!!!!!
AAAHHH!!!!!!

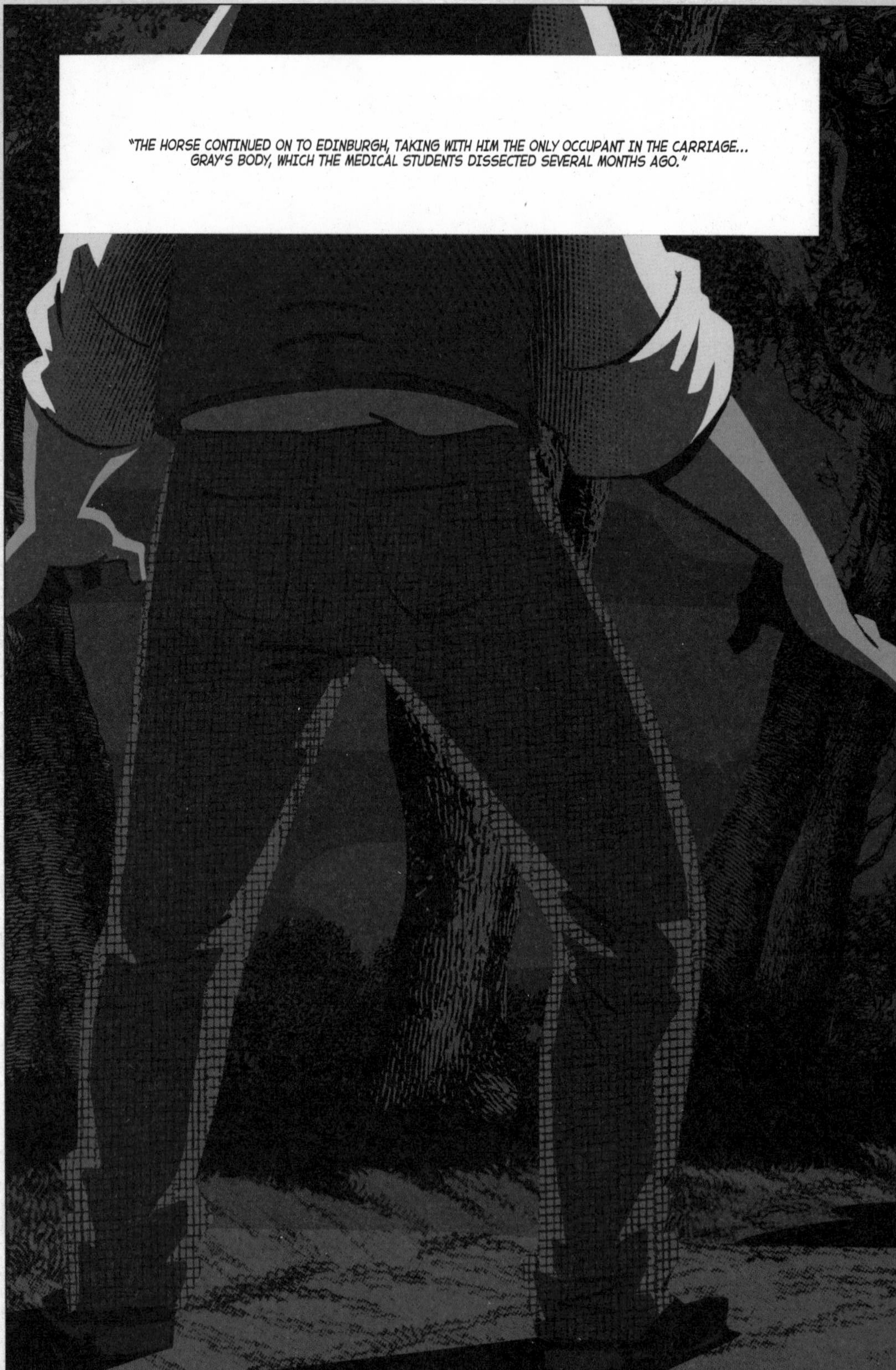
"THE HORSE CONTINUED ON TO EDINBURGH, TAKING WITH HIM THE ONLY OCCUPANT IN THE CARRIAGE... GRAY'S BODY, WHICH THE MEDICAL STUDENTS DISSECTED SEVERAL MONTHS AGO."

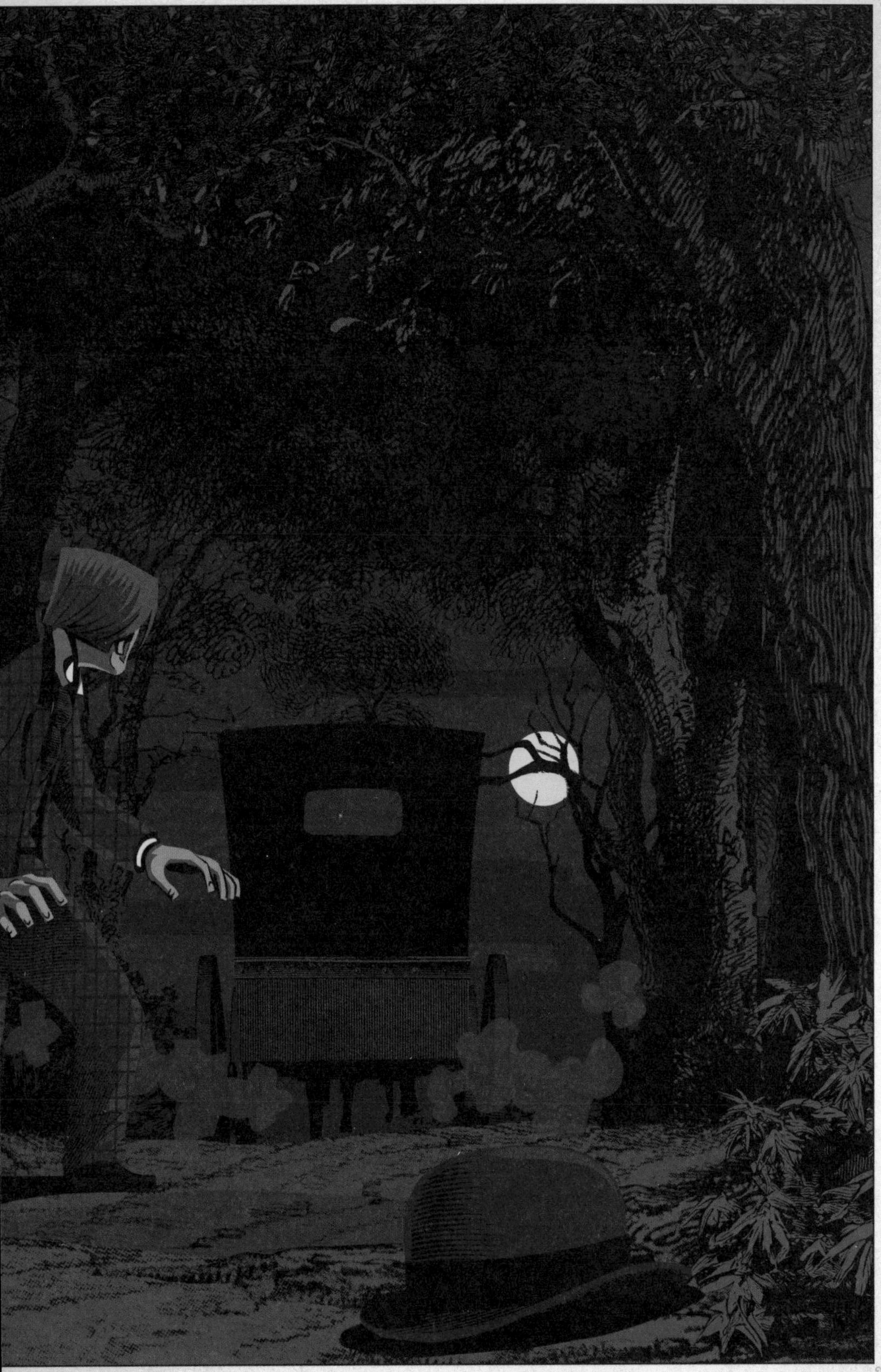

EDGAR ALLAN POE

THE BLACK CAT

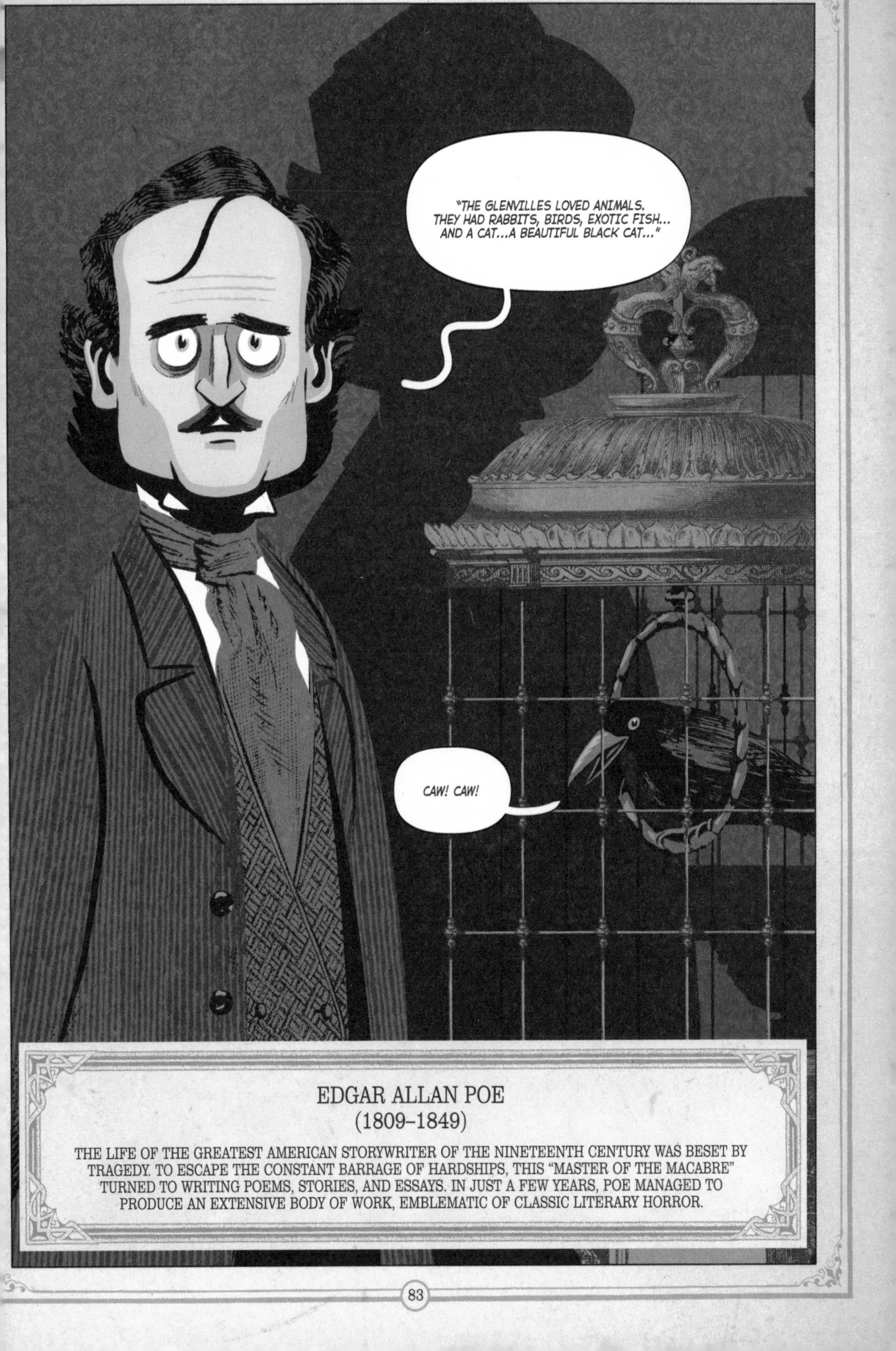
"THE GLENVILLES LOVED ANIMALS. THEY HAD RABBITS, BIRDS, EXOTIC FISH... AND A CAT...A BEAUTIFUL BLACK CAT..."
CAW! CAW!

EDGAR ALLAN POE
(1809–1849)

THE LIFE OF THE GREATEST AMERICAN STORYWRITER OF THE NINETEENTH CENTURY WAS BESET BY TRAGEDY. TO ESCAPE THE CONSTANT BARRAGE OF HARDSHIPS, THIS "MASTER OF THE MACABRE" TURNED TO WRITING POEMS, STORIES, AND ESSAYS. IN JUST A FEW YEARS, POE MANAGED TO PRODUCE AN EXTENSIVE BODY OF WORK, EMBLEMATIC OF CLASSIC LITERARY HORROR.

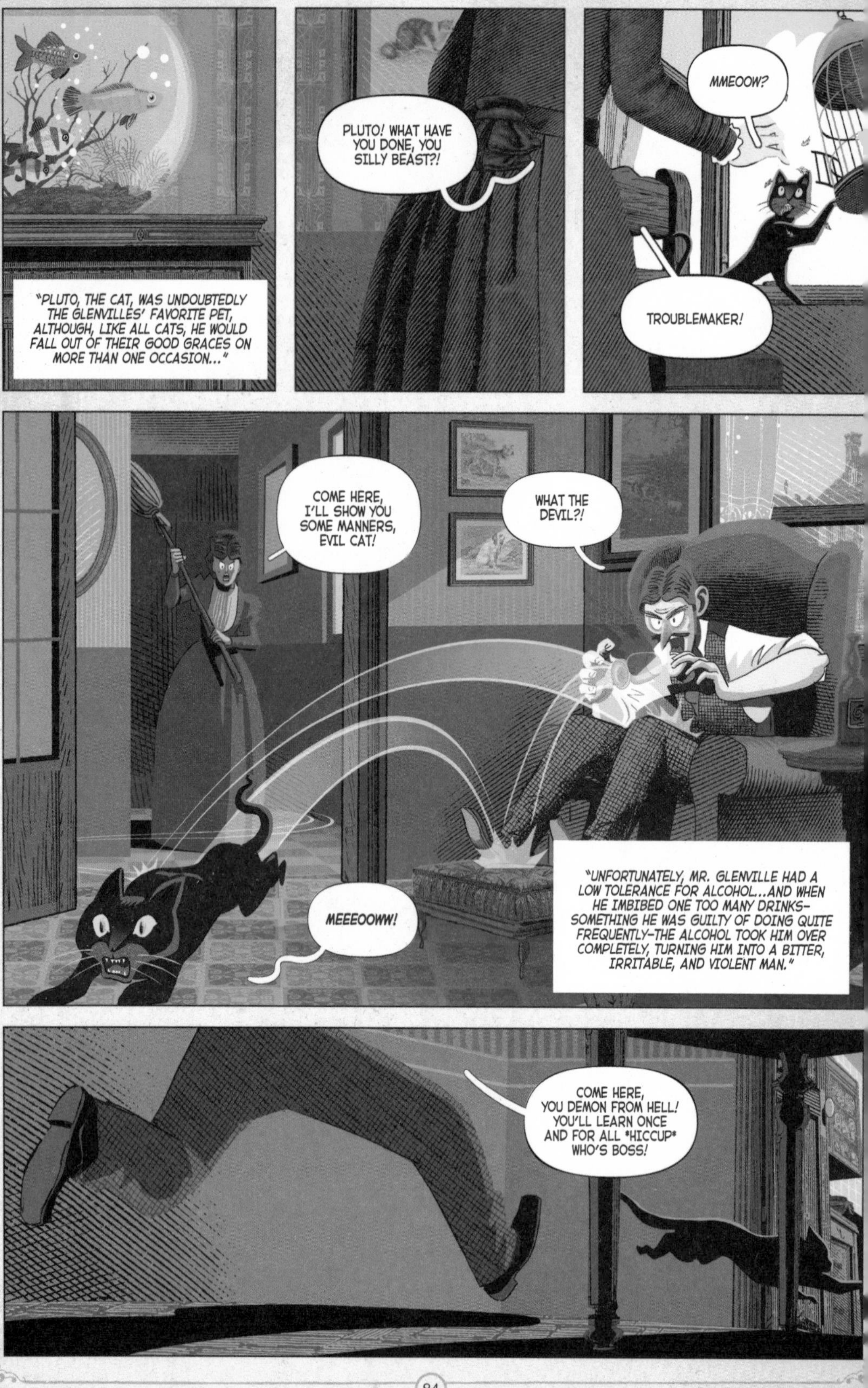
"PLUTO, THE CAT, WAS UNDOUBTEDLY THE GLENVILLES' FAVORITE PET, ALTHOUGH, LIKE ALL CATS, HE WOULD FALL OUT OF THEIR GOOD GRACES ON MORE THAN ONE OCCASION..."
PLUTO! WHAT HAVE YOU DONE, YOU SILLY BEAST?!
MMEOOW?
TROUBLEMAKER!
COME HERE, I'LL SHOW YOU SOME MANNERS, EVIL CAT!
WHAT THE DEVIL?!
MEEEOOWW!
"UNFORTUNATELY, MR. GLENVILLE HAD A LOW TOLERANCE FOR ALCOHOL...AND WHEN HE IMBIBED ONE TOO MANY DRINKS–SOMETHING HE WAS GUILTY OF DOING QUITE FREQUENTLY–THE ALCOHOL TOOK HIM OVER COMPLETELY, TURNING HIM INTO A BITTER, IRRITABLE, AND VIOLENT MAN."
COME HERE, YOU DEMON FROM HELL! YOU'LL LEARN ONCE AND FOR ALL *HICCUP* WHO'S BOSS!

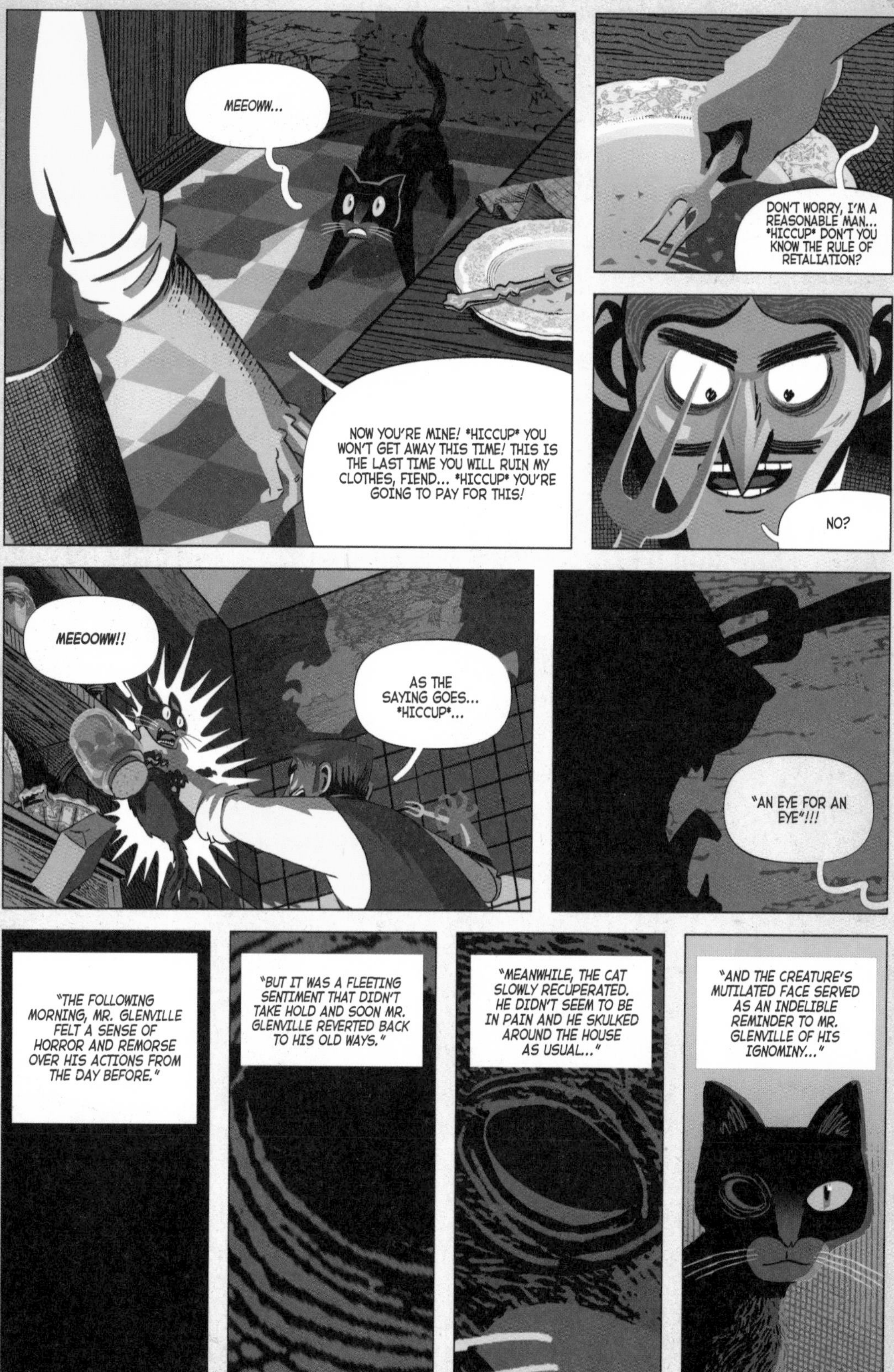
MEEOWW...
DON'T WORRY, I'M A REASONABLE MAN... *HICCUP* DON'T YOU KNOW THE RULE OF RETALIATION?
NOW YOU'RE MINE! *HICCUP* YOU WON'T GET AWAY THIS TIME! THIS IS THE LAST TIME YOU WILL RUIN MY CLOTHES, FIEND... *HICCUP* YOU'RE GOING TO PAY FOR THIS!
NO?
MEEOOWW!!
AS THE SAYING GOES... *HICCUP*...
"AN EYE FOR AN EYE"!!!
"THE FOLLOWING MORNING, MR. GLENVILLE FELT A SENSE OF HORROR AND REMORSE OVER HIS ACTIONS FROM THE DAY BEFORE."
"BUT IT WAS A FLEETING SENTIMENT THAT DIDN'T TAKE HOLD AND SOON MR. GLENVILLE REVERTED BACK TO HIS OLD WAYS."
"MEANWHILE, THE CAT SLOWLY RECUPERATED. HE DIDN'T SEEM TO BE IN PAIN AND HE SKULKED AROUND THE HOUSE AS USUAL..."
"AND THE CREATURE'S MUTILATED FACE SERVED AS AN INDELIBLE REMINDER TO MR. GLENVILLE OF HIS IGNOMINY..."

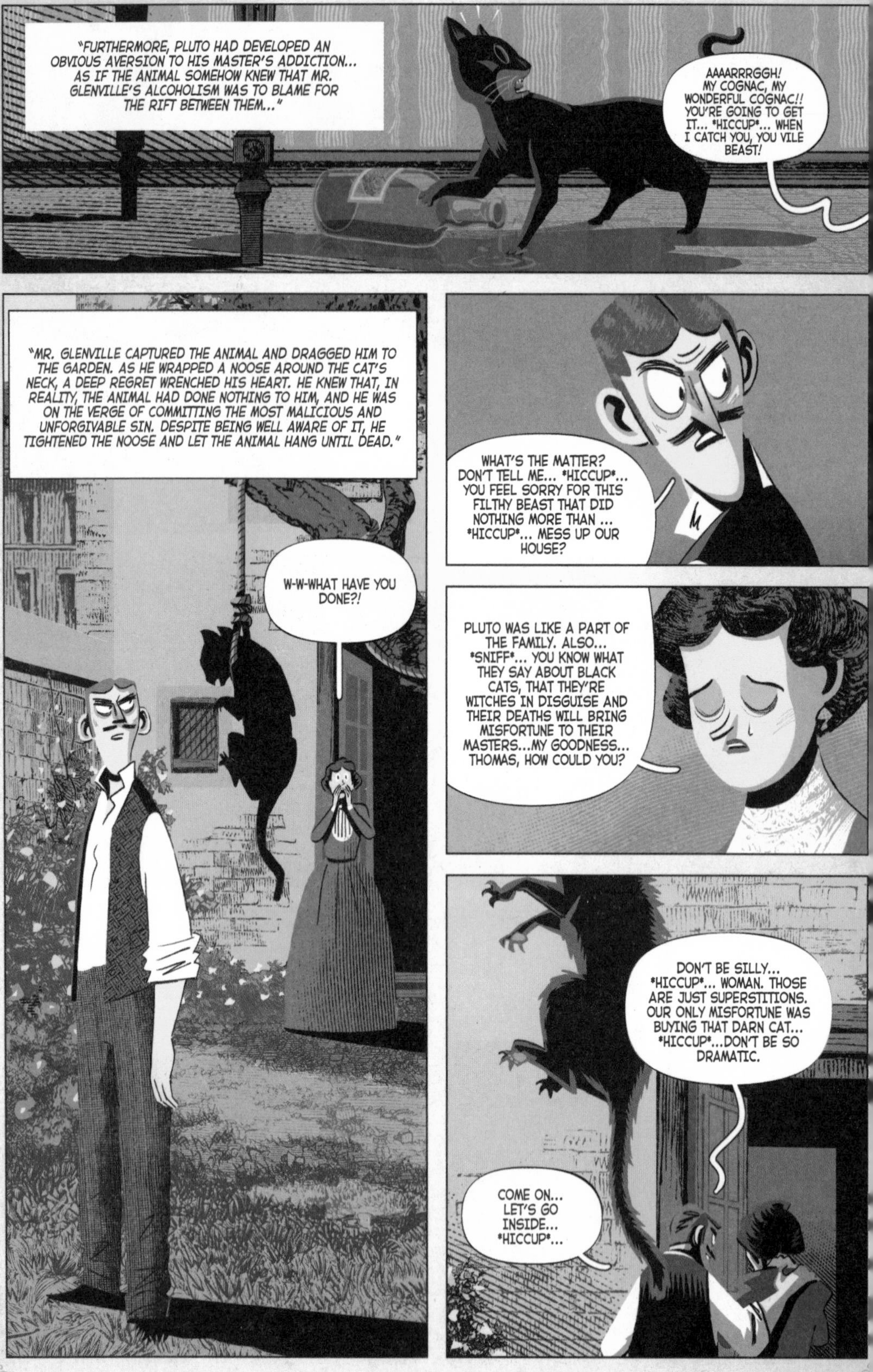
"FURTHERMORE, PLUTO HAD DEVELOPED AN OBVIOUS AVERSION TO HIS MASTER'S ADDICTION... AS IF THE ANIMAL SOMEHOW KNEW THAT MR. GLENVILLE'S ALCOHOLISM WAS TO BLAME FOR THE RIFT BETWEEN THEM..."
AAAARRRGGH! MY COGNAC, MY WONDERFUL COGNAC!! YOU'RE GOING TO GET IT... *HICCUP*... WHEN I CATCH YOU, YOU VILE BEAST!
"MR. GLENVILLE CAPTURED THE ANIMAL AND DRAGGED HIM TO THE GARDEN. AS HE WRAPPED A NOOSE AROUND THE CAT'S NECK, A DEEP REGRET WRENCHED HIS HEART. HE KNEW THAT, IN REALITY, THE ANIMAL HAD DONE NOTHING TO HIM, AND HE WAS ON THE VERGE OF COMMITTING THE MOST MALICIOUS AND UNFORGIVABLE SIN. DESPITE BEING WELL AWARE OF IT, HE TIGHTENED THE NOOSE AND LET THE ANIMAL HANG UNTIL DEAD."
W-W-WHAT HAVE YOU DONE?!
WHAT'S THE MATTER? DON'T TELL ME... *HICCUP*... YOU FEEL SORRY FOR THIS FILTHY BEAST THAT DID NOTHING MORE THAN ... *HICCUP*... MESS UP OUR HOUSE?
PLUTO WAS LIKE A PART OF THE FAMILY. ALSO... *SNIFF*... YOU KNOW WHAT THEY SAY ABOUT BLACK CATS, THAT THEY'RE WITCHES IN DISGUISE AND THEIR DEATHS WILL BRING MISFORTUNE TO THEIR MASTERS...MY GOODNESS... THOMAS, HOW COULD YOU?
DON'T BE SILLY... *HICCUP*... WOMAN. THOSE ARE JUST SUPERSTITIONS. OUR ONLY MISFORTUNE WAS BUYING THAT DARN CAT... *HICCUP*...DON'T BE SO DRAMATIC.
COME ON... LET'S GO INSIDE... *HICCUP*...

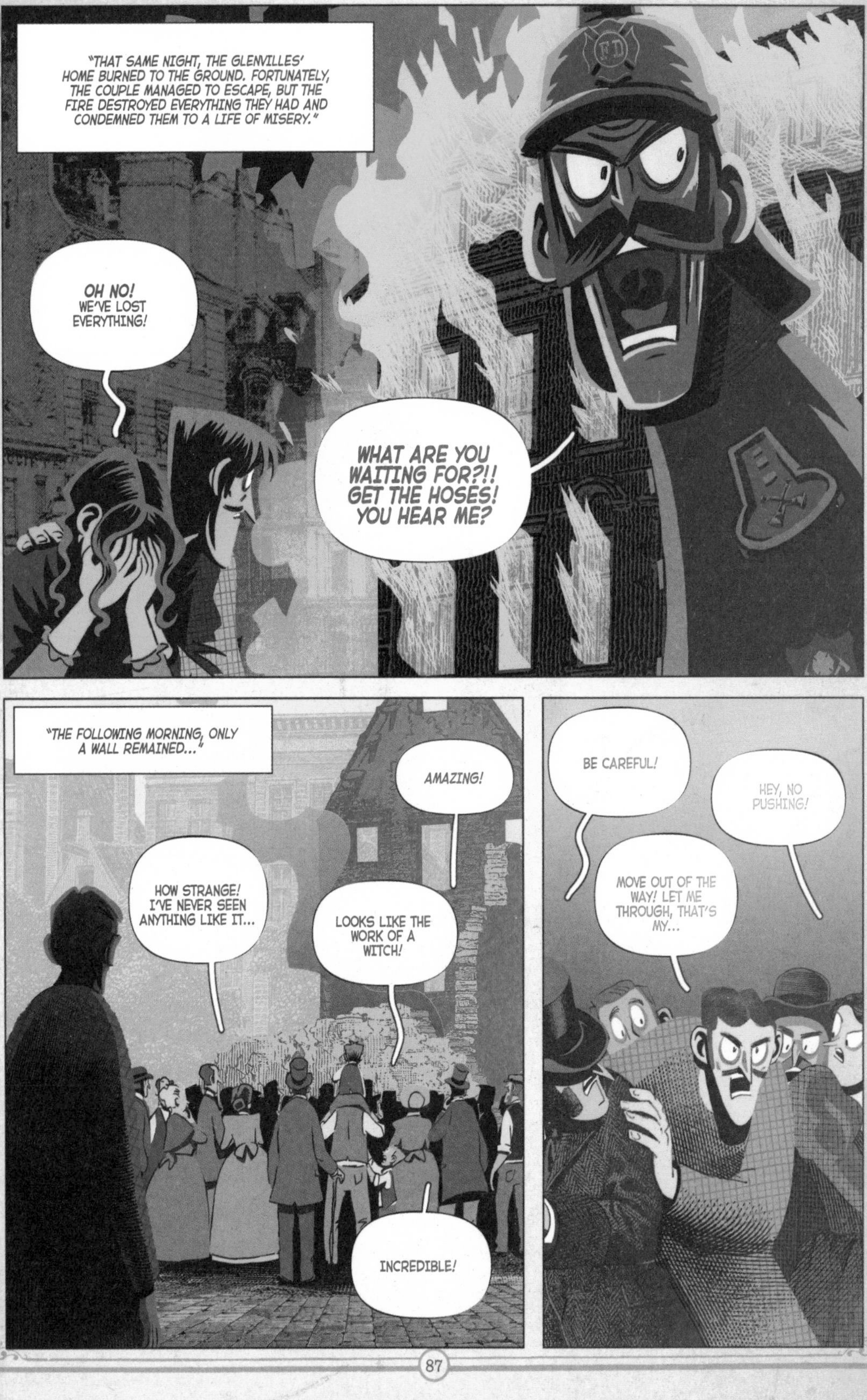
"THAT SAME NIGHT, THE GLENVILLES' HOME BURNED TO THE GROUND. FORTUNATELY, THE COUPLE MANAGED TO ESCAPE, BUT THE FIRE DESTROYED EVERYTHING THEY HAD AND CONDEMNED THEM TO A LIFE OF MISERY."
OH NO! WE'VE LOST EVERYTHING!
WHAT ARE YOU WAITING FOR?!! GET THE HOSES! YOU HEAR ME?
"THE FOLLOWING MORNING, ONLY A WALL REMAINED..."
AMAZING!
HOW STRANGE! I'VE NEVER SEEN ANYTHING LIKE IT...
LOOKS LIKE THE WORK OF A WITCH!
INCREDIBLE!
BE CAREFUL!
HEY, NO PUSHING!
MOVE OUT OF THE WAY! LET ME THROUGH, THAT'S MY...

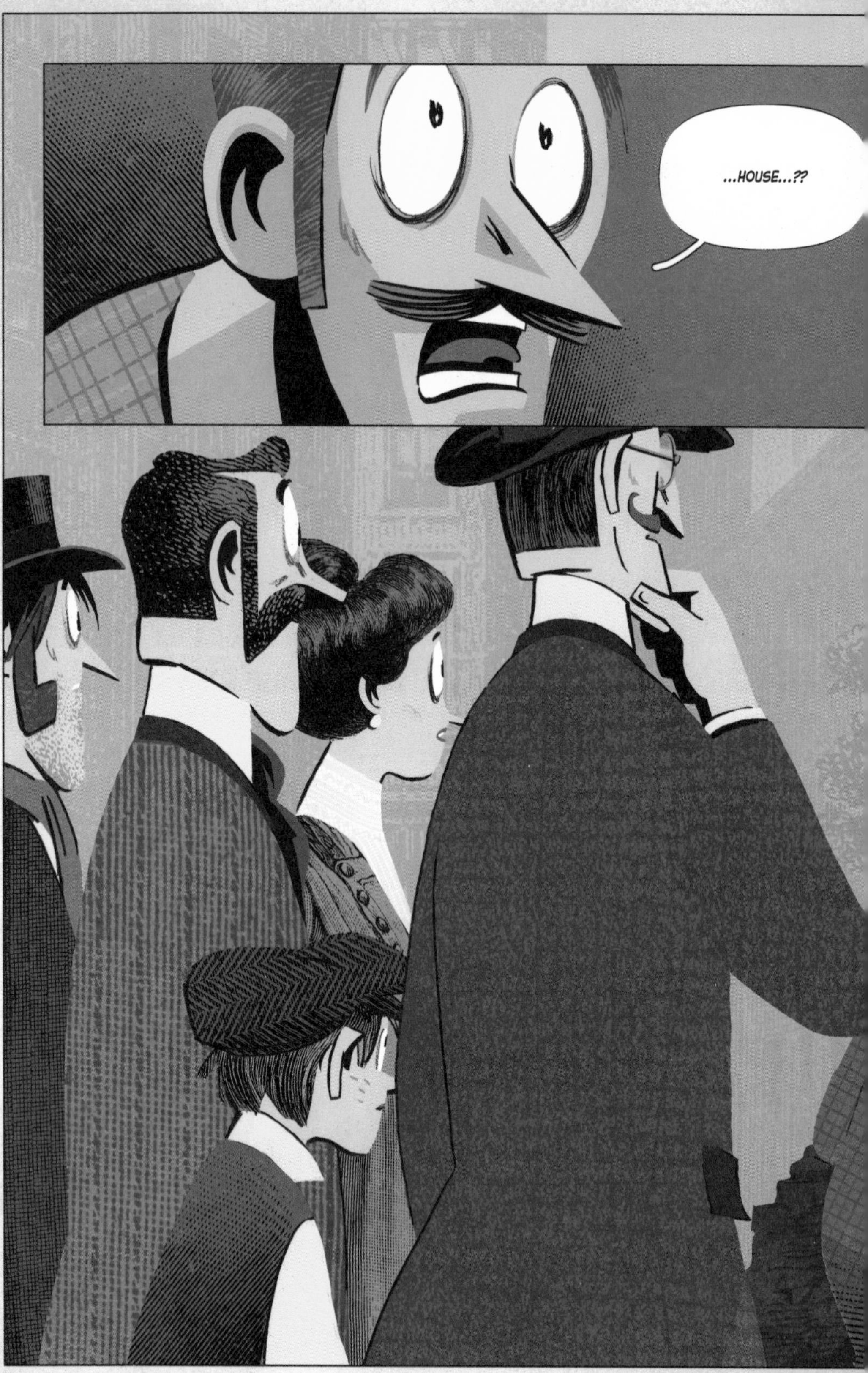
...HOUSE...??

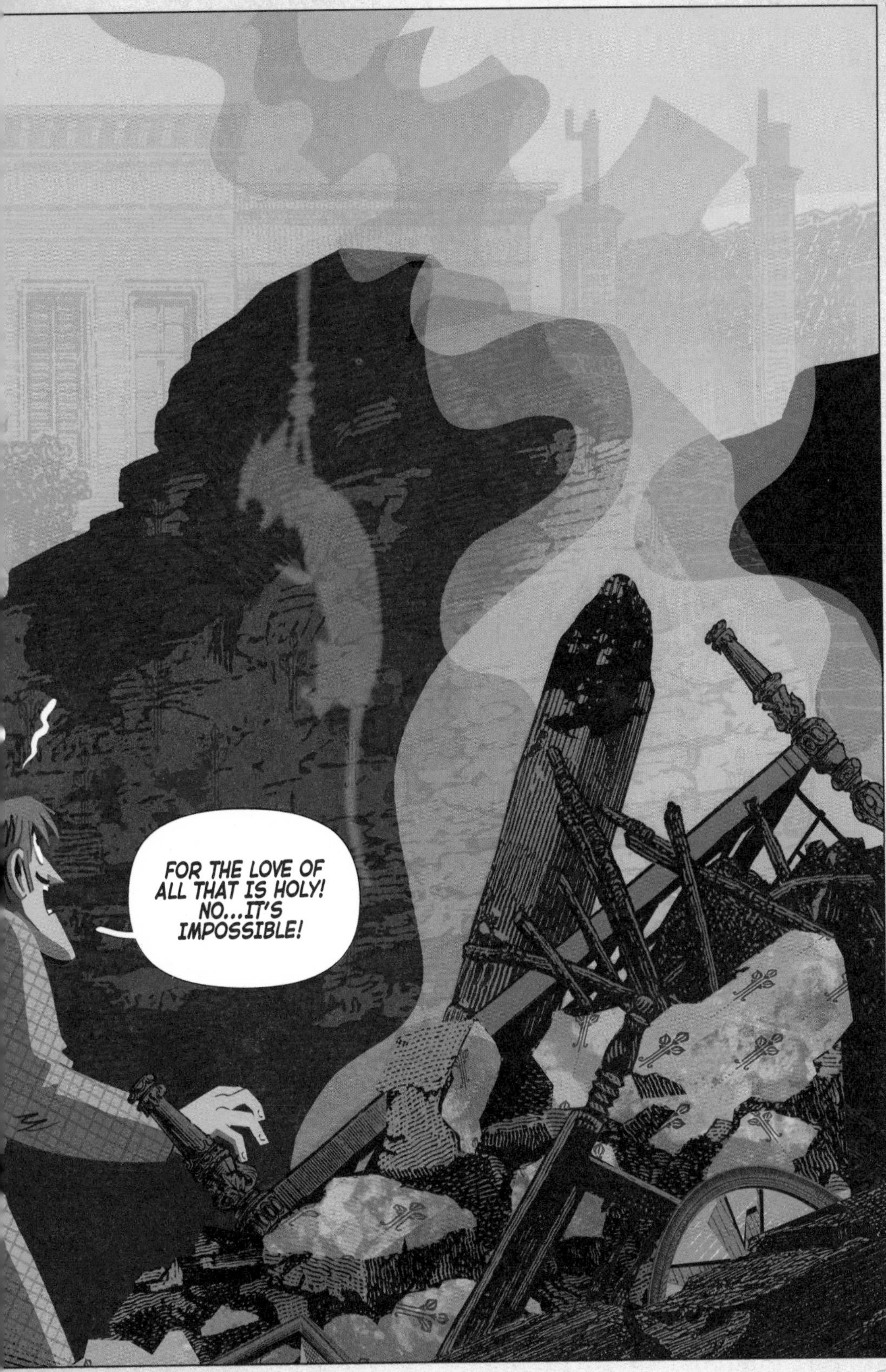
FOR THE LOVE OF ALL THAT IS HOLY! NO...IT'S IMPOSSIBLE!

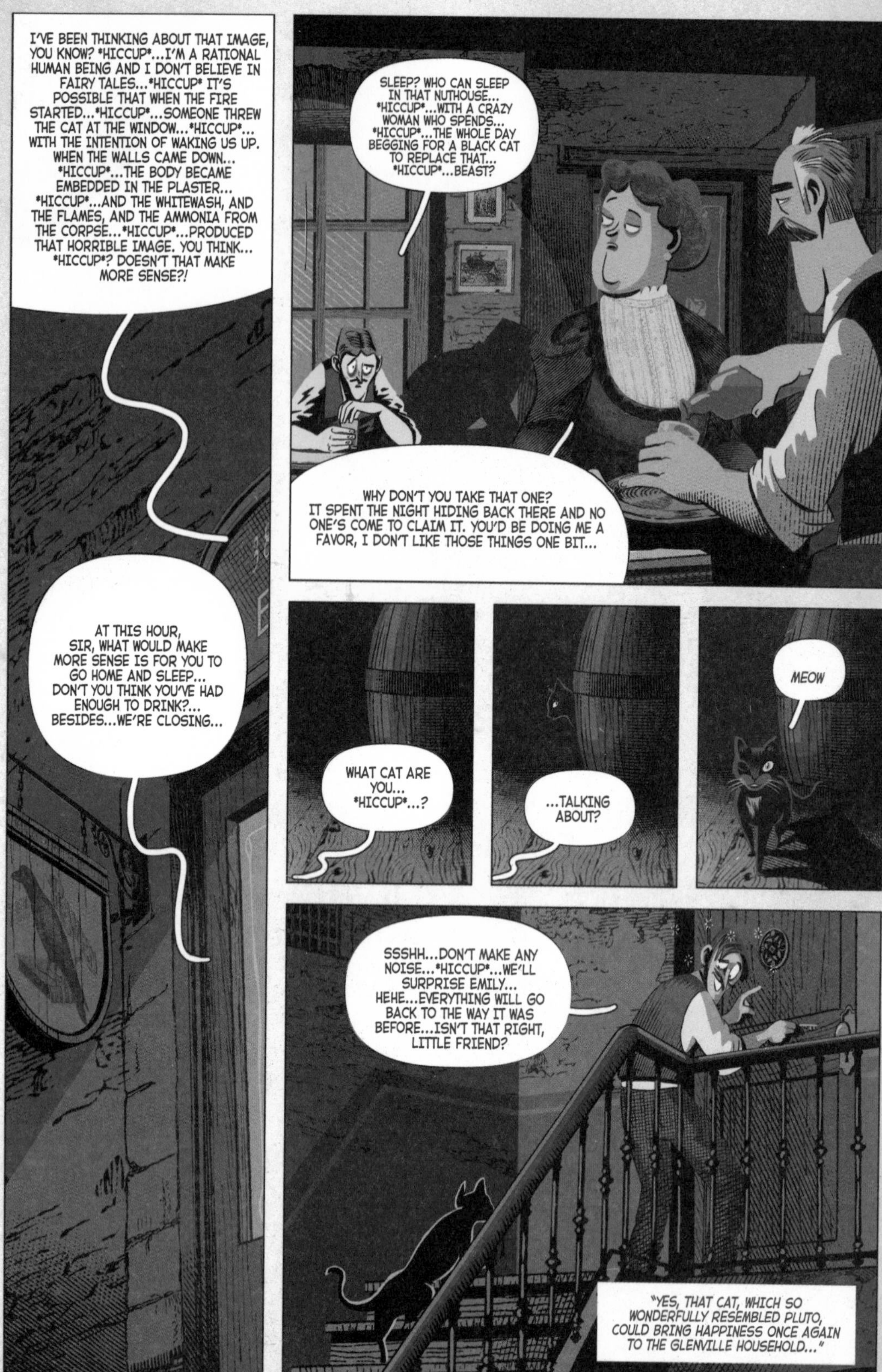
I'VE BEEN THINKING ABOUT THAT IMAGE, YOU KNOW? *HICCUP*...I'M A RATIONAL HUMAN BEING AND I DON'T BELIEVE IN FAIRY TALES...*HICCUP* IT'S POSSIBLE THAT WHEN THE FIRE STARTED...*HICCUP*...SOMEONE THREW THE CAT AT THE WINDOW...*HICCUP*... WITH THE INTENTION OF WAKING US UP. WHEN THE WALLS CAME DOWN... *HICCUP*...THE BODY BECAME EMBEDDED IN THE PLASTER... *HICCUP*...AND THE WHITEWASH, AND THE FLAMES, AND THE AMMONIA FROM THE CORPSE...*HICCUP*...PRODUCED THAT HORRIBLE IMAGE. YOU THINK... *HICCUP*? DOESN'T THAT MAKE MORE SENSE?!
AT THIS HOUR, SIR, WHAT WOULD MAKE MORE SENSE IS FOR YOU TO GO HOME AND SLEEP... DON'T YOU THINK YOU'VE HAD ENOUGH TO DRINK?... BESIDES...WE'RE CLOSING...
SLEEP? WHO CAN SLEEP IN THAT NUTHOUSE... *HICCUP*...WITH A CRAZY WOMAN WHO SPENDS... *HICCUP*...THE WHOLE DAY BEGGING FOR A BLACK CAT TO REPLACE THAT... *HICCUP*...BEAST?
WHY DON'T YOU TAKE THAT ONE? IT SPENT THE NIGHT HIDING BACK THERE AND NO ONE'S COME TO CLAIM IT. YOU'D BE DOING ME A FAVOR, I DON'T LIKE THOSE THINGS ONE BIT...
WHAT CAT ARE YOU... *HICCUP*...?
...TALKING ABOUT?
MEOW
SSSHH...DON'T MAKE ANY NOISE...*HICCUP*...WE'LL SURPRISE EMILY... HEHE...EVERYTHING WILL GO BACK TO THE WAY IT WAS BEFORE...ISN'T THAT RIGHT, LITTLE FRIEND?
"YES, THAT CAT, WHICH SO WONDERFULLY RESEMBLED PLUTO, COULD BRING HAPPINESS ONCE AGAIN TO THE GLENVILLE HOUSEHOLD..."

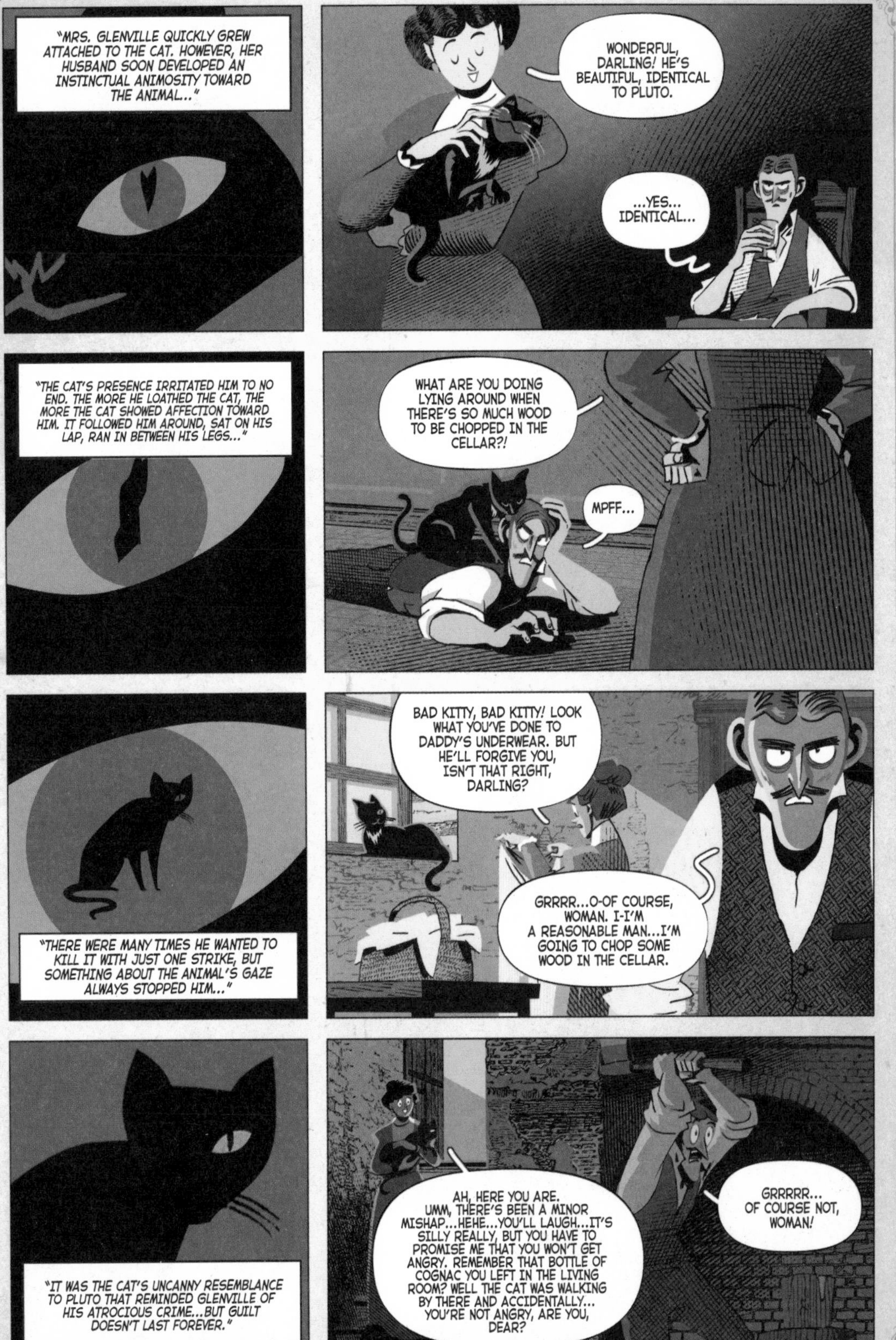
"MRS. GLENVILLE QUICKLY GREW ATTACHED TO THE CAT. HOWEVER, HER HUSBAND SOON DEVELOPED AN INSTINCTUAL ANIMOSITY TOWARD THE ANIMAL..."
WONDERFUL, DARLING! HE'S BEAUTIFUL, IDENTICAL TO PLUTO.
...YES... IDENTICAL...
"THE CAT'S PRESENCE IRRITATED HIM TO NO END. THE MORE HE LOATHED THE CAT, THE MORE THE CAT SHOWED AFFECTION TOWARD HIM. IT FOLLOWED HIM AROUND, SAT ON HIS LAP, RAN IN BETWEEN HIS LEGS..."
WHAT ARE YOU DOING LYING AROUND WHEN THERE'S SO MUCH WOOD TO BE CHOPPED IN THE CELLAR?!
MPFF...
"THERE WERE MANY TIMES HE WANTED TO KILL IT WITH JUST ONE STRIKE, BUT SOMETHING ABOUT THE ANIMAL'S GAZE ALWAYS STOPPED HIM..."
BAD KITTY, BAD KITTY! LOOK WHAT YOU'VE DONE TO DADDY'S UNDERWEAR. BUT HE'LL FORGIVE YOU, ISN'T THAT RIGHT, DARLING?
GRRRR...O-OF COURSE, WOMAN. I-I'M A REASONABLE MAN...I'M GOING TO CHOP SOME WOOD IN THE CELLAR.
"IT WAS THE CAT'S UNCANNY RESEMBLANCE TO PLUTO THAT REMINDED GLENVILLE OF HIS ATROCIOUS CRIME...BUT GUILT DOESN'T LAST FOREVER."
AH, HERE YOU ARE. UMM, THERE'S BEEN A MINOR MISHAP...HEHE...YOU'LL LAUGH...IT'S SILLY REALLY, BUT YOU HAVE TO PROMISE ME THAT YOU WON'T GET ANGRY. REMEMBER THAT BOTTLE OF COGNAC YOU LEFT IN THE LIVING ROOM? WELL THE CAT WAS WALKING BY THERE AND ACCIDENTALLY... YOU'RE NOT ANGRY, ARE YOU, DEAR?
GRRRRR... OF COURSE NOT, WOMAN!

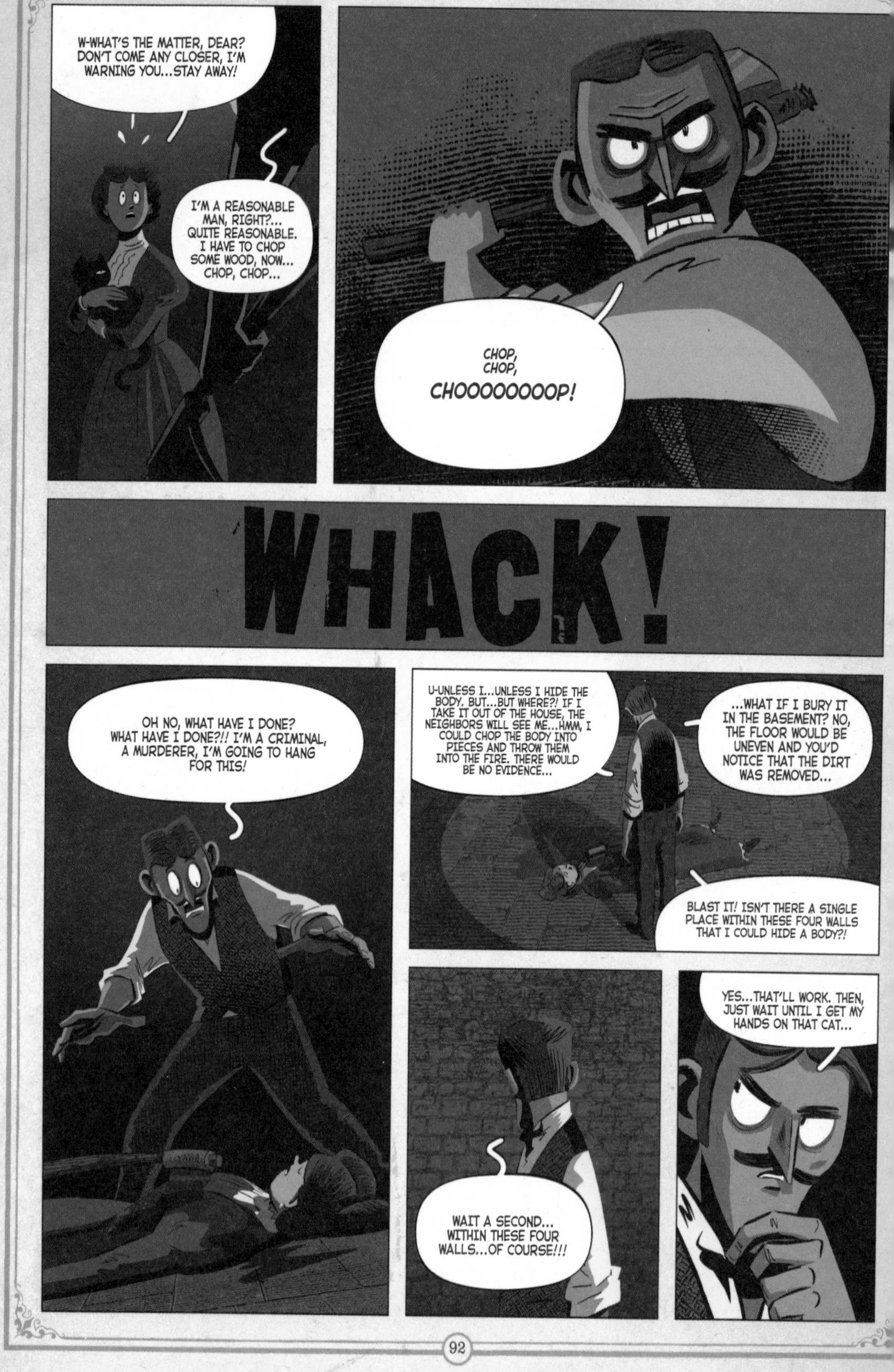
W-WHAT'S THE MATTER, DEAR? DON'T COME ANY CLOSER, I'M WARNING YOU...STAY AWAY!
I'M A REASONABLE MAN, RIGHT?... QUITE REASONABLE. I HAVE TO CHOP SOME WOOD, NOW... CHOP, CHOP...
CHOP, CHOP, CHOOOOOOOOP!
WHACK!
OH NO, WHAT HAVE I DONE? WHAT HAVE I DONE?!! I'M A CRIMINAL, A MURDERER, I'M GOING TO HANG FOR THIS!
U-UNLESS I...UNLESS I HIDE THE BODY. BUT...BUT WHERE?! IF I TAKE IT OUT OF THE HOUSE, THE NEIGHBORS WILL SEE ME...HMM, I COULD CHOP THE BODY INTO PIECES AND THROW THEM INTO THE FIRE. THERE WOULD BE NO EVIDENCE...
...WHAT IF I BURY IT IN THE BASEMENT? NO, THE FLOOR WOULD BE UNEVEN AND YOU'D NOTICE THAT THE DIRT WAS REMOVED...
BLAST IT! ISN'T THERE A SINGLE PLACE WITHIN THESE FOUR WALLS THAT I COULD HIDE A BODY?!
WAIT A SECOND... WITHIN THESE FOUR WALLS...OF COURSE!!!
YES...THAT'LL WORK. THEN, JUST WAIT UNTIL I GET MY HANDS ON THAT CAT...

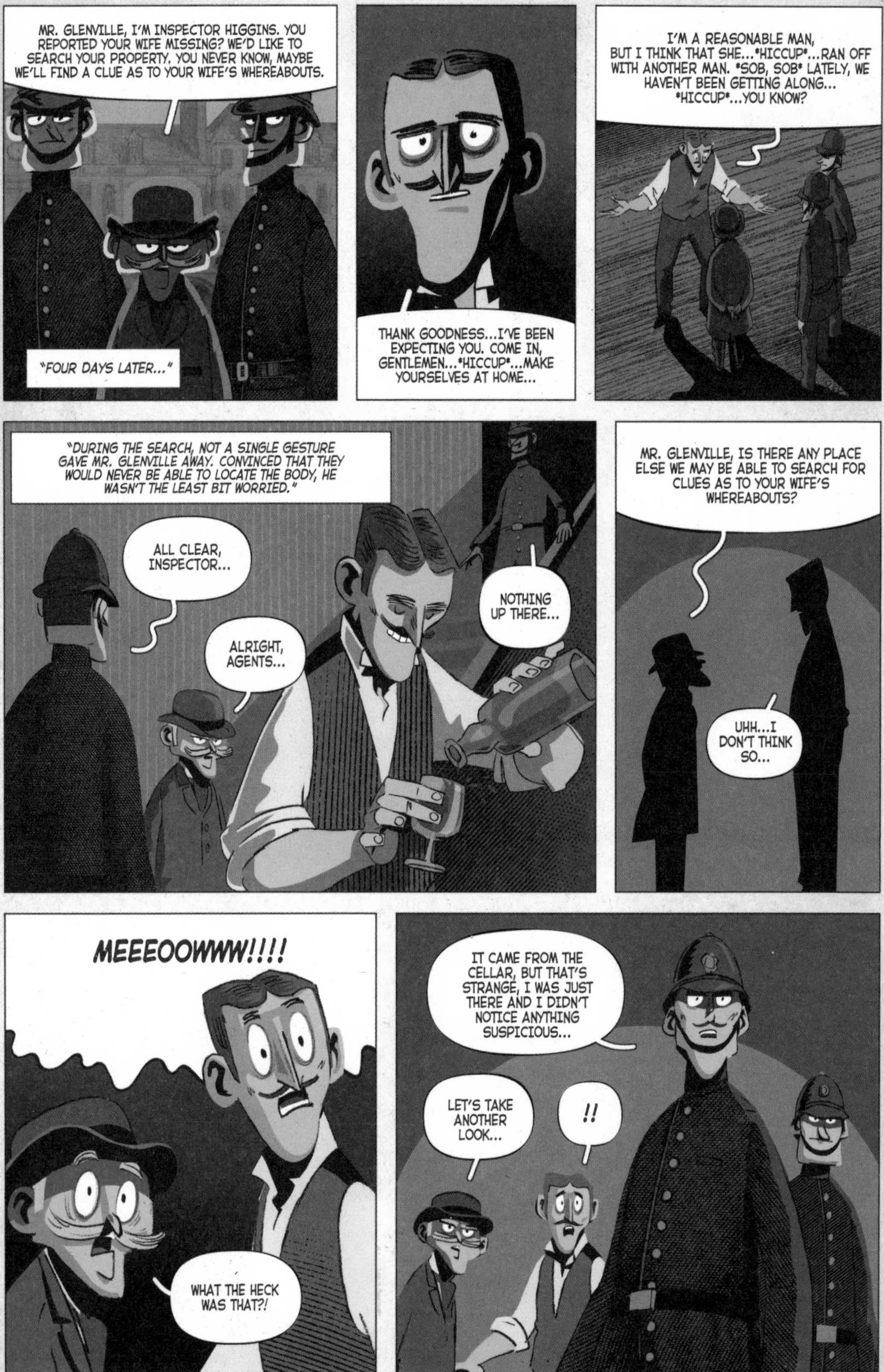
MR. GLENVILLE, I'M INSPECTOR HIGGINS. YOU REPORTED YOUR WIFE MISSING? WE'D LIKE TO SEARCH YOUR PROPERTY. YOU NEVER KNOW, MAYBE WE'LL FIND A CLUE AS TO YOUR WIFE'S WHEREABOUTS.
"FOUR DAYS LATER..."
THANK GOODNESS...I'VE BEEN EXPECTING YOU. COME IN, GENTLEMEN...*HICCUP*...MAKE YOURSELVES AT HOME...
I'M A REASONABLE MAN, BUT I THINK THAT SHE...*HICCUP*...RAN OFF WITH ANOTHER MAN. *SOB, SOB* LATELY, WE HAVEN'T BEEN GETTING ALONG... *HICCUP*...YOU KNOW?
"DURING THE SEARCH, NOT A SINGLE GESTURE GAVE MR. GLENVILLE AWAY. CONVINCED THAT THEY WOULD NEVER BE ABLE TO LOCATE THE BODY, HE WASN'T THE LEAST BIT WORRIED."
ALL CLEAR, INSPECTOR...
NOTHING UP THERE...
ALRIGHT, AGENTS...
MR. GLENVILLE, IS THERE ANY PLACE ELSE WE MAY BE ABLE TO SEARCH FOR CLUES AS TO YOUR WIFE'S WHEREABOUTS?
UHH...I DON'T THINK SO...
MEEEOOWWW!!!!
WHAT THE HECK WAS THAT?!
IT CAME FROM THE CELLAR, BUT THAT'S STRANGE, I WAS JUST THERE AND I DIDN'T NOTICE ANYTHING SUSPICIOUS...
LET'S TAKE ANOTHER LOOK...
!!

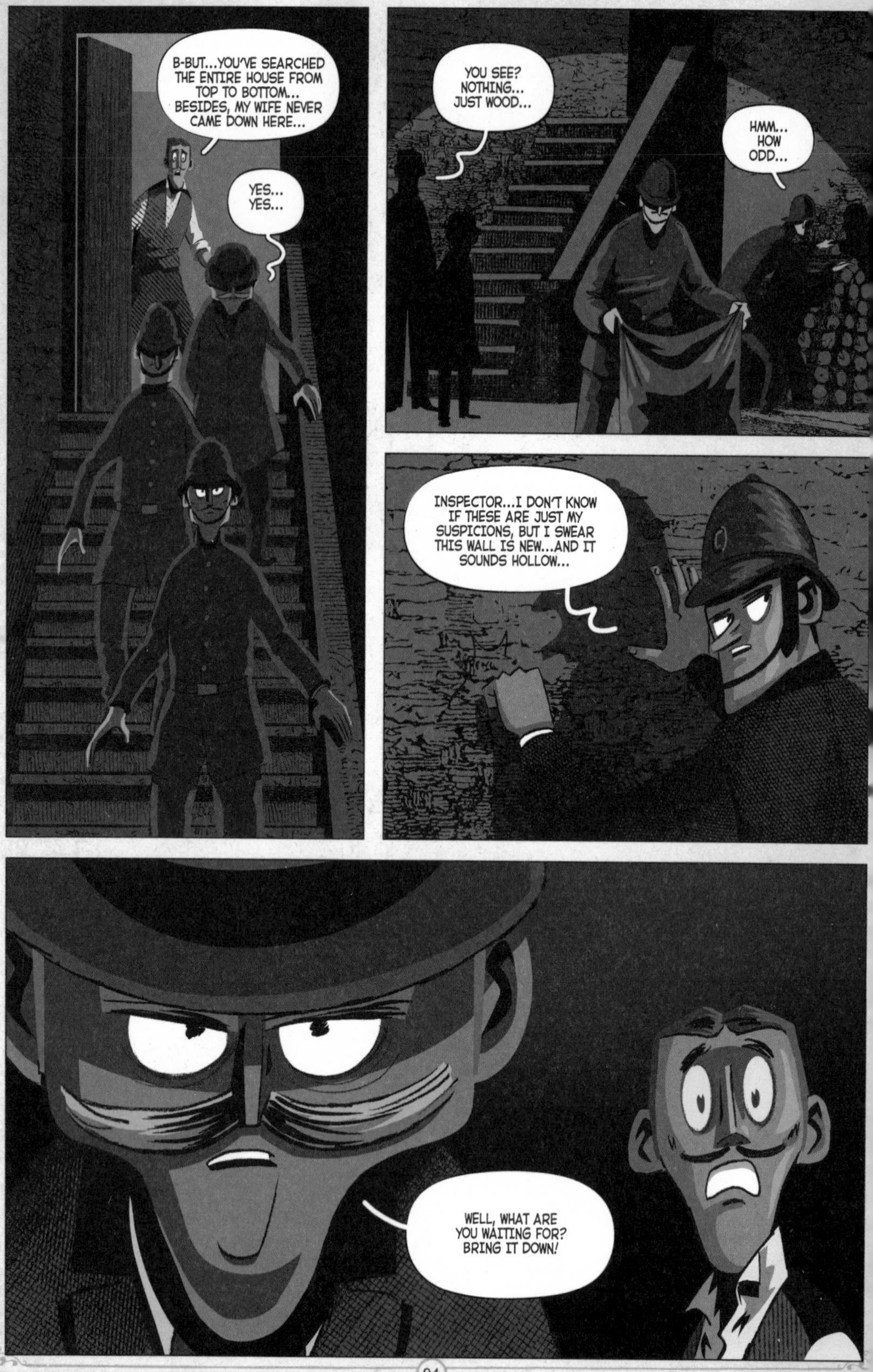
B-BUT...YOU'VE SEARCHED THE ENTIRE HOUSE FROM TOP TO BOTTOM... BESIDES, MY WIFE NEVER CAME DOWN HERE...
YES... YES...
YOU SEE? NOTHING... JUST WOOD...
HMM... HOW ODD...
INSPECTOR...I DON'T KNOW IF THESE ARE JUST MY SUSPICIONS, BUT I SWEAR THIS WALL IS NEW...AND IT SOUNDS HOLLOW...
WELL, WHAT ARE YOU WAITING FOR? BRING IT DOWN!

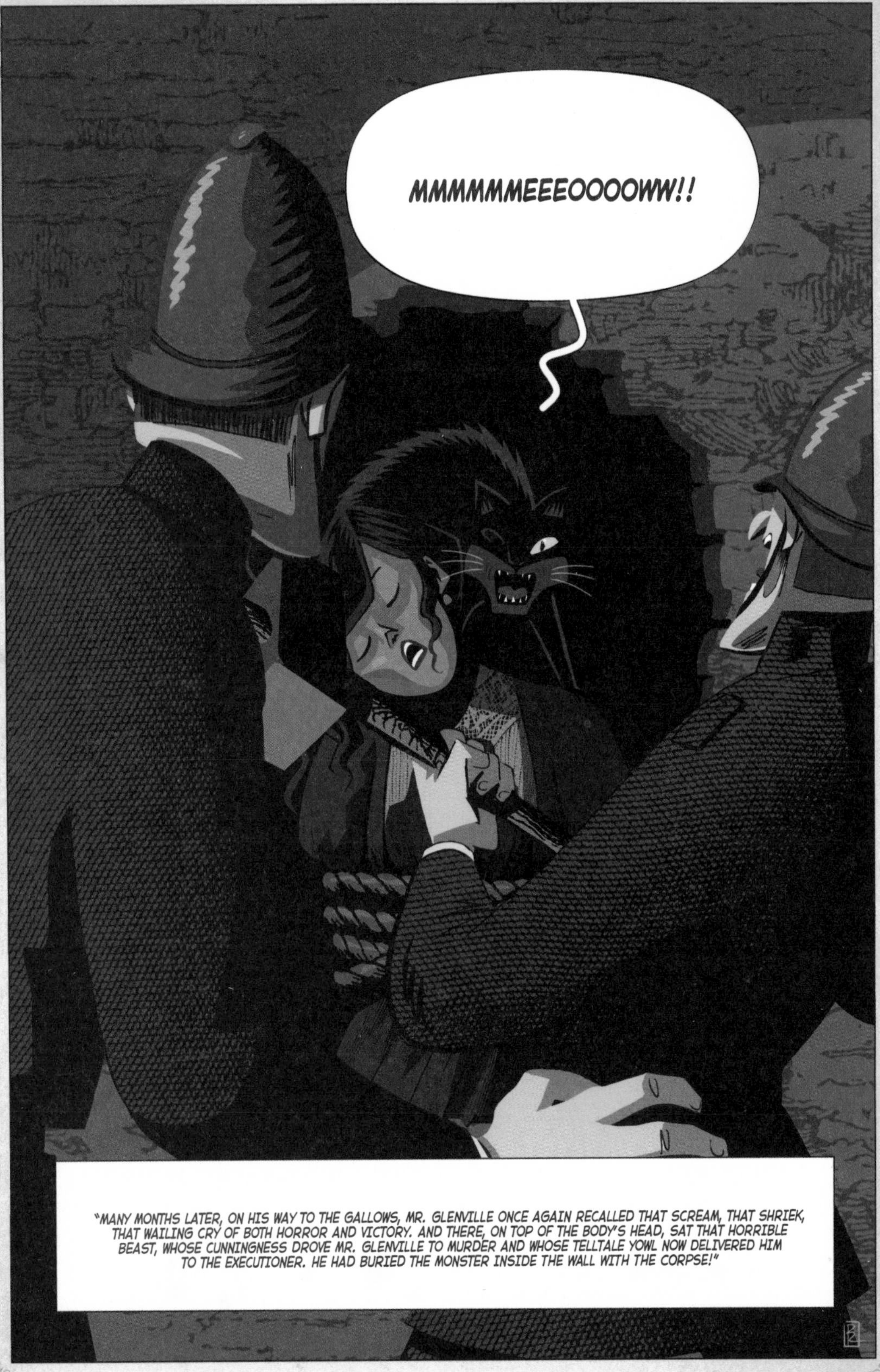
MMMMMMEEEOOOOWW!!
"MANY MONTHS LATER, ON HIS WAY TO THE GALLOWS, MR. GLENVILLE ONCE AGAIN RECALLED THAT SCREAM, THAT SHRIEK, THAT WAILING CRY OF BOTH HORROR AND VICTORY. AND THERE, ON TOP OF THE BODY'S HEAD, SAT THAT HORRIBLE BEAST, WHOSE CUNNINGNESS DROVE MR. GLENVILLE TO MURDER AND WHOSE TELLTALE YOWL NOW DELIVERED HIM TO THE EXECUTIONER. HE HAD BURIED THE MONSTER INSIDE THE WALL WITH THE CORPSE!"

FURTHER READING

BOOKS

Crowe, Catherine. *The Night Side of Nature: or, Ghosts and Ghost Seers.* London: British Library, 2011.

Le Fanu, Joseph Sheridan. *Madam Crowl's Ghost and Other Stories.* Ware, Hertfordshire, England: Wordsworth Editions, 2008.

Maupassant, Guy de. *Complete Short Stories of Maupassant, Vol. 1 of 2.* Charleston, S.C.: Forgotten Books, 2008.

Poe, Edgar Allan. *The Stories of Edgar Allan Poe.* New York: Sterling, 2010.

Polidori, John William. *The Vampyre and Other Tales of the Macabre.* Oxford: Oxford University Press, 2008.

Stevenson, Robert Louis. *The Body Snatcher and Other Tales.* Lawrence, Kans.: Digireads.com, 2009.

White, Edward Lucas. *The House of Nightmare, and Lukundoo.* Gloucester, Gloucestershire, England: Dodo Press, 2009.

INTERNET ADDRESSES

The Literature Network
http://www.online-literature.com/

The Literary Gothic
http://www.litgothic.com/index_fl.html

Robert Louis Stevenson Website
http://www.robert-louis-stevenson.org/

PoeStories.com
http://www.poestories.com/